HINT

OF DANGER

UNDERCOVER MAGIC BOOK ONE

Cover Art by Anna Spies of Eerilyfair Book Covers

Edited by ALD Editing

Proofread by Dominique Laura

❧ Created with Vellum

This one's for Bam.

Without her, none of this would have ever happened. Here's to moonlight, slow dances, bad decisions, and discovering a new beginning.

HINT of DANGER

Part One

MOONLIGHT

"*Yours is the light by which my spirit's born.*"
— e. e. cummings

CHAPTER 1

Her

Being a ghost sucked.

There was no one to talk to, nothing to do—outside of spying on those lucky enough to still be alive—and worst of all, no one to touch. Not that she hadn't tried. Once she thought she'd actually succeeded in knocking a picture over, but it had been a fluke. A gust of wind she hadn't felt was the real victor, succeeding where all she could do was fail.

It was funny that touch was the thing she missed the most about being alive, having no recollection of the last time she'd been fortunate enough to participate in such an exchange. No recollection of anything from *before,* actually.

Not even a name.

She was little more than a spectator. A spirit without a body, an identity, or even any memories of her own. For countless years, she'd been forced to watch as others lived their lives, never knowing if she had ever done the same.

It was a shitty existence, more so because there didn't seem to be any purpose to it. Why was she here? *Where* was here? Rarely was there anything to break the tedium, save new tenants who would occasionally move into the building she haunted.

Is that the right word? Can you even haunt something if you can't interact with it and no one else knows you are there?

Whatever bound her to this place would not allow her to go outside past the natural boundaries of the building. So, she couldn't leave the main entrance, but she could go to any of its balconies or even the roof. Most nights, she'd find her way up there to stare at the moon and ask the universe one of the thousands of questions whirling through her mind. Not that the universe ever deigned to answer.

Although she had mostly free rein of the building, she found herself always coming back to apartment number seven. She wasn't sure what it was about the unit. It definitely wasn't the resident—which had changed a dozen times since she'd been here—but it called to her more than the others. In a way, it felt like home. As much as a ghost could have a home, anyway.

Her current houseguest, as she'd taken to thinking of her, was some kind of scientist. She had a lab coat she'd bring home sometimes, and she was always muttering about equations and variables while putzing around the apartment. Not once had she brought someone home or done anything more exciting than play solitaire on a Friday night. In other words, she was utterly boring to her ghostly roommate who tried to live through her vicariously.

As a ghost, she may not have a life of her own, but one thing she had in abundance were opinions. After years—decades—spent watching others, she had acquired quite a collection of them.

Diets? Waste of taste buds.

Celibacy? Waste of a body.

Reality TV? Waste of time—and brain cells.

Why were the living obsessed with how other people filled their days instead of actually going out and living theirs? It was absolutely ludicrous. People were choosing to spend the time they'd been given doing what she'd been forced to do for eternity. The irony of it was not lost on her.

If she were alive, she'd devour everything life had to offer and then ask for seconds. She wouldn't waste a moment of her life on silly things like counting calories or wondering what a celebrity wore to a party.

And she certainly wouldn't pass up an opportunity to take a good-looking stranger for a ride.

Touch. She *craved* it. The sensation of having someone else run his fingertips along her skin and feeling the heat of it reverberating through her, sending her pulse racing and making her breath catch. Someone winding his fingers through her hair and tugging, causing waves of pleasure to roll down her back, or even the feather-soft press of lips against hers. Each small caress would create a ripple effect of sensation that impacted far more than just the single place they were physically connected. Not knowing if she had any practical experience in that area, she definitely had seen enough to feel confident she'd know her way around a male body if she ever got her hands on one. Or if she ever got hands, for that matter.

Certainly, she'd had her own body at one time to recall the idea of such specific feelings, if not their specific occurrences. Right?

Weary and more frustrated by her circumstances than she could remember being in a long while, she left her slumbering houseguest behind and moved through the mostly quiet apartment complex to the roof.

It was less of an actual movement and more of a willing of self that propelled her consciousness from one room to another. Usually, it was as simple as thinking of a place to arrive there, but sometimes she liked to pretend, however she could, that she was human. Even if just for a little while. And so, instead of just sending herself to the top of the building, she passed through the halls and then the stairwells, just as anyone else might if they wished to stand under the stars.

It was a beautiful night, the sky speckled with stars and the barest wisps of clouds. The moon hung low and full, its silvery reflection illuminating the world beneath it with its soft glow. Usually, the night sky was enough to soothe her, but tonight the feeling of restlessness only grew. If she had a heart, she would say it ached.

Please.

The wish was sent out into the world, filled with more meaning than a single word had any right to be.

The slightly muted sounds of a city winding down were her only answer.

Feeling defeated, she cast one last, longing look to the moon. There was a soft flare like it suddenly grew brighter. She might have missed it entirely if she hadn't been so intently focused.

Glancing down confirmed that a beam of light was now centered on the place where she hovered.

Startled, she looked back up, trying to make sense of what was happening.

The beam of light grew in its intensity, flashing until it was all she could see. It couldn't have lasted long, perhaps only a second or two until it died down enough that the rooftop came back into focus.

Lying on the ledge was a slip of something silver. Something that definitely hadn't been there only moments before. Moving closer, she realized it was a slip of thick parchment. A sense of anticipation buzzed through her as if the parchment was waiting for her. But that couldn't be. What was a ghost supposed to do with a note she couldn't even pick up?

Too curious to question herself, she moved until she was just beside the brick ledge. From this close she could make out a beautiful, looping script. 'The Monster Ball.'

She knew it was futile, but she couldn't help herself from reaching out to the piece of paper that looked like it had been crafted from moonlight. Not expecting anything to happen, she was stunned when the parchment rose off the ledge and flipped over, revealing the following words:

JUST AS THE MOON HAS BROUGHT ME TO YOU
SO SHALL THE MOON BRING YOU TO THE BALL
ALL HALLOWS EVE
THE WITCHING HOUR

IT WASN'T JUST A NOTE; IT WAS AN INVITATION—AND EVEN MORE absurd because of it. Who would invite a ghost to a ball? Was this some kind of joke?

Distractedly she realized that Halloween was tomorrow. Her houseguest had half-heartedly carved a couple of pumpkins and laid out a black cape in place of her lab coat. Even the boring human was going to be celebrating in her own quiet way.

The ghost looked up at the moon in shock as a feeling of well-being washed over her. The restless ache that sent her up here was gone, replaced with wonder and hope.

Maybe . . . maybe this wasn't a joke at all but an answer

If this was an opportunity to have an experience of her own, she wasn't going to logic herself out of accepting it. It's not like she had anything to lose.

Body or not, nothing would keep her from being ready tomorrow night.

CHAPTER 2
Nord

Holding the piece of parchment in his hand, he eyed it as if it were a snake. He trusted the bloody thing about as much as one of the venomous creatures and preferred to be holding it even less. A snake he could strangle. This . . .

Turning the invitation over once more, he scanned the elegant script. Moonbeams and bullshit if you asked him. The hell he'd be going to a ball.

Crumpling up the invitation, he chucked it into the aluminum basket beside his desk.

"What's that?" his brother-in-arms asked.

"Garbage," Nord answered.

"Mmhmm," Finley murmured, moving around the recliner Nord was sprawled in and plucking the crumpled ball of paper from the bin.

Nord knew better than to try to stop him. No one told a Guardian what to do. Not without a lot of fists and unnecessary bloodshed.

Raising a brow, Finley looked back at him. "What's The Monster Ball?"

He shrugged. "Fuck if I know."

"Where'd you get this?"

Nord remained silent, not wanting to explain how it just appeared after the moonlight played some kind of trick on him the night before. Finley would send his ass back to the Brotherhood faster than he could blink, and Nord was enjoying his vacation after several centuries of servitude.

Not that he minded being a Guardian or what it entailed, but sometimes a guy just wanted to enjoy a beer—or ten—and a pretty girl.

Shaking his head, Finley placed the invitation on top of Nord's cluttered desk. "You, of all people, should know better than to try to ignore something like this."

"You go, then."

"I'm not the one who got the invitation."

Nord shot his brother a dark look. "I'm not going."

"Yes, you are. Do you have something appropriate to wear?"

Rolling his eyes, Nord hit the volume button on the TV remote, trying to drown out the sound of Finley's pestering.

"You can borrow something of mine."

Snorting, Nord replied, "As if I could fit in one of your puny shirts."

Finley was fit—all those who served in the Brotherhood of Guardians were—but he was easily dwarfed by Nord's bulk. It would be like trying to wear a child's shirt.

Smirking, Finley gestured to Nord's black t-shirt and jersey shorts. "So you're going to risk showing up in that?"

"I already told you I'm not going."

"I don't think you have a choice, mate."

Nord snarled, which only made Finley laugh.

"Not even your bluster is going to get you out of this."

"How do you know so much about the damn thing when you hadn't even heard of The Monster Ball ten seconds ago?"

Finley's eyes shone a brilliant silver, the color replacing their usual vibrant hazel. "Some serious magic brought that to you."

Unease ran through Nord's veins as he watched Finley release his power. "You can sense it?" Nord asked, annoyed that he hadn't thought to check himself. He'd been on vacation for three weeks and had already forgotten the basics.

Finley nodded. "Not the source, but it's brimming with power. Nothing I've ever seen before. Whoever sent that to you isn't going to accept your regrets." Glancing at the clock, Finley shot him another half-grin. "You should probably find something to wear. You've only got forty minutes before midnight."

Muttering under his breath, Nord pushed himself out of his chair and stalked into his bedroom. Finley tried to follow him, but Nord stopped him with a dark look and a palm to the chest.

"I think I know how to zip up my pants, asshole."

"But what are you going to do about that beard?"

Nord froze, leveling an icy look at his friend. "What about my beard?"

Finley chuckled, shaking his head. "Mate. You look like you belong in a cave with a giant club and a bear pelt tied around your waist. Would it kill you to trim the thing? Or at least brush the crumbs out of it."

"I do not have crumbs in it!" Nord insisted, moving toward the mirror hanging over his dresser.

He was not a vain man, but Nord took great pride in his beard. Centuries ago, when he'd been a boy with his tribe, he'd been taught that a man's beard was a sign he was ready for battle; the fuller the beard, the greater a man's strength. Now an immortal warrior in his own right, the lesson had never quite left him although many other things had.

Shrewd blue eyes scanned his tanned reflection. Frowning, Nord had to admit his beard was a bit scragglier than he remembered, the longest part of it reaching his chest. Running his hands along the length of it, he muttered, "Maybe a trim wouldn't be amiss."

Throwing his hands up, Finley cried out, "Thank you!"

Nord glared at him.

"We'll do your hair while we're at it," Finley declared, already moving down the hall toward his bathroom.

"What's wrong with my hair?"

Finley shook his head. "No one wears their hair that long anymore, mate."

Nord looked in the mirror at the mess of blond hair that hung down his back, not seeing anything wrong with it. It was thick and clean. What more was it supposed to be?

Coming back into the room, Finley held up his clippers and silver sheers. "Trust me; you've been away for so long, you don't know how to blend in anymore. Let me help you."

Grudgingly, Nord nodded. If he was going to this damned ball, he didn't want to look like an ass.

Finley cast a pointed glance at Nord's hands.

Already knowing what he was going to say, Nord stopped him before he began. "The rings stay."

Finley loved to make fun of Nord's ring collection. Each band was a reminder of a long-ago battle fought and won. No matter what else he'd had to give up when he joined the Brotherhood, he'd refused to leave them behind. They were worn, ancient, and his most cherished possessions.

His father had crafted the first one after Nord had returned from his first solo hunt, a wild boar slung over his back. He'd used one of the beast's tusks to create a smooth, ivory-colored ring. It didn't fit anymore, but Nord still wore it on a chain around his neck.

The others were of various metals, each one forged from the weapon of a foe he'd slain. The last, the most important, was the one on his left index finger. His people generally saved that finger for their mate bands as it was said to be linked to the heart. Nord had no notions of being mated, having given his life to the Brotherhood. Instead, it's where he wore the ring he crafted after avenging his father's death.

Running his thumb over the smooth band, Nord frowned. Finley could change whatever he wanted about his appearance, but he'd gut the man—brother or not—if he tried to take his rings.

"Let's get this over with," Nord growled.

CHAPTER 3

Her

Time was complicated for ghosts. Days could feel like seconds in the span of the lifetimes she'd witnessed, but now that she had something to look forward to, the day crawled by. She refused to move from the kitchen clock, afraid that if she became distracted, she would miss her chance to find out if the invitation was real.

When the hands of the clock started to feel as though they were circling backwards, she gave up entirely and simply headed to the roof. She spent the hours until midnight, watching the children find their way back home after a night spent begging for candy. Tiny witches, ballerinas, and cowboys scurried across the streets, their shrieks of joy echoing off the buildings as they raced toward their next target. Their innocence touched her even as she envied them for it.

They were not the only ones wandering the streets tonight. Other, darker beings lurked in the shadows, the night just as much theirs as the children's. She eyed such a creature as she watched him peel away from the darkness and follow a group of giggling women stumbling down the sidewalk. It was probably too late, but she hoped that they would find their way safely home.

A bell tolled in the distance, signaling the start of a new day and, hopefully, her first adventure.

She looked up to the sky, to the moon that shone with brilliant light. Almost afraid to hope, she watched as a beam of light grew brighter, surrounding her with its glow just as it had the night before. It soon became blinding, and she was aware of nothing but the shine of it all around her.

The light began to fade as quickly as it appeared, and instead of a rooftop, she found herself on a sidewalk. Trash littered the street, and the foul stench of something rotting wafted toward her from the alley on her right.

"Ugh," she grimaced, freezing when the sound reached her ears.

It took her a moment to realize that she'd just heard herself. That she had a *voice*.

Looking down, she gasped. She didn't just have a voice; she had a *body*.

Shaking, she lifted her hands to her face, feeling the warm skin beneath her fingertips. Giddy laughter left her as twin tears of joy rolled down her cheeks.

There was a car parked to her left, and she moved closer to try to see her reflection in its grimy windows. It was hard to make out any detail in the foggy glass, but there was a halo of golden waves brushing against her shoulders. She caught a flash of scarlet red, which she assumed were her lips, and lots of golden skin peeking out of a black dress. Glancing down, she realized the dress had a series of intricate cut-outs that were filled with flesh-colored mesh, giving the illusion of being practically naked beneath the swirls of black fabric that clung to her feminine curves.

Toes peeked out of strappy black heels; her nails painted the same scarlet as her lips. A quick check showed that her fingers matched as well. Twisting her arm, she noticed black markings along the length of her right forearm. It was hard to make sense of the five black crystals that were connected at the bottom with some sort of looping ring inside of it.

Wondering if she had any other tattoos, she took a few steps down the sidewalk to where a streetlight flickered with a weak yellow glow.

Its harsh buzz of electricity was almost drowned out by the sound of car horns and other shouts.

She was sure she looked ridiculous to anyone who might spare her a passing glance, twisting around as she was, trying to see what she could of her back and arms under the dim light. In addition to the crystals on her forearm, she found one other tattoo.

The marking was stunning in its detail; the intricate scales of the snake on full display where its body looped around a dagger that looked sharp enough to cut her if she dared to run her fingers along its length. The snake was hissing; its tongue extended in a series of peaks and valleys she would have sworn were in the shape of the letter *M*. Just beneath its tongue, an arrow stretched out from the hilt of the dagger, and in the center, a white skull with a rictus grin stared out at her.

Beautiful but dangerous.

Was that what she was? Her fingers hovered over the tattoo, afraid to touch it and find out.

The rattle of a trashcan down the nearby alley made her jump. Eyes wide and heart racing, she stared down the dimly lit corridor, expecting something to fly out at her. When nothing happened, startled laughter poured out of her. She laughed until her stomach ached and her eyes were wet with tears.

Somehow, someway, she was alive.

No longer afraid, she began to make her way down the dark alley, a strange compulsion to see what was waiting for her at the end luring her forth, even though she could hardly make out more than the shape of her hand stretched in front of her.

She came to a stop in front of a bright red door flanked by two massive gargoyles.

What now?

Lifting a hand to knock, she froze when the gargoyles came to life, swooping down from their perch and transforming into two deliciously attractive, practically identical winged-men standing on either side of the door.

She admired their dark skin and the muscles showcased under their white button-up shirts and tailored jackets. Eyes traveling lower, she appreciated the way the slim cut of their pants hugged their legs. She finally smiled outright when she caught sight of the shiny red shoes the one on her left wore. They might be imposing, but these two clearly knew how to have a good time.

"Hello, there," she purred, fingers already itching to explore as she met the dark eyes of the man on her right.

He grinned. "First time?"

She nodded, her smile stretching further. "Promise to take it easy on me?" she flirted, leaning a little closer.

His eyes twinkled mischievously as they moved over her body. "Not on your life."

"Good," she whispered, winking at him. "I'd hate for the night to be a dud."

The twins laughed.

"I doubt you'll be bored . . ." the one with the red shoes said, trailing off at the end to indicate he was waiting for a name.

"Lina," she supplied, not sure where the name came from, only that it sounded right.

"Lina," he repeated in his deep voice.

"If there are more of you inside, I'm sure I'll find something to occupy my time," she continued, pretending to fan herself with one hand while crossing the fingers of her other.

"All we need is your ticket, and you're good to go."

There was a flare of panic as she realized she had no clue where her ticket ended up. It wasn't like she'd been holding it when the light transported her. She hadn't even been capable of it if she'd wanted to.

Whatever force had brought her would have made sure she had everything she needed. . . Hell, it had already taken care of her little corporality issue and made sure she was properly attired.

Hands patting her body, she let out a relieved "ah-ha" when she felt the edge of the paper tucked into the front of her dress. *Thank you!* She sent the thought out to whatever entity had been looking out for her thus far.

She felt the twins' eyes on her as she plucked the paper free and held it out to them with a grin.

Her friend with the red shoes took the ticket from her and held it up to his nose, eyes closing as he inhaled.

"In you go, troublemaker," the one to her right said, his smile telling her he found her amusing.

"That's the plan," she informed them, eagerly moving forward as the red door swung open. She paused for a second to ask if she'd see them inside, but the brothers were already gone.

"Huh," she muttered, shrugging it off and crossing the threshold into a long hallway.

The door slammed shut behind her, and a bright fluorescent light flickered once before plunging her into complete darkness. If she was anyone else, the darkness might have frightened her, but there was something familiar about the sense of being nothing more than consciousness floating in the abyss.

It wasn't long before the pulsing beat of music reached her. Narrowing her eyes, Lina could make out a smattering of rainbow lights in the distance.

She moved quickly, proud that she didn't stumble once for a being not used to having legs. Lina reached the end of the hallway, her eyes hungrily drinking in her surroundings. The room opened up before her, a thick layer of smoke hovering over the floor, casting the illusion of being among the clouds. The lights pulsed and changed in time with the music, looking like a massive storm cloud above her.

The majority of the space was taken up by a dance floor where guests were already grinding against each other. Lina was eager to join them; certain she'd find a willing partner easily enough. But first . . .

Her eyes had caught sight of a bar in front of her and just to the left. Metal stools stood in front of a cement slab marbled with illuminated crystals. Behind them were glowing blue shelves filled with bottles.

Licking her lips, Lina plunged forward. She'd witnessed enough drunken debauchery to know that she was more than willing to experience it firsthand. The euphoria that seemed to accompany drinking was something she would not pass up, given the opportunity.

One of the stools was free, so she slid up onto it, feeling her already short dress slide higher up her legs as she swiveled to face the bar.

"What are you having?"

Lina's eyes lifted up from the crystals that were currently a deep red and into emerald eyes that glittered like gems. For a second, Lina would have sworn she saw a hint of flame burning inside them. It was a full heartbeat before she was able to blink and remember to answer his question.

The golden-haired bartender grinned as if he knew the impact he'd had on her.

"I-uh . . . what do you recommend?" she asked.

"You good with heat, beautiful?" he asked.

Not having a clue, she lifted a shoulder in a careless shrug, feeling her hair fall back. "Love it."

That brought a smile to his handsome face. "I'm sure you do," he murmured, grabbing bottles faster than she could track.

"Nice ink," she said, gesturing toward the scales that spilled out from beneath his white t-shirt and covered his arm.

"You too. It mean something?" he asked while making the bottles flip and spin as he finished making her drink.

It was a good question, and one she didn't have an answer for.

"Maybe," she said honestly, eyes widening as he tossed a handful of marshmallows and cayenne into her glass before opening his mouth and letting out a jet of flame.

Now she knew she'd seen fire dancing in those emerald eyes.

He set the drink in front of her with a flourish and watched her expectantly as she took the glass, still warm from his fire, and lifted it to her lips. She took a sip, her eyes falling closed as she let out a low groan.

"That's delicious," she said, licking a bit of melted marshmallow from her lips. "What do you call it?"

"Dragon's Breath," he said with a grin, lifting his eyes from her mouth. "Glad you like it."

"Love it. I'm definitely going to need another."

He chuckled. "You've got it."

She drank deeply, not sure if the warmth flowing through her was because of the temperature of the drink or the potency of the alcohol.

Lina decided it didn't matter as she finished the glass and the bartender set another in front of her.

"Give me a holler if you need anything else. The name's Dec."

"Stay close, Dec. I plan to shamelessly abuse your kindness."

He laughed and winked before moving to take the next guest's order.

Alone for the moment, Lina eyed the people around her. Sexy men and women in various states of dress and undress were scattered around the warehouse. Her eyes collided with a woman wearing a tiara and a turquoise dress that showed more leg than it concealed. Lina grinned; it was the kind of outfit she would have selected for herself, given the chance.

"You'll want to pace yourself with those," the woman said, nodding at the drink Lina was still clutching.

"You've been here before I take it?"

"Every year." It was impossible to miss the note of cynicism that slipped into her voice.

She says that like it's a bad thing. Who in their right mind wouldn't love to come to a party like this?

"Cool. Any more advice from a seasoned vet?" Lina asked with a friendly smile.

"Don't trust a warlock," she answered immediately with a grimace. "And if you get into trouble, find Imperia."

Lina had been expecting something more along the lines of which other drinks to try, so the woman's tips caught her a little off guard. "Thanks," she said, wondering what constituted trouble and what this Imperia would do about it.

Before Lina could ask, a female bartender set a tall glass down in front of her new friend. Lina couldn't help but notice that the whipped cream and cherry topping in the drink matched the bartender's white hair and bright red lips.

"Brought you a double," the bartender said with a wink aimed at Lina.

Blushing, Lina wondered if she'd picked up on the trail of her thoughts. It wasn't like she was an expert when it came to supernatural creatures or their powers. As far as she knew, it was totally possible the bartender just read her mind. Possible, and mildly terrifying.

She hadn't been sure what to expect with a name like The Monster Ball, but there wasn't anything she'd classify as a monster in sight. Given Dec's little trick with the flame, she assumed many of the other guests had similarly hidden talents and perhaps even forms.

Which begged the question, if all of the other guests were 'monsters' of some fashion . . . what was she?

Lina might have a body now, but she was no closer to remembering who she really was. If she'd ever been anybody before tonight at all.

Her temples started to throb, and a frown tugged at her lips. This was not the time or place to have an existential crisis. It was a party, and it was time to make the most of it. Who knew how long she had before it was over and she was returned to her ghostly state?

Taking another sip of her drink, Lina turned to face the man who'd just sat down next to her. He had inky black hair and skin that suggested he spent long hours in the sun. Feeling her gaze on him, he turned black eyes framed with thick lashes her way.

"A woman as lovely as you shouldn't be sitting at a bar by herself," he said in a rich, slightly accented voice.

Lina smiled and leaned closer, lowering her voice as if sharing a secret. "But I'm not alone, am I?"

His eyes had dipped to the cleavage exposed by her barely-there dress. "I suppose not." Grasping the edge of her stool, he pulled her closer until her knees brushed the side of his silk-clad leg.

Lina took another sip of her drink, loving the way the warmth moved through her body. "You have a name, handsome?"

CHAPTER 4
Nord

He saw her the moment she'd stepped into the warehouse. The beauty's blue eyes were wide with delight and a determination he didn't fully understand until she beelined for the bar, her hips luring him like a siren as they swayed provocatively beneath her clingy dress.

If you could call that scrap of fabric anything more than temptation.

She could have been wearing swirls of paint for all the snaking black lines of her dress actually concealed. From the way other men and women's heads turned as she passed them, he wasn't the only one who noticed.

Nord was moving before he'd realized it, trailing her as she sat down at the bar. Eyes never leaving her, he crossed the dance floor, weaving through the crowd easily. A hand tinged light blue reached out and grasped his arm. Nord turned his head and offered a polite but dismissive smile to the fairy who was trying to coax him into dancing. She pouted playfully as he eased out of her grip, her lips painted with silver glitter that changed color with the pulsing lights.

Free again, Nord sidled up to the bar, squeezing himself into the empty space between two metal stools. There was barely an inch of space between the left side of his body and hers, her back turned to him as she chatted up a man sitting on the other side.

He caught the bartender's eye and held up one finger, pointing at a frosty glass filled with amber liquid another patron was sipping. Nodding, the bartender moved to the tap and began pouring his drink.

Laughter met his ears as the blonde tilted her head back and wiped at her eyes. "You're a scoundrel," she teased.

Nord grit his teeth, something about the calculating gleam in the eyes of the man she was talking to setting off all kinds of warning bells inside him.

The click of glass pulled his attention just long enough to offer the bartender a hurried, "thanks," as he set Nord's drink down.

Leaning against the bar, Nord angled his body towards the couple again, taking a sip to disguise his blatant perusal. He could easily see over the top of her blonde waves. The man was leaning in close to her, his hand brushing the bare skin of her knee as he waved a small bag of glittering dust in her face.

Nord had only been in this world a short time, but he'd lived long enough to come across the drug in his other travels. *Faerie dust.* A potent mind-altering substance that even the strongest supernaturals avoided. Consuming even the barest amount created powerful halluci-nations that could trap someone in the prison of their mind and leave their bodies completely vulnerable.

A low growl rattled in Nord's chest as the primitive need to protect consumed him. The girl had no clue how much danger she was putting herself in. Nord may not know who, or what, the man was, but he recognized a predator in any form.

He would not allow her to be prey.

Feigning clumsiness, Nord spilt some of his beer straight down her back.

Gasping, the woman spun around.

Nord felt like he'd been struck. She was even more stunning up close. Her skin smooth and unblemished; her cheeks flushed, sending all sorts of thoughts tumbling through his mind. Golden hair fell over her forehead, half-concealing wide ice blue eyes ringed with the darkest sapphire. They reminded him of the glaciers of his homeland.

It took him half a second to remember himself.

"I'm so sorry," Nord apologized, napkin already in his hand, moving to dab the amber drops off her golden skin. He purposefully allowed his fingers to brush against her spine, needing to touch her.

Goosebumps erupted along her back and arms and he heard her startled intake of breath. The leech behind her was all but forgotten.

Mission accomplished.

"It's all right," she finally said, giving him an easy grin that he felt straight in his groin. "It was getting a little hot in here."

Damned if it wasn't.

Nord took a deep drink, all but draining his glass. Beside him, she did the same.

Now that he had her attention, he found himself at a loss of how to proceed. "I'm Nord," he finally said, holding out a hand.

Her smile stretched as she set her now empty glass down and placed her much smaller hand in his. "Lina."

Brushing his thumb along the back of her hand, Nord surprised himself by lifting it up to his mouth and pressing his lips against it in the barest hint of a kiss. The move was filled with formality and tradition that was out of place here, but the urge to honor her in the way that came most naturally to him was irresistible.

It had been a long time since he'd had a woman. Longer still since he'd met one he wanted to keep.

Where the fuck did that come from?

Nord dropped her hand as if he'd been scalded.

Her eyes were hooded and slightly dazed as she stared up at him. The blush in her cheeks bloomed darker. It would appear he wasn't the only one affected here.

Interesting.

"So, what do you think of all this?" he asked, gesturing vaguely to the rest of the warehouse.

"I love it," she answered with the eager energy of a puppy.

There was an innocent joy about her that didn't quite fit with her edgier sex-kitten looks. Nord was more than a little intrigued. She was a riddle he had every intention of solving.

They both turned and looked towards the sounds of a band taking stage above them. Excited cheers rang out from the crowd as the black-haired guitarist strummed the first note on his blood-red guitar.

"Do you want to dance?" she asked, excitement lending her voice a breathless quality.

Nord laughed and shook his head. "I don't dance."

She didn't quite hide her disappointment. "Oh, well . . . I didn't come here just to sit at the bar all night."

Realizing he would lose her if he didn't give in, Nord picked up a half-empty glass on the bar and drained it, not caring whose it was. "In that case," he said, stepping away from the bar and holding out a hand to her, "let's go."

CHAPTER 5

Lina

She couldn't quite believe she'd heard him correctly when he held out his hand to her. Lina didn't know where the Viking of a man had come from, but she was beyond pleased he'd found her.

When she'd arrived tonight, her only plan had been to experience everything, flirt shamelessly, and hopefully find a decent enough man to pass the night with. That plan had solidified in the last ten minutes, Nord replacing the faceless stranger in her mind.

She must have felt the moment he'd stepped up to the bar, although she'd miscalculated the cause of the fission of electricity that raced down her spine. She'd thought it had been because the dark-haired man at the bar was touching her knee. Her first, real touch from another since acquiring a body.

But she'd been wrong. So wrong.

As soon as she'd spun around in her chair, the icy drink dripping down her back, the sheer force of Nord's presence had overwhelmed her.

The room was filled with attractive men, but none of them had affected her with a single look like he had. His piercing eyes were a blue so light they were practically white, shards of azure surrounding his pupils. The pulsing light in the room shone off his light blond hair; the sides shaved close and long on top, parted over his right eye. His face was comprised of sharp angles, a broad forehead, and chiseled cheekbones which were further emphasized by the perfect line of his beard. A beard that obscured his upper lip, but only made his lower lip appear even fuller.

It was hard to pull her eyes away from his face and drink in the rest of him. He was an imposing figure, standing heads taller than many of the others in the room. Not even the formal wear he'd donned had tempered the air of violence that surrounded him. His tight gray shirt and fitted black jacket strained over the muscles in his arms and chest. His pants fared a little better, hugging the thick muscles of his legs.

The light shifted, changing between yellow to green, and for a second Nord flickered. A second image superimposing itself over his towering frame. Instead of the suit, he was shirtless, leather pants slung low on his hips, blond hair long and blowing in the wind, hiding most of his face as he hefted a massive hammer high over his head. It passed as quickly as it had appeared, but Lina knew that the man standing before her was rarely, if ever, dressed formally.

He was a creature of the wild, tamed only by circumstance. If given the chance, he'd run free, more at home surrounded by nature than he'd ever be in polite society.

And then he touched her, just the brush of a finger along her spine, and that same bolt of energy speared her, stealing her breath and sending her heart racing.

No one else would do. Not when he could make her feel all of that with the simplest graze of skin over hers.

Without hesitation, she placed her hand in his once more, allowing him to help her to her feet. He tucked her hand around his upper arm, and Lina couldn't help but give his bicep a testing squeeze. The muscles beneath her fingers flexed, feeling as unyielding as iron. She allowed herself a small, satisfied smile, eager to feel those strong arms wrapped around her.

The band started playing a hauntingly beautiful song that was at odds with the thumping beat from moments ago, but perfectly fitting all the same. Couples moved around them, their swaying bodies wasting no time to take advantage of the slower, more seductive beat.

Nord's eyes were glued to her as he lifted his arm and spun her around slowly, pulling her body tightly against his. The smell of a storm about to break met her nose as she rested her head against his chest and closed her eyes. She wasn't entirely sure if that was part of the magic of this place, or Nord himself.

His hands rested at the base of her spine and seared her with their heat. The couple moved together perfectly, as if they had been made for it, the rolling of their hips completely in sync as they moved in a slow circle.

The singer's voice washed over her, ensnaring her even deeper in the seductive spell she was weaving. Feeling bold, Lina let her right hand wander, sliding down over the satiny lapel of Nord's jacket to rest on his chest by her cheek. She could feel the steady beat of his heart beneath her palm.

"For someone who doesn't dance, you're certainly good at it," she murmured.

Nord laughed, or maybe it was more of a grunt. "It's not that hard to sway."

"You might be surprised."

"An expert, are you?"

It was Lina's turn to laugh. Considering this was the first dance she could actually remember, she hardly thought she constituted an expert. However, she'd watched many couples dance and it was always easy to tell which ones had the spark of something real.

"You only need to watch to see what I mean."

Opening her eyes, she pulled away slightly to find a couple that would prove her point. Not more than a few feet away, she found what she was looking for.

"There," she said, jutting her chin in the direction of a woman with long lavender hair and an iridescent gown that hugged her body like thousands of shimmering scales. "See how she moves separate from him?"

She waited for Nord's grunt of agreement before continuing.

"A true partner would be more in tune with what their partner's body is doing and effortlessly match it, rather than focusing solely on their own movements."

"Hmm," Nord murmured, his chest rumbling beneath her hand.

"She's more interested in putting on a show than enjoying the moment spent with her mate. Those two will not last past the night, I expect."

Nord shifted to meet her gaze. "Harsh assessment from one who seems so optimistic."

Lina's lips lifted in a sad smile. "When you've been around as long as I have, you learn to spot things like that."

"Oh?" he asked, lifting a brow. "And how long has that been?"

Lina shrugged. "I lost count," she answered honestly, if not evasively. No need to complicate their evening with an explanation of her past. It was doubtful she and Nord were likely to last past the night either. That didn't mean she had to muck things up by mentioning it.

"Me too," Nord said, his eyes luminous under the pale blue lights. "It's rare I come across other, true immortals."

"I think there are plenty surrounding you right now," she said.

One side of Nord's mouth lifted in a smile. "Touché."

Her eyes dropped to his lips as the music swelled, her heart pulsing in time to the throbbing beat. Nord was being a perfect gentleman, his hands never straying no matter how much she wished they would. Had she been any other girl, she might have appreciated it. But Lina wasn't here to be good. This might be her only shot to experience what she'd seen so many others do.

Besides, as far as Lina was concerned, she'd known Nord for the better part of her life. Technically that was only about an hour at most, but she'd hardly been alive for longer than that. A fan of her math, Lina didn't give herself time to second guess herself.

Moving her hands to his shoulders, Lina lifted herself up while simultaneously pulling him down a little so that she could press her lips against his.

Nord stilled beneath her, his breath washing over her lips in a startled whoosh.

She pulled back slightly and looked up at him. "Is something wrong?"

A muscle twitched in his jaw before he shook his head to the side. The music around them faded as Nord slid his hands up her sides until they were cupping her face. "Not a damn thing," he breathed before brushing his lips against hers.

The metal of his rings was cool against her cheeks, and the soft hairs of his beard tickled her chin. Lina didn't care. She was utterly lost to the feel of his lips moving over hers. She knew it would be good, but her imagination hadn't come close to the reality of what it was like to be kissed. *Really* kissed.

It had always look so rushed from the outside. A little wet and sloppy, and more of a means to an end than the main event, but with Nord . . . he took his time and there was nothing sloppy about it.

Lina had no idea that just a touch of his lips would cause this sort of reaction within her. There was a full-on energy storm raging inside of her which greatly surpassed the small flash of electricity she'd experienced when he'd first touched her. Was this normal? This buzzing beneath her skin?

Each hot press of his mouth over hers hinted at something more. Something that if unleashed would consume her completely. She wanted to know what that something was more fiercely than she could recall wanting anything.

Nord pulled away first and she whimpered, her lips immediately seeking his again.

He chuckled, his fingers brushing her cheeks.

"Come on, let's find somewhere a little more private."

She opened her eyes. It should have been impossible for someone with eyes the color of ice to hold quite so much heat, but Nord could have burned her with a glance given the way he was looking at her.

Licking her lips, she nodded. "Good idea."

Nord dropped his hands from her face and she immediately missed his touch. She wasn't disappointed for long as one of his hands sought out hers. Lina never knew such pleasure could be derived from something as easy as weaving her fingers through someone else's. Humans were fools to take sure, simple intimacy for granted.

Lina knew better. She was going to savor each glorious moment with Nord while she could.

For all she knew, they were the only ones she would ever get.

CHAPTER 6
Lina

Nord led her through the warehouse and up a flight of glowing stairs to the second floor. He moved fast, his stride long and purposeful. Lina almost felt like she was running beside him as she attempted to keep pace.

He looked over his shoulder and grinned apologetically when he realized he was moving a bit faster than he realized.

Despite overlooking the party below, the loft area was shrouded in shadows. There were lots of dark areas with interesting sounds emanating from them. Seems they weren't the only pair sneaking away.

They passed a few occupied white couches before finding one that was free. Nord gestured for her to take a seat.

Lina glanced around. "Here? I thought you said you wanted to go somewhere private."

He raised an amused brow. "How private were you hoping for? If you hadn't noticed, we're at a rave. This is as good as it's going to get."

She looked around the loft area, seeing a couple walking out of an illuminated room at the far end. Following her gaze, Nord's eyes glittered when they met hers.

"No need to rush things, Kærasta. Just because the Ball only lasts for the night doesn't mean we have to."

Her heart sped up even as her brows puckered at the unfamiliar word. Given the tender way he uttered it, she guessed it was some kind of endearment. "Kærasta?"

His eyes softened and he ran his knuckles along her cheek. "Its definition got muddied over time, but for the people of my homeland, it would be the same as calling you sweetheart."

Lina swallowed, guilt swiftly replacing her other more amorous feelings. If he thought there was the possibility of a future between them, she owed him her honesty. No need to get his hopes up.

"What if we don't?" she asked, her voice soft.

His brows furrowed as he pulled her down to sit beside him. "What do you mean?"

Sighing, Lina squeezed her hands between her knees. This was not how she imagined things going when he'd led her from the dance floor.

"Nord," she started, having to look away from the concern blazing in his eyes. It was easier to talk if she didn't have to look at him. "Before tonight, I didn't exist. I mean, not in this form."

"What?"

"I . . . I was a ghost. Or maybe just a spirit. I don't actually know if I was ever alive. I have no memory of it," she rambled.

"A ghost?" he repeated.

Lina nodded. "Whatever magic brought me here crafted this illusion," she explained, gesturing to her body.

"Lina, look at me."

She managed to resist for a second before obeying, her eyes slowly lifting back up to his face. Her mouth fell open as she noticed his eyes blazing a bright azure.

"I see no sign of illusion about you," he told her as his eyes returned to normal.

"H-how can you tell?"

"I'm assuming you aren't familiar with the Brotherhood of Guardians?" he asked.

Lina shook her head.

Taking one of her hands in his, he brushed a piece of hair off her face. "That's what I am. A Guardian. One of my powers is the ability to see the essence of every living thing. When I look at you, I see nothing to suggest that you are anything but wholly alive."

The possibility of it made her head spin. "But how can you tell that it's not just some kind of spell."

"Magic—all magic—leaves a trace. If you were bespelled into this body, I would sense it."

"So, this . . . is real? It's, I mean . . . *I'm* not, temporary?"

Nord's smile was transformative. His eyes crinkling as he moved closer to her. "As far as I can tell."

It was too good to be true. Lina was struggling to wrap her head around the implication of truly being alive. She let out a joyful whoop and threw her arms around his neck.

He laughed, wrapping his arms around her. "I take it that's good news."

"You have no idea," she said. "There are so many things I've wanted to do."

"What's at the top of your list?" he asked, tilting his head as he studied her.

Lina gave him a wicked grin. "Getting in your pants."

Nord laughed. "I'm not one for putting on a show, Kærasta. But let's see if we can't reach a compromise."

"I guess I can work with that," she whispered as his lips met hers.

The energy storm was still there, but it was less frantic now. Contained, at least for the moment. She shifted her body until she was straddling his lap, wanting to be as close to Nord as she could.

He let out a low groan as she slid over his legs and she smiled, distantly thinking she might still be able to get him to change his mind about letting her get inside his pants.

Lina practically melted when one of his hands worked its way into her hair, tugging her head back so his lips had access to her neck.

"Yes," she hissed as he worked his way down and over the top of her breasts.

Arching into him, Lina was aware of every part of her body that pressed into his; the places she was soft where he was hard.

No amount of voyeurism prepared her for the truth of being with someone. She'd had no way to know about or expect the sheer number of overwhelming sensations racing along her skin and causing heat to pool low in her belly.

She squirmed, a nameless need begging to be answered.

Nord's hands flexed over her ass, holding her still. "You keep doing that and I'm going to forget my compromise," he groaned.

"Good," she whispered, gently biting his bottom lip.

"Lina . . ."

She loved the way her name sounded when he said it. "I'll take whatever you're willing to give me," she said against his lips. "Just please, don't stop touching me."

One of his arms banded about her waist, anchoring her body to his while the other moved to her leg, sliding up the exposed skin until his fingers brushed the bottom of her dress, and then further still.

All she was aware of was the pounding of her heart and the progress of his hand until the backs of his fingers brushed along her center. She had no words to describe the sound that came out of her mouth at his featherlike stroke.

Looking pained, Nord moved his hand so that it was clenching her thigh.

"You don't have to stop." *Please, don't stop.*

Expression clearing, he brushed the hair off of her face, lingering to cup her cheek. "I wish there were a way to ensure no one could see us," Nord murmured against her ear. "I don't want to risk exposing your body or your pleasure to the eyes of others."

As if the magic swirling through the warehouse had been waiting for his request, the area around their couch darkened, blocking out all but the faintest of pulsing rainbow lights.

Lina hadn't realized it was possible for the hint of possession in his words to make her burn even hotter.

"Is that what you're a Guardian of?" she teased. "My virtue?"

She'd been joking, but his eyes were serious as they bore into hers, the azure flecks in the center seeming to swell in size. "I've lived many lifetimes, Kærasta. I know better than most the power of fate. There's no doubt in my mind that you are what brought me here tonight. A Guardian is nothing without a charge. So yes, Lina. Your virtue, your body, your life . . . they are all mine to protect."

The intensity of his words and what they implied should have shocked her. They barely knew each other, but there was no mistaking the sincerity of his vow. Nord meant every word.

She ran her hand along his beard, loving how the soft blond hairs curled around her fingers. "Even from yourself?" she asked, already knowing the answer.

"Especially from me," he grinned, nipping her fingers as she moved them over his bottom lip.

Lina expected to feel disappointed, but that couldn't be further from the truth. If what he said earlier was true, they had time to discover each other properly. Whatever was growing between them was too important to rush and she had to admit the possibility of countless days—and nights—appealed to her.

One night with Nord would never be enough.

"All right then, Guardian," she sighed. "I guess we should probably get back to the party."

He nodded, holding her tighter when she shifted to stand up. "But first, just one more kiss," he growled, pulling her lips back to his.

CHAPTER 7

Nord

One kiss turned to hundreds and it was hours later before they finally pulled away from each other and made their way up to the roof to cool off.

It was all he could do not to drag her off to one of those damn cubes and finish what they'd started on the couch, but she deserved better. He would wait and satisfy himself by learning everything he could about the woman who, after a single glance, had captivated him completely.

"So, you really don't have any memories of who you might have been?" he asked, memorizing the way Lina looked surrounded by moonlight. She had an ethereal quality that made it easy to believe she was not truly of this world.

Lina turned away from the moon to look at him. "None," she answered, her eyes luminous.

"Do you think it's important?" she asked, sounding worried.

Nord shrugged. "I don't believe in coincidence."

"So, my being here, this time, this place—"

"That body," Nord cut in, running a hand along the tattoo on her upper arm.

"—it serves a purpose," she finished.

Nord nodded. "I believe it does. Why else go through the effort of creating meaningless details?" he asked, gesturing once more to her tattoos. "Memory or not, I believe they are clues about who you are, or were."

Lina bit her bottom lip, still painted a deep scarlet despite the kisses they'd shared. "I don't even know how to go about deciphering them."

Taking her hand, he brought it to his lips. "Lina, you don't have to do it alone. I will help you."

Her face was soft; her expression unguarded as she lifted her free hand up to his face. "What if it takes years? I can't ask this of you."

Nord shrugged. "I find myself with a lot of free time on my hands as of late. I could use a hobby."

Lina snickered. "You want me to be your hobby?"

"Definitely."

She shook her head, still laughing. "But what about your other responsibilities? Doesn't the Brotherhood keep you busy?"

"I just finished an extended assignment. I've earned some time away from the Brotherhood. It won't be an issue. Besides," he said, turning his face to kiss the palm of her hand, "you are my new assignment. I already told you, Lina. A Guardian knows when they've found their charge. My place is here now, with you."

It was true. He'd been drawn to her the second she'd stepped into the warehouse, all the noise and chaos of the party raging around him was drowned out by her presence. He'd heard of such things happening to other Guardians when they found their true charge, but had yet to experience it himself. Even so, there was no doubt in his mind that he was supposed to find her here. The feeling of relentless ennui that had plagued him for the better part of the last century had dissipated entirely as soon as she was in his arms.

Guardians were gifted with immortality and the ability to traverse worlds, all in the search of their divine purpose. He'd served with others across countless lifetimes and realms with the hope that one day he'd know the peace of finding out where he belonged.

Tonight, in the middle of a ball he hadn't wanted to come to, she finally walked into his life.

He'd be eternally grateful that Finley had pushed him into going—and had helped him look presentable. From the way Lina was staring at him, she appreciated the effort as well.

"Well that's convenient, then," she said, wrapping her arms around his waist and resting her head against his chest. "Because I don't think I could let you go."

He kissed the top of her forehead. *You'll never have to.*

He may not have spoken the words out loud, but he had a feeling she understood all the same. He'd already said more than he should have about being her Guardian. Nord would scare her away with too much talk of lifetimes and eternal service. Better to focus on getting to know each other and helping her uncover her past and deal with the rest of it later.

"Lina," he said, a thought occurring to him.

"Hmm?"

"What abilities do you think you have?"

She pulled away to look at him. "What do you mean?"

"Well, you must hold some kind of power, otherwise you never would have been invited here."

Eyes wide, she shrugged. "I have no clue."

"That might be a good place for us to start. Once we can figure out what power you possess, we might be closer to learning who you are."

She looked excited. "Do you think I could fly? Or maybe turn myself into something else—like a bird or a wolf or something?"

Nord grasped the back of her dress, the image of Lina hurling herself off the roof to test the theory sending him into a momentary panic. "Let's not start with that."

She must have picked up on his concern because she laughed and agreed. "Probably a good idea to start small."

"I don't think you're a shifter," he said, once his heart returned to a normal tempo.

"You don't? How can you tell?" she asked, her eyebrows lifted in surprise.

"I would have sensed it when I looked at you."

"Magic leaves a trace," she repeated, recalling his earlier words.

Nord nodded. "That and there's something in their essence; a duality that would be impossible to hide from one of my kind."

"Okay," she sighed, sounding a little wistful. "Not a shifter, then."

"You sound disappointed," he said, studying her.

Lina shrugged. "After spending so long trapped in that building, the thought of being free like that . . . it was appealing."

When she said that she'd been a ghost, he never imagined she'd been confined. He'd always thought ghosts were wanderers, capable of traveling wherever they wished. The thought of Lina being caged in any capacity made Nord want to punch something. Hard. Repeatedly.

"Do you think I was being punished?" she asked, her voice small.

His answer was swift and fierce. "No. I have trouble envisioning you doing anything worthy of such a cruel punishment."

Her voice was playful, but her eyes were earnest as she asked, "How can you be so sure? Maybe I was one of the bad guys."

Nord laughed.

Lina pulled away, her hands on her hips. "Hey. It wasn't that funny. A snake and dagger tattoo hardly seems like something a sweet girl should have."

"Kærasta, your heart is pure. There is far too much light in you for you to ever be truly cruel or evil."

"You sensed all that with just one look, huh?" she asked, not sounding convinced.

"I've spent my life around monsters. It doesn't take long to learn the difference between a warrior that fights to protect, and one that fights to destroy."

"You think I could have been a warrior?"

Nord tried to picture Lina with her waves of blonde hair and bright blue eyes wielding a sword. The image didn't quite fit, although he had no doubt she was the type of woman to fight tooth and nail to defend someone she loved.

"If you're a fighter, I don't think you use weapons in the traditional sense."

She glanced down at her hands, turning them over in the pale moonlight. "These don't look like the hands of a fighter, but I hate the thought of just standing on the sidelines and letting someone else fight my battles for me."

Nord ran his scarred and calloused fingers over her exposed palms. "Maybe you're a mage of some kind; your power acting as your weapon when needed."

"So, spells? Like a witch?"

Nord nodded.

She pressed her lips together while she mulled the idea over. "That seems more plausible."

Flinging out her hands, Lina shouted, "Abracadabra!"

Nothing happened.

Nord tried not to laugh.

He failed.

She looked at him sheepishly and shrugged one of her bare shoulders. "It was worth a shot."

"Maybe you just need to find the right magic word," he suggested, his shoulders still shaking with laughter.

She nodded thoughtfully. "Maybe."

Lina stared up at the moon, looking so earnest his heart ached a little. Knowing it was unlikely they'd solve the riddle tonight, Nord couldn't help but try to help her anyway.

"Close your eyes," he said, moving to stand behind her, his arms wrapped around her waist.

He couldn't seem to keep himself from touching her, but she didn't seem to mind. If anything, she welcomed his touch.

"Why?" she asked, snuggling into him.

"Just do it," he ordered, kissing the top of her head. "Are they closed?"

"Mmhmm."

"All right, I want you to imagine you are calling your power to you. Like it's locked away inside of you and you need to coax it out."

"How do I do that?"

Nord was silent for a moment as he considered what it felt like when he used his power. It was second nature after centuries and it took longer than he expected to find a way to describe it.

"For me, it's like giving permission for it to take over. I have to keep my power tightly contained at all times. So, I have to consciously loosen that control. It's like taking a deep breath and letting every muscle in my body relax."

"Why do you have to control it so tightly?" she asked.

"Because while my power is active, not only can I see the essence of all living creatures, I can manipulate it. If I'm not careful, I could accidentally change something's very nature without meaning to."

She stiffened in his arms, trying to twist to look at him. He held her in place. "We're not here to talk about my power," he said. "Now close your eyes and focus."

"You're bossy."

Nord smiled. "Shh. Concentrate."

He felt her relax in his arms, her shoulders drooping and the rise and fall of her chest slowing.

"Can you feel it?" he whispered, dipping his face so his lips were by her ear.

"No," she said softly.

Nord chuckled, squeezing her. "It was just our first attempt. We'll figure it out."

Turning to face him, she wound her arms around his neck. "Thanks for trying."

"Of course."

The band had taken a break and something with a heavy beat played in the background, but Nord barely heard it, his focus wholly on the woman in his arms.

"Is there anything else on your list I could help cross off tonight?" he asked.

"Well, I already told you about item number one," she said, giving him a seductive smile.

"Besides that, you little temptress."

Lina pursed her lips, her eyes narrowing thoughtfully. "Well, I have always wanted to know what it was like to be well and truly drunk."

Nord laughed, having not expected that answer. "Is that what you were trying to do at the bar when I found you?"

Lina nodded. "It seemed like a good place to start."

"You're going to need a lot more than two drinks if your goal is to get wasted."

"How do you know I only had two drinks?" she asked, raising a brow. "Were you spying on me, Guardian?"

"I don't spy."

"Liar," she teased. "You were totally spying."

"I was doing my duty."

"Hey!" she said, eyes widening as she picked up on something he hadn't said. "You spilled that drink on me on purpose. Didn't you?"

Nord refused to incriminate himself, so he did the only thing he could to distract her. He kissed her.

CHAPTER 8

Lina

"You're probably going to regret this in the morning," Nord told her as they waited for one of the rooftop bartenders to notice them.

"Worth it," she said.

"You say that because you've never had a hangover," he muttered.

Lina grinned. She couldn't wait. Feeling *anything* meant she was alive, and she'd never regret a decision that reminded her of it.

The dark-haired bartender saw them first.

"What are you having?" he asked in an accent she recognized as Spanish thanks to one of her previous roommates.

Nord looked at her. "You sure about this?"

"Oh yes."

"Shots are the way to go, then." Nord eyed her thoughtfully before turning back to the bartender. "Can you bring us six shots of Fireball?"

With a little salute, the bartender spun and performed a series of dance moves as he grabbed the right bottle and began pouring the shots. The bottle flew through the air, moving around his body and under his leg as he entertained them.

"Enjoy," he said, sliding the six overflowing glasses to them.

Suddenly nervous, Lina glanced at Nord. "Are these all for me?"

"Fuck no," Nord laughed. "I'm not trying to kill you. Half for you, half for me. That should be enough to get a good buzz going for you without making you pass out."

"And you?" she asked.

Nord looked almost offended. "I've drank men twice my size under the table. Three shots aren't going to do anything to me."

Rubbing her hands together, Lina gave him a wide grin. "What is it people are always saying? Bottoms up?"

Nord handed her the first little glass. "Cheers, Lina."

She clinked her glass with his and slammed back her first shot. The alcohol burned as it slid down her throat, but it was sweeter than she'd anticipated and she licked her lips as she set the empty shot glass back on the bar.

"One."

Nord was smiling as she grabbed the next and made quick work of it. "Don't suppose there's any point in telling you to slow down."

She made a face at him and grabbed her third shot. "Hurry up, slowpoke."

The shot glass looked absolutely minuscule in his hand, but Lina loved the way his throat worked as he swallowed the amber liquid. The sight of him made her far warmer than the alcohol had.

He'd finished his last shot while she'd been busy staring at him.

"Who's the slowpoke now?"

Not looking away from the challenge in his icy gaze, she took the last shot and slammed her glass down next to his.

It didn't take long for a delicious numbness to settle into her limbs. "I think it's working!" she shouted happily.

Her Guardian rubbed his ear. "You're more of a lightweight than I thought."

Lina grinned. "Come on, let's dance."

Nord shook his head, but followed her as she led him to the other dancing couples. The music was fast and energetic. Lina glanced down at her heels and pursed her lips. Those would not do at all.

She grabbed onto Nord's shoulder and lifted up her foot to start undoing the tiny buckle.

"What are you doing?" he asked.

"Making sure I don't kill myself!" she shouted back, shoving the strappy heel into his hands.

Nord glanced at the shoe dangling from one of his fingers. "What am I supposed to do with this?"

"Don't lose them!" she ordered, handing him the next one before moving deeper into the dancing crowd and losing herself to the beat.

She turned, immediately spotting him at the edge of the crowd. Her heels were cradled in his hand as he watched her dance, his eyes glowing white-hot as she lifted her arms over her head and rolled her hips in a figure-eight, never breaking eye contact with him.

Heart racing and joy unlike anything she'd ever known flowing through her, Lina danced. She lost track of time as she bounced and spun to the beat, strands of her hair sticking to her neck and cheeks.

Warm hands grabbed her hips and Lina spared only a second to confirm the fingers were covered in rings before leaning back into Nord.

"My shoes?" she asked over the music.

Nord bit her earlobe, his beard tickling her. "Fuck your shoes. I'll buy you as many as you want, but if you keep dancing like that, I'm prone to start murdering people for the way they're looking at you."

Lina giggled, spinning in his arms.

"Whoa there, tipsy girl," he said, catching her as she teetered to the side. "Looks like item number two on your list is completed."

She grinned at him, pushing back as she grasped his forearms and swung her head from side to side, her hips swiveling in time with her serpentine movements.

"Fuck, Lina," he groaned, pulling her hips until they were flush with his, his arousal unmistakable where it pressed against her.

"We can always go back to item number one," she cooed, hoping she sounded sexy and not demented. It was hard to tell when she had to shout over the music.

He shook his head. "You're impossible."

"Just determined."

The music died down as they heard the band come back for their final set.

"Are you having fun?" she asked him.

Nord nodded. "More than I ever expected."

"Me too," she told him.

"Good," he said, his voice soft now that they didn't need to yell.

She blamed the alcohol, but her heart swooped inside of her chest at the look burning in his eyes. Never did she allow herself to hope that someone like him might be waiting for her. That there was a person out in the world who would look at her like *that*. Like he'd destroy entire worlds if she asked him to.

"Thank you for giving me this," she said.

His smile was confused. "I didn't do anything."

She laughed. "Tonight could have ended up so much differently if you hadn't been here."

A shadow passed over his face and his fingers flexed against her hips.

"Thank you for being my safety net so that I could learn to fly without fear of falling."

She wasn't sure where the words came from, only that it was desperately important to her that he hear them. That he know how much it meant to her that he was helping her do the things, little as they were, that she had always ached to try.

If he thought her words silly, he didn't let on. Instead, he leaned down until his eyes were level with hers. "Sweet Lina, I will always catch you."

The sweetness of his words overwhelmed her and unexpected tears prickled her eyes. Not knowing what to say, she pressed her lips to his and clung to him. Hoping her body could say all that she could not.

When she pulled away she laughed and wiped the stray tear off her cheek. "Okay, no more serious stuff. We don't have much time left! Let's party!"

Nord laughed. "What do you have in mind?"

Lina pressed her lips together and scanned the crowd, looking for their next adventure. Her eyes widened as she spotted a jet of purple flame in the shape of a mermaid who was swimming through colorful clouds that rolled across the sky-like waves.

Pointing to the place where the flame came from, Lina started moving.

"Come on!" she called over her shoulder.

"Lina! Lina, wait!" he shouted, but she was already half-way there.

CHAPTER 9

Lina

The amazed gasps of the crowd grew louder as she found her way to the two men responsible for the fire show. One spewed jets of multicolored flame into the sky, the colors ranging from the deepest red to the palest blue. The other tossed cards high above them, which disappeared as neon-colored smoke took on various shapes and moved through the crowd in response. Together they created the fabulous illusions wafting through the air.

The smoke dissipated slightly, giving Lina a clear view of the performers and a woman with stunning purple hair. One of the men—she thought his name was Milo based on the crowd's cheers—was holding the woman by the wrist. He was smirking, his brown eyes crinkled with laughter as he attempted to scribble in her palm with a golden pen. Before he made contact, she twisted out of his grasp, causing him to laugh and lean in close to whisper something only she could hear. Then, deck of cards back in his hands, he resumed his show as if nothing had happened.

Lina was entranced as butterflies exploded from emerald green flame and flew around the partygoers. She held her arms high above her head, laughing when one of the fluttering creatures landed on her outstretched fingers.

She lowered her hand slowly, afraid the illusion would dissipate. Up close, she could see the glowing creature was animated by a tiny ember and that its wings were filled with swirling smoke.

The tiny flame started to flicker, the magic wearing off.

"No, you don't," she whispered, close enough that her breath brushed over the butterfly's wings. Puckering her lips, Lina blew a gentle stream of air over its shivering body, the green flame burning brighter as it took flight and returned to the sky.

"How did you do that?" Nord asked, his arm slung around her waist.

"What do you mean?" she asked.

Instead of answering, Nord narrowed his eyes and studied her for a moment. "How are you feeling?"

She smiled so hard her cheeks ached. "Great!"

"Not feeling a thing, are you?" he asked, amusement lacing his voice.

"I feel you."

The azure specks in his eyes appeared to glow. "Do it again."

"Do what?" she asked, her brows veeing. "You aren't making any sense."

"The next time they send one of their creatures into the sky, I want you to take control of it. Transform it if you can."

"Nord," she sputtered, "I can't do that."

"Do you trust me?" he asked.

"Of course, I do."

"Just try it. Actually, don't *try* to do anything. Just imagine what you want the colorful flame to be in your mind."

"Oo-kay, if you say so."

The crowd was chanting the names of the performers.

"Rake!"

"Milo!"

Milo's brown eyes shone with confidence. He gave the crowd a cocky smile. "You want more?"

"Yes!"

"Something bigger," a slurring girl with silver hair demanded.

"I'm not sure your man would like it if I showed you something bigger," he said with a flirtatious wink.

Roars of approving laughter sounded at his innuendo.

"Here you go," Nord whispered in her ear as Rake let out another colorful flame.

Milo's cards flew through the air, the hot pink flame twisting and twirling until it became a giant phoenix.

Like their other creatures, this one dipped and floated in the air, a combination of fire and smoke.

"Know what you want it to be?" Nord asked softly.

Lina nodded, her eyes narrowing as she stared at the soaring bird.

"Take that image and believe in it with every fiber of your being."

Lina's eyes fluttered closed. She was so focused on the picture in her mind, it felt like she was holding her breath.

"Lina," Nord breathed as the crowd let out shouts of delight. "Open your eyes."

As she did, she gasped. The bright yellow snake she'd imagined was now slithering along a bed of smoke, the pink phoenix nowhere to be found. As new pictures entered her mind, the smoke and flame obeyed.

The bed of wispy clouds coalesced into a shining dagger of cobalt blue, and the snake coiled around it, hissing with a tongue of purple flame.

It was her tattoo . . . sort of.

Shocked laughter bubbled forth. "Nord, do you see that?"

"I do."

There was another spray of cards and her illusion scattered, turning into dozens of tiny birds.

"I guess someone didn't like me stealing his thunder," she murmured.

Nord chuckled. "Guess not."

Milo's dark eyes met hers over the crowd. He walked toward her and Nord took her hand in his, moving so he was standing slightly in front of her.

Milo's smirk said that he hadn't missed the movement.

"Nice work. You ever need a . . ." he trailed off and glanced at Nord, "job, just let me know."

Lina laughed. "Will do."

With a wink and a nod, he disappeared back into the crowd.

"Do you think anybody else noticed what I did?" she asked, turning to look at her Guardian.

"Does it matter if they did?"

Lina was about to shrug, still riding high on the giddiness of discovering her power—or perhaps that was just the side effect of the alcohol. Either way, she didn't have a care in the world. Before she could, a feeling of ice water ran over her body, causing her smile to falter.

"Lina? Something wrong?" Nord asked, missing nothing.

"I—" she started, her unease growing by the second.

Twisting her head, she scanned the crowd, trying to identify the source of her agitation. At first she saw nothing; just more drunken revelry.

"Lina," Nord pressed, concern giving his voice a sharp edge.

"I'm fine," she said, turning back to him, only to stop short as a sense of déjà vu washed over her.

There, just behind two partially shifted werewolves, a pair of familiar gray eyes stared at her looking as if they'd just seen a . . . ghost.

CHAPTER 10

Nord

Lina had lost her happy flush, her skin bone-white and practically translucent in the moonlight. Beside him she started to shake, her fingers fluttering rapidly at her sides as if they were trying to spell something out on the air.

He sensed danger, although he couldn't tell which direction it was coming from. His instincts were screaming at him to protect, to defend, but it was impossible when he didn't know where the threat was.

"Talk to me, Kærasta."

She blinked, her pupils wide with terror as she stared, transfixed at something to his right. Nord twisted, trying to ascertain what frightened her so badly.

"I-I remember," she whispered, her voice cracking.

He jolted, his attention snapping back to her. "Remember what?"

"How I died." Her voice was hollow and dry, sounding more like the skittering of leaves over concrete than the vivacious girl he was coming to know.

Placing his hands on her shoulders, he turned her until she was looking at him, hoping that the sight of something familiar and safe would help her find her way back from the horrific memory she was lost in.

"How did you die?" he asked, his own voice hoarse.

She looked confused, as if trying to make sense of whatever she was seeing. "It's a bit of a blur—a series of images more than the event itself. There was a . . . ritual," she fumbled over the word, as if not certain it was accurate. "It was a trap. I was"—her brows dipped low and she looked up at him, her eyes wide and filled with pain —"betrayed."

Her anguish hit him like a blow to the gut. She looked lost. Nothing like the woman who'd been dancing barefoot on the dance floor mere minutes before.

"By who?" he growled, the need to avenge her giving his voice a savage quality he barely recognized as his own.

Lina shook her head looking frustrated. "I'm not sure. I only remember his eyes, just before—" she cut herself off, looking like she was about to be sick.

"Just before what, Lina?" he asked, his voice soft as he squeezed her hand in his, trying to reassure her that she was safe.

Blinking, she licked her lips. "Just before he slid the dagger into my heart."

Nord snarled.

"It wasn't . . . it wasn't the first cut, Nord," she said, rubbing her free hand up and down her other arm.

"What do you mean?" he demanded, his heart pounding like a war drum signaling the start of a battle. Or a hunt. Either way, the murdering bastard's days were numbered.

A bit of color had returned to her cheeks and there was a flash of rage burning in her eyes when she spoke again. "I think he carved something into my skin first."

A vein throbbed in his neck. *Yes. Definitely numbered.* "I look forward to returning the favor."

"If we can find him again in this crowd, he's all yours," she muttered, more of the life returning to her as she searched behind him.

"Wait. The fucker that murdered you is *here*? You didn't think to start with that?" he asked, not really upset with her but furious that they missed their chance.

Lina nodded; her eyes narrowed as she scanned the rooftop. "He was over there," she pointed, "staring right at me like he couldn't believe what he was seeing."

"Probably didn't expect to see the woman he murdered however long ago to show up at a party very much alive," Nord said dryly as he looked in the direction she pointed.

He didn't see anything more than oblivious party goers, losing themselves to the music and their partners. Nord let out a frustrated breath. He should have thought to ask her what triggered the memory. Maybe then he could have caught the little rat before he'd had a chance to hide, but he'd just assumed it was a result of accessing her power for the first time. Now it was too late. Lina's murderer would be long gone, especially if he realized she spotted him.

"I guess someone did recognize my sigil in the sky," Lina added as an afterthought.

"On the bright side, if one person is familiar with it, others will be too. That gives us something to start our search with," Nord said, trying to shake off his frustration.

Being upset wasn't going to do either of them any good. Their hands were tied . . . for now. The only thing he could do tonight was make sure his charge was cared for.

"You okay?" he asked, focusing on her once more.

If not for the drunken sparkle missing from her eyes, Nord wouldn't have known she'd just received the shock of a lifetime.

Lina shrugged, giving him a wan smile. "As good as I can be, all things considered. It was a hell of a memory to resurface out of nowhere."

"I'll bet. Is there anything I can do? Get you some water or something?" he offered lamely. He was a little out of his element trying to figure out how to help someone deal with recovered memories of their death.

"No." She smiled more warmly, moving back into his arms to rest her head on his chest. "But it's sweet of you to ask."

He ran his hand over her head, pressing a kiss to the top of it and loving the way she fit against him so perfectly.

"Do you remember anything else?" he asked.

Lina was quiet for a second before shaking her head. "No, nothing."

"There's no rush. The memories will come when they're ready."

"It's funny. I spent years wondering who I was and what had happened to me. Not once did I stop to consider that the memories might be bad ones."

"They won't all be bad, but no one's life is comprised of only good times. The only way we learn to savor the sweet moments is because we've known the bitter."

"Speaking from experience?"

Nord's finger brushed over his father's ring. "I am."

She snuggled closer and squeezed him, offering more comfort than she probably realized. "I know that you're right. It's just . . . I'm not so sure I really want to remember anymore. If those are the kinds of things waiting for me, I might be better off just creating new memories and leaving the past buried."

Nord's fingers caressed the length of her face before tilting up her chin. "Do you really think you could do that?"

"No," she sighed. "Especially not now. Someone wanted me dead, Nord. I need to find out why."

Her bravery touched his warrior heart, filling him with pride. He leaned down to brush his lips over hers.

"We will, Lina. And when we do, we'll face it together."

CHAPTER 11

Lina

She knew the night was coming to a close as people flocked to the roof. Part of her was sad to see the night end, but another part of her was exhausted. Who knew having a body could be so draining?

When she'd arrived tonight, all she'd wanted to do was have fun and live while she could, but the night had other plans. Not only had she gotten her body back, she'd learned she'd been murdered, discovered her power—sort of; she was still a little iffy on the details of how it worked—and found a man who claimed he was destined to be her Guardian.

Lina smirked. So not all bad, really. Having powers was pretty cool, and not something she ever thought was a possibility. And more time with Nord could only be a win as far as she was concerned.

"What's that look for?" Nord asked, handing her a drink as he returned to her side.

She smiled gratefully, accepting the offering and taking a sip of the warm liquid. "I was just thinking that tonight was not anything like I expected."

"Oh?" he asked, lifting a brow. "What did you expect when you heard 'The *Monster* Ball'?"

"I never really focused on that part. It was more about the adventure of getting to experience things for myself instead of through somebody else."

"And was it what you hoped for?" he asked, his eyes warm and his lips lifted in a small smile.

"Oh yes," she murmured, kissing him. "And no."

"No?"

"Feelings are exhausting. I had no idea."

Nord's head tipped back and he laughed. "They can be."

"I would never trade it, you know. Being alive. No matter the consequences of reality, it's worth it to be alive . . . to be standing here with you."

His expression softened, and he tightened his arm around her waist.

Before he could answer, the lead singer's seductive voice came over the speaker. "We hope you've all found love, even if only for a little while . . ."

She continued speaking, saying goodnight and introducing their final song, but Lina's attention was wholly focused on Nord. It was too soon to tell if love was what was building between them, but she was looking forward to finding out.

For all the bad that might be waiting for her, there was a lot of good too. Best of all, tonight was only the beginning.

A haunting song with a thumping beat started seconds before the first of the fireworks exploded in the sky.

"What do you say? One last dance?" Nord asked.

Lina feigned shock as her mouth fell open. "Is the big tough Guardian actually *asking* me to dance?"

"Wait too long and the moment will be lost," he warned, his eyes glittering with amusement.

"As if I could ever turn down an offer like that," she said, stepping into his arms.

Nord pulled her close, one hand rested just above the swell of her backside, while the other lifted to cradle her head where it rested against him.

Everyone else's faces were turned toward the sky watching the vibrant colors explode above them.

Except theirs.

They were focused only on each other and didn't immediately realize that their surroundings had changed. The last, bright flash of light must not have been a firework, after all. Or not *just* a firework.

Not letting go of Nord, Lina glanced around. "Where are we?"

"Hmm?" Nord asked, his eyes closed.

"Guess you had a good time," a man said, appearing in a doorway behind them.

Nord's eyes flew open, his body strung like a bow beneath her arms. "Finley."

The stranger grinned. "Expecting someone else, mate?"

"Fucking moonlight," Nord muttered.

Lina lifted a hand to cover her laugh.

"You going to introduce me to this gorgeous creature?" Finley asked, leaning against the doorframe as if he had no intention of going anywhere.

"Nope," Nord said. "Fuck off, Fin."

"You got it, mate," he said with a little salute. Turning to Lina, he winked and added, "Looking forward to meeting you properly in the morning."

Lina gave him a little wave before Nord grunted and pulled her back to him.

"What are you doing?" she asked, still chuckling.

"I'm not done dancing with you yet."

Heart melting, she couldn't help but point out, "But there's not any music."

"Lina?"

"Yeah?"

"Shut up and dance with me."

Grinning, Lina rested her head on him once more. Some battles were worth losing, and she had to admit, the sound of Nord's heartbeat steady and true beneath her ear provided a lovely beat. Even though she did miss the seductive lure of the siren's melodies.

As if the thought conjured the women, the haunting refrain from the band's last song swirled around her.

Nord's amused voice had her eyes fluttering open. "The lack of music bothered you that much?"

"What do you mean?"

The side of his mouth curled up. "Well I'm certainly not the one doing it."

It took a second for her to realize the song she'd revisited in her mind was *actually* there in the room with them.

"Huh."

"You must have been the one to dim the lights around us at the ball too. Seems like part of your power allows you to alter reality to suit your needs," he murmured thoughtfully. His eyes had a devilish twinkle when he added, "Or wants."

It was too much for her to process right then, the thought of bending reality to her will and all of the endless possibilities it created. She shoved it aside, along with the single memory of her past—and her murder. Those were both mysteries she'd solve another day.

Instead she gave Nord a flirty grin, pulling his lips to hers. "There's only one thing I want right now, and that's to be right here with you."

"Works for me," he rumbled, tucking her in closer before continuing to sway to the siren's sultry voice.

Nord and Lina danced as the sun came up, their soft voices and hushed laughter soon replacing the music. Despite all that had happened, contentment unlike anything Lina ever felt filled her and she couldn't help but look out at the clouds and whisper, "Thank you."

Her eyes closed before she saw the flicker of answering light.

Part Two

MEMORIES

"Memories are bullets.
Some whiz by and only spook you.
Others tear you open and leave you in pieces."

RICHARD KADREY, KILL THE DEAD

CHAPTER ONE

Lina

She sprinted forward, her heartbeat louder than the roar of thunder. The black walls of the alley were illuminated only by brief flashes of lightning.

Still she ran, feet stumbling over themselves in her haste, water from the storm splashing her already drenched legs.

Someone was coming.

Heart in her throat, she pumped her arms faster, not seeing the wall looming before her until she was crashing into it. There was no time to check her momentum. Bouncing off the wall, she fell to the floor and scrambled to get back up.

It was too late.

"Please." The word was a ragged cry. A sound born from true terror.

The next few seconds came in flashes. The soft click of metal striking metal. The hiss of flame meeting the rain. A face cast into being by a small orb of light. Gray eyes peering down at her.

With nothing left to lose, she opened her mouth and screamed.

LINA SAT UP, BLANKETS TANGLING AROUND HER LEGS LIKE COTTON

shackles as the terror from her dream held her captive. It was a struggle to draw breath, to suck in air that felt like equal part fire and blades as it scraped against her throat.

Is breathing supposed to be this hard?

Blinking, she glanced around, her mind still scrambling to separate dream from reality. *Where am I?* It was hard to make out much except shapes of furniture in the shadows of early morning, but one thing was obvious; she didn't recognize this bedroom.

Fuzzy memories swam to the surface and she began to recall how she'd arrived in this place that felt both strange and safe. An invitation that was delivered by moonlight. Supernatural creatures of both fantasy and nightmare disguised by formal wear. Her—solidly human. Drinks . . . a lot of them. Slow dancing with a Viking under the stars . . . wait, that couldn't be right. *Do Vikings even exist anymore? And would a werewolf really wear a tuxedo? How much of last night was real?*

Lifting a trembling hand, she rubbed at her chest, the feeling of the sweat-dampened T-shirt dragging across her skin a foreign sensation, as was the frantic pounding of her heart. She paused, reveling in the novelty of it. A heartbeat—*her* heartbeat. Not only that, but a body.

Holding out her hand, she wiggled her fingers. They were there. Real. Not the incorporeal form she'd been unable to see for she didn't know how long.

Her breath left her in a whoosh.

"I'm . . . I'm alive."

A high-pitched burst of hysterical laughter turned into a stunted scream as the door to the room crashed against the wall.

A man stood framed by the doorway; his ax held high, ready to eliminate the threat. His hair was plastered to his head, the light blond strands appearing almost bronze as water dripped down his chiseled face. Pale blue eyes glittered like twin pieces of arctic frost as they swept across the bedroom. His lips were pulled back in a snarl of potent rage, his thick beard only serving to emphasize the promise of impending violence rolling off of him.

That answers my question about Vikings.

The sight of him sent her heart rate spiking once more, but this time it had nothing to do with fear. He, at least, was familiar. Very familiar. If her foggy recollection of the night before was correct, they'd done more than dance . . . they'd kissed. Repeatedly. The memory of those kisses sent a wave of heat through her new body. Was it normal to feel this attracted to a man she'd just met? One whose name she barely knew?

"Nord," she whispered hoarsely, her eyes following the path created by dozens of tiny water droplets cascading down his body.

My scream must have interrupted his shower, Lina realized absently. Not that she was complaining.

Not with that view.

Even Nord's muscles had muscles. Muscles that bunched and flexed delightfully as he lowered his weapon and gave the room a final scan.

Lina's eyes drifted further south, heat flooding her cheeks as her mouth went dry. Ink covered almost every visible inch of his tanned skin. Her fingers itched to trace the thick black lines that swirled in dozens of intricate shapes, to discover the story written on his body as if she'd be able to decipher the hidden message etched into his flesh through touch alone.

She wasn't sure whether he realized he was naked or if he simply didn't care. There were many things she didn't know about the man she'd gone home with last night.

Or about herself, for that matter.

Amnesia was fun that way. She might have a body again, but she was still lacking all of the memories that should accompany it. The only past she could recall was her time as a ghost. And there wasn't much in the way of memories worth recalling from that lonely part of her life.

Nord's grip shifted on his weapon, and she caught the flash of metal catching light. But it was not the sharp blade reflecting the moonlight. It was his rings—one for each finger.

Heat raced through her body, and Lina dragged her eyes back up his towering form, her gaze snagging once more. This time on the thick silver chain around his neck and the small white ring that hung just below the hollow of his throat.

"Lina?" he asked, his voice a deep rasp she barely heard over her still racing heart.

It took more effort than it should have to force her eyes to finish their journey to Nord's face. This time they focused on the shape of his lips as he spoke.

"Lina?" he asked again, his low and lightly accented voice tinged with concern.

Licking her lips, Lina blinked and managed to croak, "Yeah?"

"Are you all right?"

She let out a shaky laugh. "Hard to tell." It wasn't like she had much to compare it to. As far as her mind was concerned, she'd just woken up from her first night's sleep. Ever.

Nord frowned, clearly disturbed by the answer. "I heard you cry out. Nightmare?" he guessed.

"I-I think so," she managed, lifting a shoulder, and causing wisps of shoulder-length blonde hair to tickle her skin. "I didn't realize dreams could feel so . . . real." *Terrifying*, she mentally corrected. If real was what it felt like to be sitting here talking to him, then what she'd experienced in that dream had been so much more.

He studied her, his face unreadable in the soft light of early morning. "Why don't you come get some coffee? Fin made a fresh pot."

Fin . . . Finley. The name dredged up the image of a smiling man she'd met only briefly when she'd arrived here after the ball. He was a friend of Nord's and a charmer to be sure. But if she was being honest, her interest was piqued by the promise of coffee. She'd always wondered what the fuss was about.

"Unless you'd rather try to go back to sleep," Nord added, pulling her attention back to him.

Lina's eyes shifted to the small clock by the side of her bed. Seven thirty-six. She hadn't been asleep for more than a couple of hours.

"No," she said, as she swung her legs over the side of the bed. "I don't think I could fall back asleep even if I wanted to." Then she kicked her legs out a couple more times just because she could.

I have legs! Now she knew what that mermaid had felt like.

"Kitchen is just past the bathroom on the left," he said, stepping out of the room. "Join us whenever you're ready."

Lina felt a small smile tug her lips up as she got an eyeful of Nord's retreating figure. A massive tree spanned the full length of his back;

thick, twisting roots curling down his spine and tapering off as they reached the taut globes of his ass. The Viking wasn't tattooed everywhere, after all.

Once he disappeared from sight, Lina fell back on the bed, a low groan escaping as she scrubbed her hands down her face. Her head was pounding. Likely from the barrage of hazy images her brain was still trying to sort through. That, or all the alcohol she'd had the night before.

It had seemed like a good idea . . . at the time.

What better way to give her new body a real test drive? Especially if she didn't have to worry about the consequences. She'd been convinced that whatever magic brought her to The Monster Ball would return her to her ghostly state as soon as it ended. Lina couldn't have been more excited that she'd been wrong.

The absurdity of her current situation struck her then. Alive for less than eight hours and she'd already gotten drunk and gone home with a stranger. If that wasn't bad enough, said stranger actually owned and knew how to use an ax. Weren't there movies about girls as dumb as her? One of her old 'roommates'—her nickname for the humans whose apartments she haunted—used to love watching them.

What other option did she really have though? It wasn't like she had an actual home to go back to. Or a family she remembered, for that matter. Wouldn't that have been a hell of a reunion? *Surprise! I'm not dead anymore, do you have a place I can crash for the night?*

She didn't even know if this body matched the one she'd lost when she died.

Besides, if she was being honest, she'd have chosen Nord regardless. Everything about their time together had felt like it was meant to happen. Like he was the reason she'd been at the party last night in the first place.

Lina chuckled to herself. "Okay, so in hindsight, not the smartest call. Try to remember not to do anything else that might kill you before you get a chance to actually live."

Still laying back with her eyes closed, more moments from the night before sparked to life behind her eyelids. Standing on the rooftop of a building that had been her prison as much as her home.

Brilliant green butterflies brought to life by magic. The scrape of Nord's beard against her cheek and the husky sound of his voice as he whispered in her ear. And then . . . a pair of haunting gray eyes.

Her murderer's eyes.

Lina jerked upright as the reminder crashed into her. She hadn't just died; she'd been murdered.

Other moments from last night might be fuzzy, but that one was crystal clear. No one, no matter how drunk, could forget something like that.

As much as she wanted to focus on the more pleasant aspects of the evening—like the part where Nord pretended to spill his drink on her, or how his body molded against hers as they danced—she couldn't deny there was another reason she was here. If she'd actually seen those eyes in the crowd last night, her murderer was still out there. She needed to find her killer before he found her. That meant she had to find a way to get her memories back, and fast.

Thankfully, Nord had offered to help her. It was time for him to start making good on his promise.

Surging to her feet, Lina stumbled a little at the rapid shift in position. She slowed and looked down at her legs, still in awe that they were really there. Seeing what she wore, Lina plucked at the borrowed shirt that hung to mid-thigh. It was appropriate for sleep maybe, but probably not breakfast. She didn't have much in the way of options, she realized, biting on her lower lip. The only piece of clothing she owned was a skimpy black dress that showed off as much as it concealed, and she was pretty sure there was a name for it when a woman wore last night's dress the morning after. Something about shame. Morning of shame? Cone of shame? That didn't seem right, but best not to risk it. Just in case.

"T-shirt dress it is," she said, standing in front of the mirror.

It was a shock, seeing herself clearly for the first time. Last night she'd only managed to catch glimpses of her reflection. Now that she had a chance to look her fill, Lina couldn't quite wrap her head around the fact that she was looking at herself and not some pretty stranger.

She took in her reflection, noting her makeup smudged blue eyes and pursed lips, trying to marry the image in front of her to her mental picture of herself. It was impossible. Lina tilted her head, her eyes narrowing as she tried to get a better look. The woman in the mirror copied the movement.

Lina stuck out her tongue. So did the mirror-woman.

She poked a finger in her nose. Danced a little jig in a circle. Grimaced as her boobs bounced up and down, the heavy weight of them more than a little uncomfortable.

The woman in the mirror shared her discomfort, both of them reaching up to hold their jiggling breasts in place.

"Who knew boobs were such a pain in the ass?" she asked.

Her reflection didn't have an answer.

Head shaking at her silliness, Lina grabbed her tangle of hair and twisted it up into a knot that listed drunkenly on top of her head. The epitome of women's fashion, she was not, but she was presentable, and her hair was out of her face. That was a win as far as she was concerned and more than enough to give her a little confidence boost.

It lasted as long as it took to step into the hallway. Glancing both ways, Lina frowned as she realized Nord's directions were of no use to her.

She had no idea where the bathroom was, which meant that the kitchen might as well be in another country. Recalling a game kids used to play on the street outside the building she'd resided in, Lina was about to shout the word 'Marco.'

Thankfully, before she could embarrass herself, she made out the low cast of voices coming from the right. She turned in that direction. Straightening her shoulders, she took a deep breath, remembering something else the kids on the street used to say.

With a small smile, Lina whispered, "Ready or not, here I come."

CHAPTER TWO

Lina

Lina couldn't deny the small thrill of victory she felt when she successfully reached her destination. Not that following the straight line of the hallway had been difficult, but it felt like a test, and her arrival signified that she'd passed it.

Her eyes roamed the industrial-looking kitchen with its exposed pipes and floating shelves before landing on the two men standing on the far end of the rectangular room.

"Morning, beautiful," Finley said, his eyes giving her an appreciative sweep as he looked up from his phone.

Lina jumped, not used to people actually noticing her, let alone talking to her. A blush warmed her cheeks, although whether it was in response to the attention or simply embarrassment, she wasn't sure. She might have discovered a hereto unknown preference for wild Viking men, but compliments—lighthearted or otherwise—were new, and she was far from immune to them.

Especially when delivered by insanely attractive men.

If Nord embodied a wild Viking, Finley screamed billionaire playboy. He casually leaned against the counter, as he smirked at Lina over the rim of his coffee mug. His carefully styled brown hair emphasized the neatly trimmed dark stubble lining his jaw, and his hazel eyes sparkled with mischief as his full, pouty lips lifted in a teasing smile. Even his outfit conveyed a sense of refinement laden with irreverence. The perfectly tailored navy suit showcased his powerful build, and the loose top button of his shirt solidified his playboy vibe. He knew *exactly* what effect he had on women and reveled in it.

Finley winked as if reading Lina's mind.

Nord threw a roll of paper towels at Finley's head. "Knock it off."

Chuckling, Finley returned his attention to his phone.

"Hungry?" Nord asked, glancing back over his shoulder at her.

Lina considered the question. Was she hungry? How did someone know if they were? She placed her hands on her stomach, half-hoping through the power of osmosis, it would fill her in. Then a smokey scent hit her nose and her stomach gave a low gurgle. She didn't need any help translating that reaction.

"Definitely," she said.

"Take a seat at the bar," he said, gesturing to the area behind her. "I'll bring you a plate."

Lina's stomach clenched with anticipation for her first real meal. That, along with the comforting presence of her two newest room-mates, was enough to soothe away some of the lingering disquiet caused by the terror-filled dream with those haunting gray eyes.

She turned and took a seat as directed. There was no wall sepa-rating the bar from the open living area just beyond it, which allowed her to look through the floor-to-ceiling windows at the city coming to life outside them. The view was stunning, but Lina was more intrigued by the presence of the shiny black piano in the corner of the living room. Did one of them play?

There wasn't time for her to voice the question before Nord set a plate in front of her, a steaming cup of coffee in his other hand.

"I wasn't sure if you preferred it with cream or sugar," he said, setting the cup down.

Her lips twisted in a wry smile. "Me neither."

Nord's eyes raked over her face, the expression in their icy depths unreadable. "It must be overwhelming."

"Not knowing how I take my coffee?"

"Not knowing who you are," he corrected, pushing away to go grab his plate and mug before returning and taking a seat beside her.

Lina was thankful he wasn't sitting across from her. It was hard to focus with those intense white-blue eyes boring into her like they could pierce her soul. Not that it was any less of a distraction, having his arm and thigh brush against hers.

"Everything's a little overwhelming at the moment," she finally replied, picking up her coffee and taking a tentative sip. The heat of it scalded her tongue, causing tears to prick her eyes before the drink's dark, bitter flavor hit her. Making a face, she quickly set the cup back down. *That is what everyone raved about? Were standards really that low or did food just taste awful in general?*

She hadn't realized she'd asked the questions out loud until Nord and Finley both laughed. More heat flooded her cheeks. She'd need to be more careful about voicing her thoughts. It hadn't been an issue when no one could hear her . . . now though, it might get her into trouble.

Nord chuckled. "I guess that answers that. Fin, can you bring us the cream and sugar? A lot of people prefer it that way," he added in a softer voice just for her.

She eyed the cup warily, not seeing how anything could make it taste better.

Ignoring the bitter brew, Lina picked up a fork and took a small bite of the eggs. The texture of it was odd, both fluffy and squishy, she wasn't sure she was a fan until the flavor exploded on her tongue. Making a happy sound, she scooped up more and immediately took a second, much larger, bite.

She made quick work of her meal, especially once she discovered the glory that was bacon. Lina went so far as to snatch a piece off of Nord's plate when she'd finished the slices he'd given her. Other people might have faltered at his frown, but Lina just grinned as she brought her prize to her mouth.

"A woman after my own heart," Finley said with a smile.

"I never knew what I was missing," she said, returning the grin.

"So, it's true, then. You can't recall anything about your life before last night?" Finley asked, his expression turning serious.

"You mean before I was a ghost? No. Nothing."

"That's got to be one hell of a mindfuck," he said, taking a sip of his coffee.

Lina shrugged as she chewed. Yeah, it was weird, having no memory of who she was or where she came from, but . . . there were worse things. Like not being able to live at all. So why waste time worrying about it?

"Not even your name?" Finley pressed.

"Nope."

"What made you go with Lina?"

"First thing that came to mind when someone asked," she replied honestly.

"You look like a Lina," he said, smiling.

"Do I?" She frowned down at her body. "I don't even know if this body was mine before . . ." She held up her right arm, flashing the five crystals connected by a ring that had been inked there. "Or that I had tattoos. You think a girl would remember something like that."

"Tattoos, plural?" Finley asked, studying the markings on her forearm with interest.

Lina nodded and twisted a little in her seat as she pulled up the shirt sleeve on her left arm to show him her bicep. "There's this one, too."

Once again, the design stunned her with its detail. The hissing serpent, lethal dagger, and grinning skull all intricately tied together. The blade's edges looked sharp enough to cut her if she dared to run her fingers along its length. The snake's tongue extended in a series of peaks and valleys that looked like the letter M to her. And just beneath its tongue, an arrow stretched out from the hilt of the dagger, with the skull in the center.

Lina shivered, tugging her sleeve down. She couldn't put her finger on it, but something about the tattoo filled her with restless energy. It wasn't fear exactly . . . but there was definite apprehension.

Finley made a low humming sound as he pulled away. "I feel like I've seen that somewhere before."

"Really? Where?" she asked, nibbling on another stolen piece of bacon.

He shook his head, appearing annoyed that he couldn't remember. "I'm not sure, but maybe it will come back to me."

Beside her, Nord was tense.

"I think you're scaring your food," Lina whispered, giving him a soft smile.

His expression softened as he lifted his gaze back to her. When their eyes met, the sapphire specks ringing his pupils seemed to glow.

Lina's breath caught, heat spiraling through her. Now *he* was a mystery she wanted to solve.

Every time he looked at her it felt like he was the sun and she was trapped in his orbit. Had it really been less than twenty-four hours since they'd met and he'd sworn his allegiance to her? She was still a little unsure what had actually happened last night and how much of his vow to protect her was wishful thinking. It was the first thing she intended to ask him about once they were alone.

Whatever the time frame—one day, one year, a whole lifetime—this connection between them was hands down one thing she didn't question. Their bond was as real to her as the body she'd been gifted. One look at him, and she'd known, without a doubt, that they had been destined to find each other.

"I think I might have a solution to your problem," Finley said, reclaiming their attention.

"Which one?" Lina asked. "I have a handful."

"Your missing memories. I don't suppose you know anything about the Brotherhood?"

Lina gave him a wry grin. "I don't know much about anything."

"That was probably a stupid question, considering. My apologies."

"If you stop to apologize every time you put your foot in your mouth, we're never going to get anywhere," Nord said.

Lina failed to contain her snort of mirth, and Nord shot her a smile.

Finley rolled his eyes in a good-natured way and said, "Nord and I are both part of the Brotherhood of Guardians."

Lina vaguely remembered Nord mentioning something about that the night before. "Guardians? So, you guys are like bodyguards or something?" Lina asked, trying to connect the fuzzy dots in her mind. Hadn't Nord mentioned being her Guardian?

Finley laughed outright. "Not quite, although I doubt you'll hear any of the Brothers admit even that much. While we do protect people, we're more of an intelligence network. We keep an eye on the supernatural world and make sure no one is causing too much trouble."

Even after last night's ball and seeing all the creatures there, hearing him say supernatural world felt surreal. More concerning was the fact that such a world needed a special network to keep it in line.

"And if someone does cause trouble?" she asked.

Finley's eyes glittered. "Then we end it."

And them.

The words were unspoken, but the message was clear.

Lina cleared her throat. "What's that got to do with me?"

"Well, the North American branch is located here in Bell Falls, and our bureau is known for its records room, better known as the archive. If there's anything about your past to be found, you should be able to discover it there."

"Fin, I don't even know where to start," she protested.

He shrugged. "Why should that stop you? It's not like you have anything to lose. Start by looking at pictures of other magic users, like you."

Lina glanced at her hand, wiggling her fingers a little as she tried to call forth the power she discovered the night before. There wasn't so much as a tingle in response. Whatever magic she might possess; it was staying hidden for the moment.

As if he could sense her confusion, Nord placed a large hand on hers and squeezed gently. "We'll figure it out," he promised, his voice low.

Finley was oblivious to their exchange as he waved her concerns away.

"Maybe someone will spark a memory."

She tried hard to clamp down on the burst of excitement his words set off within her. It was way too soon to get her hopes up.

"And I what? Just walk in and ask to look at your records?"

Finley laughed. "Not exactly. I'll have to put in a request for you, but we have graduate students who do that all the time. It's standard procedure."

"Just one problem. I'm not a student. As far as I know, I'm not anything."

Well, that wasn't exactly true. If her memory was to be believed, she possessed a fair bit of magic herself. "That's just a matter of paperwork. Give me an hour and you'll be a master's student finishing your degree in Supernatural Criminology with all the appropriate documentation to support it."

"Just like that?" Nord asked, seeming as dubious as Lina felt.

"Give me some credit, mate. It's not like I've never made a paper trail before. Leave it to me. Before the day is over, Lina will be just another one of Bell Falls' upstanding citizens."

"How long do you think it will take to get facility access?" Nord asked.

"A day, maybe two. This kind of request is fairly straightforward."

Energy thrummed through her at the thought of answers to her questions finally being within reach. The archives might be a long shot, but . . . it was more than she had now.

Nord nodded, draining the last of his coffee from his mug. "Then while you're at the bureau today, I'll take Lina shopping."

Her eyebrows flew up at that. "Shopping?"

"Don't exactly think you can show up to the bureau wearing that T-shirt, love," Finley said with an appreciative smirk. "No matter how lovely you look in it."

Lina would have sworn she heard Nord growl beside her, but Finley was laughing and moving away from them before she could question it.

"See you two later," Finley called, his voice still ringing with laughter as he strolled out of the kitchen.

"Ass," Nord muttered, almost inaudibly.

"For someone who's supposed to be your friend, he sure seems to annoy you," Lina commented lightly, helping Nord carry their dishes to the sink.

A smile ghosted his lips. "Give it time. It'll be the same for you."

Lina chuckled. "Uh-oh. Should I be afraid?"

He tossed her a dry look. "I've only been back in town for three weeks. You tell me."

Lina hummed, trying to find a way to learn more about her mysterious Guardian without being obvious. "Only three weeks?"

"I was on a mission."

That told her basically nothing. Where had he been? What had he been doing? The lack of forthcoming reply was clue enough that those weren't questions he was going to answer, although . . . maybe it was less an unwillingness to tell her and had more to do with what he was *allowed* to divulge. That seemed in keeping with belonging to an 'intelligence network.'

"Hey, Nord?"

"Hmm?" he asked, attention on the dishes he was rinsing in the sink.

"Can I ask you some questions? About what happened last night?" she rushed to clarify. "Things are a little foggy."

His brow lifted with amusement. "I think those last few shots you insisted on were probably a mistake."

Lina shrugged. "I'm not sure I'd go that far."

"Says the girl who can't remember what happened last night."

"I didn't say that, I just said things were foggy. Like, did I really make butterflies out of smoke and air?"

He nodded. "You did."

"And I made music play without any instruments or anything?"

He nodded again.

Lina frowned at her hands, trying a second time to summon her supposed power. "Then why can't I do anything now?"

His eyes shifted to her, and his lips dipped in a small frown. "I'm not sure."

Figuring a lack of magic was the least of her worries, Lina carried on. "And the part where you spilled a drink on me to get me to stop talking to that other guy?"

He fought a smile. "Accident."

"Liar."

"I'm the one with the perfect recall."

She made a face at him. "Making a fool of myself dancing?"

He shook his head. "Didn't happen. You're a natural."

A smile stretched across her face at the frank admiration in his assessment. "Dancing with you under the stars?"

"Real."

She held her breath for a second before forcing the next question out. "You vowing to protect me?"

He turned his full attention to her. "Real."

Lina blinked a few times, flustered by the weight of his undiluted regard. Nothing in the handful of experiences she could recall prepared her for the palpable electricity that raced across her skin from a single, scorching look.

Heat stained her cheeks, and it took conscious effort not to fling herself into his arms. Maybe if she were still wearing her gown, and they were still surrounded by the magic of the ball, it would be different. But here, now, even though they were only standing mere inches from each other, she hesitated to act on her desire.

Licking her lips, she asked, "You called me something—"

"Kærasta," he supplied.

"What does it mean?"

"That I'm a fool," he said under his breath.

"Besides that," she pressed.

"It's what my father called my mother whenever she looked at him the way you're looking at me," he said, eyes dropping to the floor as he shifted uncomfortably.

Feeling a flicker of hope, she asked, "And the kisses?"

His eyes lifted to her lips. "Real, but Lina—"

She may not have much experience with men or dating, but every woman instinctively knew nothing good ever followed the word 'but.' She tried hard not to let herself drown in disappointment.

Despite the connection they'd shared, the simple truth was they were little more than strangers. Strangers brought together by fate certainly, but fate nonetheless. Perhaps he'd just been caught up in the moment and regretted getting so close so fast. Could she blame him? Under any other circumstances, she wouldn't even *be* here right now. So what was she expecting? A declaration of love? They'd just met. He'd already promised to help her find out the truth of her past, and to keep her safe. She couldn't ask more of him. No matter how he made her feel.

Embarrassed by the confusing tangle of emotions his proximity caused, Lina looked away, needing that brief reprieve to collect her scattered thoughts.

"Lina, last night was incredible," he started, "but it can't happen again. Not until you get your memories back."

The rejection stung almost as badly as if he'd slapped her. "Why not?" she asked, brows drawing together in a frown.

"Because we don't know if you belong to someone else."

She opened her mouth to protest the absurdity of it, but Nord stopped her with a look.

"I made a vow to protect you. A Guardian doesn't make such a vow lightly. In fact, a Guardian only makes two such vows in their lifetime. The first, when we join the Brotherhood, and the second when, and if, we find the one we are meant to serve. We are bound to that vow above all others. It is our true purpose. So when I say I'll protect you, Lina, that doesn't just mean physically, but in every possible way. Us being together would only complicate things down the line for you if we learn you're tied to someone from your past. I won't put you in that position."

She wanted to tell him that was the stupidest thing she'd ever heard, but she was still caught up on the part where he'd just said protecting her was his true purpose. By the time she was able to form a sentence, he was already talking about something else.

She would let it go for now, but this conversation was far from over.

"We're going to have to start a list of the things you like so we can keep them in the house," he said, his voice thoughtful.

"Excuse me?" she asked, her mind not fully caught up to the conversation he'd carried on without her.

"Food," he explained. "So bacon was a yes."

"Top of the list," she agreed.

"And eggs?"

She nodded. "Not bad."

"Coffee?"

"That's a hard pass. It was better with the cream and sugar, but I'm not sure anything will erase that first impression."

He laughed. "Fair enough. We'll stop for lunch while we're out today, see if we can't find anything else to add to your list."

True excitement blossomed at the prospect of going out and exploring the world she'd only ever seen through movies or from the top of the building she'd haunted.

"Sounds amazing."

"I'll go grab you something to wear so we can head out."

She offered him a smile that felt a little wobbly at the edges.

"Thank you, Nord. For everything. Breakfast. The clothes. A place to stay. I don't know what I would have done without your help. I really appreciate it."

Something flickered in his eyes, but it was gone before she could decipher it.

"I already told you. Whatever you need, I'll take care of it. You don't have to worry about a thing. Not even a nightmare."

The reminder of her dream caused her excitement to fade, and she regretted that fifth helping of bacon as her stomach rolled. "I'll try to remember that." Trying to play off the shift in her mood, she added, "Seems silly that a dream frightened me so badly. Barely even remember what it was about."

Lie.

Each detail of that dream was emblazoned upon her mind, but she wasn't about to admit it. People had bad dreams; it didn't mean anything.

He grinned, clearly relieved by her answer. "I'm glad to hear it. Be right back."

"I'll be here," she said, offering him a smile that didn't reach her eyes. "Not like I have anywhere else to be."

If he noticed the note of melancholy, he didn't comment. Instead, he gave her arm a soft squeeze as he left the kitchen.

Lina stared after him, her heart clenching painfully in her chest. One thing was becoming uncomfortably clear.

Being alive was exhausting.

CHAPTER THREE

Lina

Lina walked beside Nord, her eyes wide as she tried to take in everything all at once. It was overwhelming, but in the most invigorating possible way. The screech of the brakes and honking of car horns were the perfect accompaniment to the throng of people and loud shouts of street vendors peddling their wares.

When she'd been a ghost, she'd split her time amongst the apartment complex's residents and the rooftop, always confined from the world she existed in. A part of her wished she could go back there now, to see if any of the residents recognized her or if she could learn something about her past, but she didn't even know where it was located in relation to her current whereabouts.

Lina craned her neck up, trying to find the top of a skyscraper Nord was ushering her past when the tiny hairs on the back of her neck stood on end. The sensation was so unexpected, that she stopped right in the middle of the sidewalk.

"Oof," she grunted, bouncing off a rogue pedestrian.

"Watch where you're going," the woman shouted angrily.

"Sorry," Lina called after her, but the woman was already distracted by her cell phone. "Maybe you should take your own advice," she added, watching a mother and daughter narrowly avoid the woman's path.

Lina rubbed her arm where the woman crashed into her, the odd feeling that had caused the collision in the first place already gone. Nord's eyes focused on the place where she cradled her arm.

"Are you hurt?" he asked.

"More surprised than anything. If you would have told me an hour ago that a shoulder could do this much damage, I would have laughed at you. But she almost knocked me over."

Nord's lips twitched. "You should see what I can do with a finger."

Lina flushed. She was pretty sure he hadn't meant that the way it came out.

"I'll bet," she managed.

"What about this place?" Nord asked, gesturing to the shop next to them.

Mannequins lined the windows, in various abstract poses, holding signs that promised all of winter's must-have essentials were inside.

Lina shrugged. "Looks good to me."

He held the door open, and she moved in, the scent of something delicate and floral reaching her at the same time as the strains of an electric guitar. It was an assault on her senses, and she wasn't sure where to even start.

Nord solved the problem by waving down a teenage salesperson.

"Yes, sir? Can I help you find something?"

"Our luggage was lost. We need to replace everything. It would be a huge help if you could help us pick out items."

Lina was pretty sure she saw dollar signs in the young man's eyes.

"Absolutely, sir. Right away, sir. What sizes do you need?"

Lina had no clue. She pointed to her body, mostly hidden in Nord's shirt. "This size."

The guy laughed, like she'd told a joke. "Right. You can look around while we start pulling things for you in the dressing room," he said, already selecting items as he started walking toward the back of the store.

Lina watched him walk away and shook her head. "I know I'm new here, but I'm pretty sure that guy is going to try to rob you blind."

Nord shrugged. "I can afford it."

"Miss?" a young woman with purple hair called. "If you would follow me?"

Seeing a dress made entirely of sequins and yellow feathers, Lina turned horrified eyes on Nord. "What if they try to put me in something like that?"

"Now that I'd pay to see."

"Traitor."

Nord laughed and sat down in one of the chairs near the dressing rooms.

"See you on the other side," she said under her breath as she headed into the small room the woman was standing next to.

"Go ahead and start with whichever outfit you want. If you need something in a different size, let me know," she said with a bright smile before closing the door.

Lina eyed the forty-something articles of clothing already hanging in the room.

"Oh boy." She lifted a strappy shirt that looked more like a torture device than something she was supposed to wear. "What did I get myself into?"

Twenty minutes later, she was red-faced and sweating, as she fought with the hooks of a bra she was trying to put on.

"This is bullshit," she grunted, confused that one of the arm straps was hanging around her neck. "How did that even happen?"

"Lina? You okay in there?"

She froze, one arm angled behind her, the other up in the air, trying to detangle herself from the strap attempting to strangle her. Both her boobs were on full display while a pair of dark-denim jeans that were only half-buttoned revealed her new lacey pink underwear.

"Yup," she squeaked, desperate to figure this out before he tried to come in and help her. "Almost done."

"Guess you're hanging free," she told her reflection, managing to pull off and toss the stupid bra on the floor with one hand, while grabbing a ribbed tank with the other. Then she selected a black leather jacket, zipping it most of the way up to hide the fact that she was braless—not because she was worried about flashing some boobage, but because she didn't want to raise any questions about the battle she'd just waged and lost in the dressing room.

Once again, Lina was certain she'd missed the mark when it came to women's fashion, but at least she was properly attired.

She stepped out of the dressing room, a couple of shirts and two pairs of jeans in her hand. The salesgirl looked crestfallen. "That's all you liked?" she asked.

Lina looked between her selection and the girl. "Yes?"

"We'll take the pants in every color. Same with these shirts and the jacket," he said.

The girl looked at him like he was her personal savior. "You got it. What about the undergarments?"

Before Lina could vehemently protest, Nord was nodding. "Those too."

She scowled at him. "This isn't nearly as fun as I thought it would be."

He looked confused. "Why did you think it would be fun?"

She threw her arms up. "I dunno, people are always going on about shopping, and how much they love it, but this sucks. I'm sweaty. I'm sore. I'm pretty sure I have some kind of strap burn from that damn bra. And I don't know why, but it feels like a small animal is squishing my insides." She rocked on her feet uncomfortably.

Nord pressed his lips together. "I wish I could say we're done, but we still need to get you some shoes and a few other necessities."

Lina groaned.

"How about we check out that chocolate shop next door first?"

Her curiosity was piqued. "That might be agreeable."

"Might be?"

"It'll have to be pretty damn good to make up for the pain and suffering you just subjected me to. Tell me the truth, is this shopping trip really just a weird human hazing ritual in disguise?"

Nord snickered. "Not an intentional one."

"Mmhmm. Right. Totally buying that. Can't help but notice you're not jumping up and down at the chance to try things on."

"It's a woman's clothing store."

She narrowed her eyes playfully. "How convenient for you."

He shook his head, laughter sparkling in his eyes as he led her to the counter where the woman had taken the items she selected. Nord helped her remove the tags from the clothes she was still wearing.

While they waited for the saleswoman to finish ringing them up, Lina turned to Nord and said, "Fair warning, if this chocolate thing falls through, I'm demanding payback."

"Is that so?" he asked, handing the woman a stack of bills.

"Yup."

"Dare I ask what you have in mind?"

"Only seems fitting that you have to play the real-life doll for a while."

Nord smirked. "Never gonna happen."

"You really that confident in your peace offering?"

"Just trust me."

―――――

LINA STEPPED OUT OF THE CONFECTION STORE, HER EYES HALF-closed in delight as she took another bite of her chocolate-raspberry cupcake. Because of her fascination, she almost missed the pins and needles feeling that tickled over her nape.

Nord studied her with interest, the flecks in his eyes seeming to shine.

"Good?" he asked.

"Oh yes," she moaned around a mouthful. "You were right. Chocolate is officially at the top of the list."

He smiled. "Glad you like it."

He led her to their next stop as she ate. Lifting a hand, she rubbed at the tiny hairs standing on end, no longer able to ignore the tingling sensation crawling up her neck. This time, she was able to associate the sensation to a feeling, and she didn't like it. She felt watched. Her stomach gave a nervous flutter, and she looked around. People were everywhere. Maybe, after being a ghost for so long, being seen by so many people was getting to her?

Nord noted her discomfort.

"Something wrong?"

Lina's frowned deepened, not sure how to explain what was going on.

"Yeah, just tired I guess."

He looked at her for a beat before nodding. "We're almost done. First, we need to get you a phone," he said, pointing to a small electronics shop. "In you go."

She wanted to tell him that she didn't need one. Who was she supposed to call? But the sudden desire to get off of the street surpassed the need to argue. She followed close behind him, accidentally stepping on his heel in her haste to get inside.

"Sorry," she said, wincing on his behalf. He gave her a curious look but didn't comment on her odd behavior.

Nord explained what he was looking for to a salesman, while she pretended to look at the shop's offerings in the display window. She scanned the faces in the street. Maybe that tingle meant someone she knew was nearby. Or maybe it was a warning. Her pulse increased, and she half-expected to see a pair of pale gray eyes out there. But that was crazy.

Right?

"We're all set," Nord said, brushing her arm a few minutes later.

She almost flew out of her skin at the brief contact, and he frowned.

"Everything okay? You've been jumpy ever since we came out of the chocolate shop."

She was about to tell him, the words on her lips, when the sensation vanished. Feeling foolish, she let out a little laugh and shook her head.

"Just still getting used to this whole having a body thing." She waved her arms around. "It's a lot to process."

"I'll bet," he said, sympathy flashing in his eyes. "We have one more stop to make before heading back to the penthouse. Think you can manage?"

"Yeah, no problem."

"Come on," he said, his hand resting on her lower back as he escorted her outside.

This time, the pins and needles feeling didn't return.

———

THEIR FINAL STOP OF THE DAY WAS A LITTLE BOUTIQUE A FEW blocks away. Lina stood outside, eyeing a pair of heels with more than a little longing.

"Guess we're getting those ones, huh?" Nord asked, coming to stand beside her.

"No," she said. "You've already been more than generous."

Nord shrugged. "So?"

"I cannot even begin to repay you for all of this," she said with exasperation, gesturing to the colorful bags he was already holding.

"You need clothes. I can provide them. What's the problem?"

Lina sighed. "A pair of stilettos are hardly a necessity," she said, her eyes darting back to the red, peep-toe darlings in the window.

Nord studied her, his lips pulling down in a small frown. "Your words say one thing, but your face says another. Come on, let's go."

"No, Nord . . . wait," she called after him, but he was already pulling the door open for her and he was wearing the same determined face he'd had at every other stop.

Shopping had turned out to be a battle of wills she couldn't win. Even if losing felt a whole lot like winning.

Shaking her head, Lina walked inside.

"Hello?" a saleswoman called, stepping out of the back.

Her steps faltered as her gaze landed on Nord, and her painted lips fell into a stunned 'o.'

"Can I help you?" she asked.

"Hi there," Lina interrupted. *Back off, lady, I have dibs.* "I was wondering if you had these in a size eight?" she added, holding out the red heels.

The woman blinked, coming out of her daze, and turned to Lina with her polite, insincere smile back in place. But as her eyes lifted from the shoes to Lina's face, her smile fractured.

A deathly white blanketed her face, and her body trembled as her eyes grew round.

"Ma'am, are you all right?" Lina asked, setting the shoes down and stepping forward to help.

The woman flinched violently away from Lina. She was shaking, her breath barely more than shallow gasps. "No. No, this . . . this can't be," she said, shaking her head.

"Ma'am?" Lina tried again, ready to catch the woman if she collapsed.

"You shouldn't be here. You *can't* be here."

Lina froze.

"Why the hell not?" Nord demanded, his voice sounding like the first dangerous roll of thunder before a storm.

"B-b-because she's . . . she's dead."

CHAPTER FOUR

Nord

Bags spilled onto the floor as Nord surged forward, grasping the stuttering woman by the neck and jerking her just hard enough to grab her attention.

"You will tell me what you know," he demanded in a savage whisper.

The woman's eyes began to bulge, her hands curling around his much larger one, scratching pathetically. He wasn't holding her nearly tight enough to cut off her breath, not even hard enough to mark her. Lost as she was to her fear, however, the woman—Rachel, according to the silver name tag on her blazer—didn't realize that. Which had been the point. Right now, the scenarios she was picturing were far worse than anything Nord planned to do to her.

People always underestimated the power of illusion. A man his size, with a snarl twisting his lips and the promise of a painful and bloody death burning in his eyes? That was more than enough to send a dozen men to their knees, pleas for their lives falling from their mouths faster than water surging through a dam.

It was the unknown people truly feared. The implied threat, the danger simmering under a thin veil of restraint. It caused the mind to play all sorts of tricks on itself. For that reason, the mind was his favorite battlefield.

When it came to psychological warfare, Nord was a master. He'd lost count of how many battles he'd won, without ever spilling a drop of blood. He was no stranger to bloodshed, not by a longshot, but every warrior had a weapon they preferred. It just so happened that *he* was the weapon, forged by his enemies' nightmares and baptized by their tears.

"I-I . . ." Rachel gasped. "You don't know what you're asking."

Nord drew on his power, letting it infuse his voice. "How do you know her?" he demanded, tilting his head back to gesture at Lina.

Rachel was shaking so badly she was struggling to remain upright. If not for his hand holding her in place, she would have collapsed at his feet.

"I-I can't," she tried again, tears splashing down her cheeks.

"Tell me," he practically purred, but this was no domesticated, contented sound. It was a feral warning—a blade wrapped in velvet, although its edge was already piercing the skin.

Blood vessels burst in Rachel's eyes as her face turned a mottled red.

"Nord," Lina called from behind him.

He ignored her.

"Don't make me ask again."

Rachel let out a terrified little squeak. "M-mo-mo—"

That was all she managed before she started choking, her words cut off by a wet, burbling cough.

"Nord!" Lina cried as blood sprayed out of Rachel's mouth and all over his chest.

Her eyes rolled back, and her knees sagged, Nord officially supporting all of her weight as she started to convulse. Blood and spittle flew from her mouth, her body contorting wildly as Nord helped lower her to the floor, suspicion taking root within him.

"Is she going to be okay?" Lina asked softly, not even a second before a final agonized scream rent the air.

"No," he replied, matching Lina's tone. "But at least she's not suffering anymore."

Nord knelt down beside her now still body, his eyes glowing a blinding azure as he unleashed more of his power. The store transformed under his gaze, the colors blurring until all that was left were the pulsing, golden threads that existed inside all living things. Already Rachel's were fading as her life force drained out of her.

"What are you doing?" Lina asked.

"Searching for signs of magical foul play. That was no natural death."

"Is it safe? To touch her, I mean. If it was magic that did this to her, can it be transferred?"

Nord glanced over his shoulder, his chest growing tight at the brilliant glow that was Lina. "No, whatever did this to her was specifically triggered. But you don't have to worry, no touching required," he said with a forced smile before returning to his investigation.

"And you'll be able to tell? Just by looking?"

"All magic leaves a trace. You just have to know how to search for it," he replied as he scanned the body.

It didn't take long to find what he was looking for.

Just inside of her mouth, a dull lavender smudge stood out against the woman's waning luminescence. He zeroed in on the spot, just barely making out a few loops and swirls, the edges of which were already starting to blur. It was almost reminiscent of a calligraphy character, although not any letter he recognized. Still, it was as damning as a fingerprint at a crime scene.

With it, he and Finley might be able to dig up information in the Brotherhood's archives about who was behind this. Not that he'd mention it to Lina until he knew something concrete. No need to get her hopes up without good reason.

Nord let go of his power and pushed to his feet.

"Well?"

"She was cursed."

"Cursed?" Lina asked, her sapphire-ringed eyes going wide. "Can you tell how or by who?"

"Nothing that specific for now," Nord said. "Someone went a long way to ensure that she'd never be able to speak about what she knew."

Lina glanced from him to the prone body on the floor, a visible shudder working its way down her slender frame. "This is all my fault. That woman is dead because of me."

"No, Lina," Nord moved, wrapping his arms around her and shielding her from the body. "The blame lies with whoever cursed her."

"But seeing me alive when I should be very much dead is what set off whatever that was."

Nord frowned. What were the fucking odds that the first time she leaves the house they ran into someone that recognized her?

"No, my pressing her to share what she knew triggered the curse. Your presence surprised her, but it wasn't until I pushed for information that true harm was caused. If there's any fault here, it is mine."

"You were just trying to protect me," she protested, her words muffled as she spoke into his chest.

Nord fought the urge to brush his lips over the top of her head. *She could belong to another*, he reminded himself. He'd been selfish last night, touching and kissing her as if she was his, but clarity came with the dawn.

Lina didn't remember her life before the ball, which meant that there could be someone out there, mourning her. So even though everything in him raged against it, he would keep his distance. He'd sworn to protect her, and he would, even from himself. He would not let them go down a path that she may eventually regret. Not until they knew for sure that she was free.

Nord sighed and let her go, taking a careful step back. "We should call Finley. He'll want to see this for himself."

"What are we going to do in the meantime? I mean, anyone walking by could see her."

Nord frowned, debating for a second, before using his power once more and casting a glamour over the front of the store, making it look like an extension of the bricked-up building on the left.

"You couldn't just flip the sign over?" Lina asked with a little laugh.

"Wouldn't do much to keep people from looking in the window."

"I suppose not."

Nord pulled out the cell phone Finley had gifted him and punched a button. The phone rang once before his friend picked up.

"Everything okay?"

"There's been a situation."

"On my way."

"Do you need the—" Nord started, but Finley had already hung up. "He's on his way," Nord said, pocketing the phone once more.

Lina was busy shoving clothes back into the bags he'd dropped. He watched her for a stolen moment, trying hard not to notice the curve of her ass in her new jeans. Biting back a growl, he shifted his eyes to her face. It had a determined set to it, one he recognized because he'd worn it so often himself. In the days immediately after his father had died, Nord focused on a series of small tasks, throwing himself into the mundane as a way of regaining control in a world that was spiraling out of it.

He couldn't blame her. Life as she'd known it had been upended entirely over the course of a single day. All things considered, she was holding up quite well, seemingly rolling with the punches, but he'd seen the truth in her eyes. She may have been the ghost, but she was the one that was haunted.

Haunted by a past she couldn't remember.

Needing to offer her some sliver of comfort, Nord found himself saying, "We did learn a couple things from our friend Rachel here."

"We did?" she asked, peeking up at him. Her hair had fallen and was spilling over her back and shoulders in golden waves.

His fingers itched to run through the silken strands. To tangle themselves in the thick locks and tug her head back so he could— Nord swallowed and forced himself to look away. Keeping his distance from her was going to take more effort than he'd anticipated.

Nord gestured to the body, using it to distract from the fact that he couldn't meet her gaze. "She recognized you, which means your body definitely belongs to you and you're from the area."

Lina was silent for so long that he risked another glance at her. She was standing again, staring at herself in the mirror with her brows furrowed. A note of wonder filled her voice as she replied, "I guess it does."

"Perhaps Fin's suggestion of looking through pictures has merit. Maybe there are some of you floating around somewhere."

Turning away from her reflection, she nodded. "It's something."

Then glancing at the illusion he'd cast, she asked, "So what else can you do?"

"What do you mean?"

"Well, your eyes went all glowy, and you were able to tell that someone had used magic on that woman. And you managed to turn this window into a brick wall—"

"It only appears that way. It's just an illusion."

"An illusion," she repeated.

Nord nodded. "Guardians are gifted with the ability to see the strands of nature, but we can also manipulate them."

"You lost me," Lina admitted with a soft smile.

"When my eyes go 'glowy,' that's me using my power to find the strands that are woven into the fabric of the world. When I cast an illusion, I am modifying those strands, making them appear to be something else or changing their true nature entirely. The most talented Guardians can even tie two separate places together and create a portal between them."

"That's . . ." she trailed off, searching for a word, "incredible. Is that everything?" As soon as the question left her mouth, her cheeks went rosy, as if she was worried she might have offended him.

"Well, those are the main things. We also have some mental abilities, but those are rarer and more nuanced."

"What do you mean?"

Nord debated how much to reveal. "Well, for example, all Guardians have telepathic links that allow us to speak to each other mentally if we're within range."

"That seems convenient."

"It definitely can be, especially when we need to keep conversations private."

"So if Finley had been 'in range' you could have just spoken through your link instead of calling him?"

"Exactly."

"Can you speak in other people's minds? Or just to each other?"

"It depends," Nord said. "Like with any skill, some of us are stronger in certain areas then others. Some Guardians can project their voices to non-Guardians, but not all. As a general rule, we tend to avoid it. Most people consider it an invasion."

"An invasion? Why?"

"People don't like other's playing around inside their heads."

"Talking is hardly playing," Lina protested.

"True, but once you've made a connection to someone's mind, it's not impossible to dig deeper."

Lina mulled that over, her eyes bright with interest. "Will you show me? Some of your magic?"

"Like what?"

She shrugged. "Anything."

Nord glanced around, looking for something he could use. Picking up the heel she'd been eyeing, he drew up just enough power to change the color from red to black.

"Illusion or—"

Before she finished the question, he turned the shoe into a dagger. "Not illusion," he answered, handing it over.

She held the dagger in her hand, her mouth falling open in shock. "That's amazing," she breathed.

"I'm much better with my illusions," he said, feeling the inexplicable need to show off for her. "In fact . . ." he let his words trail off as he turned himself into a perfect replica of her.

"Holy shit," she breathed, her hand outstretched. "You're me."

That was how Finley found them. Twin Linas, one smirking, and the other tracing her fingers down her duplicate's face.

"Am I interrupting something?" he drawled.

Nord let go of his hold on the illusion, not bothering to explain what they'd been doing as he filled his partner in on what had happened.

Finley frowned as he inspected the body, his glowing eyes lingering on the marking in her mouth. "It's already fading. The amount of power required not only to cast a curse of this nature, but to have the evidence of it dissolve . . ." He stood, dropping his power. "It shouldn't be possible."

"Do you recognize it?" Nord asked.

Finley shook his head. "No, and in less than an hour there won't be anything left to trace, which is going to make it damn near impossible to track the caster down."

"Whoever did this knows how to cover their tracks," Nord murmured. "Not just with the curse itself, but by finding a way to make the residual magic dissipate."

"Whoever it is, they've got access to some serious magic," Finley said, his expression grim.

Nord found his eyes traveling to Lina, his lips dipping into a frown. People don't waste this kind of magic on something insignificant. *Who were you and what were you involved in?*

She'd moved off to the side when Finley started his investigation so as to be out of the way. At the moment, she was staring at the shoes lining the walls, but it was clear that she wasn't really seeing them.

As if she could feel his eyes on her, Lina looked over her shoulder and caught him staring.

Nord knew his questions must be reflected in his eyes, but he couldn't make himself look away.

There was something about this woman, more than just sheer beauty, that drew him to her. It was some indiscernible quality that bound them more tightly than he'd been to any person he'd ever known.

Other Guardians had mentioned it could be like that when you found your true purpose. The one you were meant to safeguard. Nord hadn't believed it until he'd witnessed it firsthand. Instead of fearing that kind of bond, he'd craved it for himself. What would it be like, he'd wondered, to find the one person in all the worlds you were created for?

After Lina, he'd hoped that they would be one of the rare few where the bond went deeper than mere duty, but then . . . Nord had always known hope was a dangerous thing.

Once again, it was Finley who pulled him out of his retrospection.

"Oh, Lina. Before I forget. I have something for you," he said, holding out an ID to her. "Happy belated birthday."

"Huh?"

"I had to pick a birthday for you, so I chose October thirty-first.

Seemed appropriate since that's when you officially graced us with your presence. You're twenty-three, in case you were wondering."

Lina grinned. "Any other pertinent details I should know?"

"Let's see. You're finishing your master's degree in Supernatural Criminology. You're an orphan. Your family immigrated to the States from Estonia when you were less than a year old. And you're a registered mage."

Lina blinked at Finley a few times before asking, "How in the world did you come up with all of that?"

"Criminology students are the only ones allowed research access, so that was a given. Without family to speak of, orphan was an obvious choice as well. You have an Eastern European look about you, and Estonia is relatively small, seemed like a safe bet, and with traveling here so young, it explains the lack of accent. As for the mage bit, well . . ." Finley shrugged, "just because we don't exactly know the full extent of your powers, doesn't mean we can't guess what class you belong to."

Nord had to admit, his partner was thorough. It grated though, that Finley had been able to do something for Lina that he couldn't. While it was not a lack of skill inasmuch as a lack of contacts, the knowledge still rankled because of what else it revealed. This was the first time, in centuries, he had to rely on someone else instead of his own ability. It was a humbling experience. One he did not remotely enjoy.

Lina clutched the plastic card in her hand, her smile stretching. "So, does this mean I have access to the archive now?"

Finley shook his head, giving Lina an apologetic half-smile. "Not quite. This was step one. Step two is filing the paperwork, which I'll do as soon as I get back to the office." His eyes swept the floor. "I'll place a call for a cleanup crew. They'll bring the body back to the lab and run some tests, for all the good it will do them. Actually," he paused to glance at his watch, "I should do that now and file my report while the details are still fresh. It might be best if you two aren't here for that part."

Nord and Finley exchanged knowing glances over Lina's head. The last thing they needed was Lina getting put on the Brotherhood's radar before they had a chance to find their own answers.

At Lina's confused look, Finley explained, "There will be no way around giving statements if you're here when the crew arrives. It'd be easier for everyone involved if we avoided that. Not that it would be a problem since your background is now intact, but . . . I'd rather not risk linking your name to something like this so close to filing a request for document access."

"Makes sense," she agreed.

With nothing left for them to do here, Nord started to turn toward the door. "We'll see you back at the house."

Lina eyed the bricked-up glamor with obvious distrust. "I know you *said* it's just an illusion but wouldn't one of your portals be safer, not to mention faster?"

Nord couldn't stop the amused lift of his lips. "A portal will leave a trace, and the whole point of us leaving is not to reveal that we were ever here."

Lina gave the spot where the door once stood another mistrustful glance.

"It's always hard to get your mind to dismiss what your eyes see as truth. I find it easiest when someone else goes first," Nord said.

"I'm not sure my brain is ever going to green light walking into a wall of bricks, but by all means," she muttered, her arm sweeping out to the wall, "after you."

CHAPTER FIVE

Lina

"*She's dead.*"

The words, along with the horror-stricken look on the woman's face as she uttered them, echoed on a loop in her mind.

Being a ghost was all she'd known up until midnight last night. Why then had it sounded so much more damning coming from that saleswoman? And more importantly, how the hell had she known about it in the first place?

Lina absently traced the lines of the tattoo on her forearm while staring unseeingly into the fireplace. Not for the first time, she wished that her memories had been restored along with her body. Then she felt immediate guilt for wanting more when she'd already been given such a massive gift. She couldn't begin to comprehend how or why she'd been given a second chance, she could only double down on her vow not to squander it.

"I'm surprised you're still awake."

Despite the soft rasp of his voice, Lina still gave a little jerk.

"Sorry," Nord said, coming around the couch to stand in front of her. He looked mouthwateringly gorgeous in a pair of loose-fitted joggers and a black Henley that stretched taut over the hard planes of his chest. "I didn't mean to scare you."

"You're fine," she said, giving him an embarrassed smile that had nothing to do with being startled and everything to do with the way her eyes devoured him every time he entered a room. "Just lost in thought."

"You look troubled. Want to talk about it?" he offered, crouching down so that their faces were level.

She had every intention of refusing, but when she opened her mouth, the words came pouring out unbidden. "I just can't get her out of my mind. She *knew* me, Nord. Or . . . *of* me at the very least. And now she's dead." Lina's hands fell into her lap with a little plop. "And the worst part is, I'm not sure if I'm upset because someone was willing to kill her to protect their secrets, or because it means I didn't get any answers. What am I supposed to do with that?"

He was silent as he considered her confession, the firelight playing over the sharp angles of his cheek and nose, giving him the appearance of some sort of ancient, sun-kissed warrior. His head tilted slightly to the right as his eyes searched her face.

"Are you expecting me to be repulsed by your admission? Because if you're looking for judgment, you'll find none here."

Lina's brows puckered, even as relief spread through her at his easy acceptance. "It's hardly a flattering thing to admit."

He shook his head slightly, looking perplexed. "Lina, all that makes you is normal. I'd be more shocked if you weren't disappointed that you lost such a lead."

"It seems somewhat selfish to be disappointed that another woman *dying* means that I was unable to question her."

"Perhaps," he said, his eyes never straying from hers. "Or, it just makes you honest for admitting it. We can't help our nature, Lina. All we can do is fight against it until we eventually let it win."

"So, you're saying I'm selfish by nature?" she asked, raising a brow, hoping the slight lift of her lips conveyed that she was teasing.

"Show me a creature that isn't. It's how we're hardwired to survive. In fact, it might be one of the basest of any living creature's instincts."

"One of?"

"The need to eat, sleep, f—" Nord's eyes briefly dipped to Lina's lips at her soft inhale before his lips quirked and he self-edited, "reproduce."

She tried hard to ignore the heat rolling through her body as she replied, "Yeah, but those are human needs. You can accomplish any of them without being selfish."

"Not always."

There was something about the flat tone his voice had taken that had her eyes sharpening. "You're speaking from experience."

He didn't admit it outright, but his eyes shifted to look somewhere over her shoulder as he replied, "When you haven't eaten in days and it's between you and a stranger getting a meal that night, no one is choosing the stranger. Especially not if there are others counting on you to bring them something to fill their bellies."

Nord's eyes had gone hard and distant as he spoke, matching the stripped tone of his voice.

The thought of him being in such a position had her stomach twisted in knots. Without even intending to, she'd ended up dredging up a piece of his past. A piece that cut deep and carved into other parts of him that never fully healed. In his attempt to comfort her, he freely gave her a part of himself not caring that he had to stare into a painful void within himself to do so. And he offered it, not like the gift that it was, but like something to be thrown away. As if this small offering had no value, when to her, because it was a piece of him, it meant everything.

"Nord," she whispered, her hand landing on his leg with all the frazzled grace of a bird not sure whether its new perch would support its weight.

For a second, he didn't react to the slight contact at all. He could have been carved from granite, his muscles unyielding to her touch. But then she saw it. The spark of flame burning hot in the back of his frozen eyes. It was like watching that first crack in the ice, before it splintered and fell away.

There was nothing distant about his gaze when his eyes returned to hers.

Time froze as Nord seemed to memorize her with the intensity of his stare. Lina wasn't sure whether or not she remembered to breathe as she waited for him to act on the blatant hunger she found there. She wanted to throw her arms around his neck and climb into his lap, feeling the velvety scrape of his beard against her skin as they fell into a tangle of limbs in front of the fireplace. Finally following through on what began at The Monster Ball and exploring what so obviously existed between them.

Before her body could act on the desire-fueled wishes filling her mind, his voice broke through the lustful fog.

"*Kærasta*," he whispered, the endearment tortured as he captured her wrist and turned her hand over, cradling it between his. "I cannot keep my promise when you look at me like that."

She was too busy relishing the feeling of his skin sliding against hers to process what he was saying. It was such a little thing, the touch of two hands, but for her—someone who existed without the ability to touch at all—it was something to be savored.

"Hmm?" she murmured, staring at the place their hands were joined.

He began to curl her fingers inward, gently placing her hand back in her lap, before he released her. Lina felt the loss of his heat immediately. Her brows furrowed, and her eyes darted back up to his face, seeking an explanation as his earlier words finally penetrated.

"What promise?"

"To protect you."

"Not that again," she groaned, shaking her head slightly. "What do you think you're protecting me from?"

Instead of answering, Nord lifted a hand and brushed his knuckles across her cheek. Her eyelids grew heavy with the need to close and lean into the tender caress, but something was off. Even though he was touching her, Lina could feel him pulling away. Already the fire in his eyes was little more than a dull glow.

Panic began to erode the desire inside of her. Somehow, just when she thought they were getting somewhere, she'd only succeeded in pushing him further away.

"We already talked about this, Lina. Your heart could belong to another," he whispered. "I cannot stake claim to something that is not rightfully mine."

Denial sprung forth, vehement and fierce. "No, *you* talked about it. If I recall correctly, you didn't let me say anything on the matter. If you had, I would have told you that I couldn't possibly feel everything I feel when I'm with you if I'd already given my heart to someone else."

His expression softened, but only momentarily before it was closed off once more. "You cannot know that, Lina. Not until you regain your memories. Until then . . ." he trailed off, the rise and fall of his chest the only hint as to how much his next words cost him, "we cannot be together."

"No," she said with a burst of hysterical laughter. "That's complete bullsh—"

He stopped her with a press of his finger against her lips. "I cannot be the one who causes you even a second of regret. It's not right or honorable to make you carry that burden when I can protect you from ever having to."

Irritation ignited, and she slapped his hand away, the clinking of his rings providing subtle emphasis to her indignation. "I've overheard my fair share of stupid excuses in my time, Nord, but I'm pretty sure that one tops the list. I don't want you to be *honorable*," she spat. "I just want you to be mine."

The slight tightening around his eyes was the only outward reaction he gave in response. He blew out a breath and stood, putting space between them. When he spoke next, his hands were on his hips and his head was tilted down toward the dancing flames. "Lina, I'm yours in every way that matters."

In any other situation, the words would have made her swoon, but the way he said them, devoid of any trace of emotion, it made her feel like she'd just been robbed of something precious. Irritation moved swiftly to anger, and she pushed to her feet and moved to stand in front of him, forcing him to face her. If he was going to do this, if he was going to insist on breaking her heart, he was damn well going to look her in the eye while he did.

"Except for the way that I want." She would have sworn she saw the flicker of apology in his eyes, and she couldn't keep herself from pressing. "You just got done telling me that we're born to be selfish. So *be* selfish. Why fight it?"

"Because I made a vow. I *will* protect you, Lina. Even from yourself."

She wanted to roll her eyes; the only thing that stopped her was how obvious it was that he wholeheartedly believed what he was saying. *Well, screw that.* All he was doing was wasting precious time they could have together. He thought he got to make that decision for her.

No.

No way. Not after how long she'd waited for her own chance at happiness.

"You may have made a vow, but I didn't, so let me remedy that right now," she said, frustration and desperation making her voice tremble.

His expression turned wary as he waited for her to continue.

"You told me we can only fight against ourselves for so long until we give in. So you build your walls and you fight against this all you want. But while you do, I'm going to wage my own battle, and I'm not about to play fair. Not after how long I waited for the chance."

The crackle of the fire and her ragged breaths were the only sounds as she dared him to say something. Seconds stretched as he stared at her, his face unreadable.

Lina felt something within her give and crack as she waited. A little of her bravado began to wilt the longer he went without responding, but she fought hard to keep all of that from her face. If he could do it, so could she.

"I can see your mind is made up. I guess all I can do is offer you a final warning." His voice was soft enough to be mistaken for tender, though his words were anything but. "Lina, when it comes to battles, I'm an expert. You're going to lose."

Her eyes narrowed. Let him underestimate her. It would only make her job easier. "I wouldn't be so sure about that."

"I've spent my whole life waging war."

Lina shrugged. "Maybe you have, but never against me."

His eyes thawed momentarily. "True."

She held her hand out, and he glanced at it before giving her a confused look. "You want to shake hands?"

"Isn't it customary to shake hands at the start of a battle?" she asked, recalling the sporting matches one of her old roommates used to watch.

His lips lifted slightly. "In a war? No . . . not usually. I've seen duels begin with a man slapping another in the face with his glove, but never a handshake."

Lina frowned. "Maybe I'm misremembering, but I'm certain I've seen opponents shaking hands as a sign of respect."

A chuckle escaped as Nord shook his head. "That happens at the end."

"Oh," she murmured, feeling foolish as she started to drop her arm.

Nord's hand caught hers, and he gave her a tight squeeze. "Good luck to you, Lina."

"And to you as well." Something that felt a lot like hope blossomed in her chest. "May the best woman win."

His hand tightened around hers before he dropped it. She could feel his eyes tracking her movements as she left the room, and even though she knew she shouldn't, she paused before she stepped into the hall and glanced back over her shoulder.

Nord had both hands braced on the mantle; his head bowed. But it wasn't until his whispered, "Fuck me," that Lina allowed herself a smile.

The battle may only just be beginning, but she could already tell, victory was going to be sweet.

CHAPTER SIX

Lina

P ain. So much pain.

That was the first thought that came to her when she opened her eyes. Her head throbbed and invisible knives stabbed her eyes, causing her to squint and try to shield them. The instinctive motion was halted, and panic tightened in her chest.

She couldn't move.

A furtive glance down confirmed that her arms were lashed to a chair with heavy chains. Her vision was blurred, objects appearing more as flashes of color and suggestions of shapes, but there was no mistaking the silver links that sat heavy against her frozen flesh.

She was shivering. Water dripping in icy rivers down her face and neck. Pain exploded behind her eyes as she tried to lift her aching head.

Maybe that wasn't water.

The only sources of light came from the flashes of lightning outside and from the flicker of a dozen candles laid out on the floor. At least, she assumed they were candles based on the way the golden light flickered and danced with the shadows.

Harsh whispers came from somewhere behind her. She tried to cry out, call for help. Her voice came out as a low, tortured moan.

Her thoughts were as sluggish as her movements.

The whispers fell silent, replaced by the scrape of boots over the floor.

Crack.

Her head flew sideways, her cheek smashing into the wood of her chair before the fact that she'd just been hit even registered.

Blood pooled in her mouth, dribbling down her chin as her heart began to pound.

A hand fisted in her hair, pulling her head up and back.

A grunt of pain escaped behind her lips.

"Did I tell you you could speak?" a voice asked from beside her.

She whimpered.

There was a rustle of cloth, and then the heat of someone else's breath washed over her cheek.

"I'm growing impatient. I've been waiting for this day for what feels like my entire life." A hand trailed down the side of her face in a macabre imitation of a caress. "Just a little bit longer now and then you won't be my problem anymore. In fact, you won't be anyone's problem."

LINA SAT UPRIGHT, HER BREATH COMING TO HER IN HARSH GASPS. There were no screams this time, her horror so absolute it'd stolen her voice. She was shaking hard, her muscles clenched so tightly that she knew she'd feel the ache of it for a good while after.

It was a long time before her heart began to slow and she could draw a full breath.

She almost wished she had screamed. That Nord had come running, ready to fend off the monsters that stalked her in her dreams. Somehow waking up alone in the darkness only made the nightmare more sinister.

It had felt so real.

The chains. The pain. That voice—at least those damn gray eyes hadn't tormented her this time.

Wait. That voice.

She *knew* that voice.

Her blood turned to ice, and she scrambled to her feet as bone-deep knowing consumed her.

That wasn't a normal dream.

It was a memory. *Her* memory.

Of the night she died.

CHAPTER SEVEN

Nord

Lina flew into the kitchen, beelining straight for Nord. He let out a soft grunt as she flung herself into him, ducking her head against his chest and wrapping her arms tightly around him.

"What's wrong?" he asked, not hesitating as he curled his arms protectively around her shaking body.

"Just . . . just hold me for a minute, okay?" she panted hoarsely.

The unmistakable note of fear in her voice had him going from merely protective to battle ready in an instant. He pulled back slightly, using a finger to lift her chin. "What happened?"

It was not a question so much as a demand.

Lina blinked up at him, her eyes a storm of emotions. He'd expected tears given how obviously upset she was, but her eyes were dry. She was terrified, but she was fighting it. His little ghost was a warrior in her own right.

"Lina," he pressed when she didn't immediately answer.

"I had another dream," she said finally.

Nord bit back a growl. He could fight anything . . . except night-mares. Give him an opponent he could touch, and he would end them. But what match was he to a phantom of her mind? He tried to keep his expression free of his frustration, but by the way Lina's eyes dipped, he must not have been entirely successful.

"Kærasta, what aren't you telling me?"

Her eyes softened at the endearment, and Nord internally scolded himself. He hadn't meant to slip, not last night and not now, but when faced with her fear he couldn't seem to help himself. All he wanted to do was protect her.

"I don't think it was a dream. Well, *just* a dream," she corrected.

Nord could feel his eyebrows dropping low as he frowned. "A dream but not a dream?" And then his body stiffened as what she was trying to say became clear. "A memory?" he guessed.

She swallowed and nodded. "Of the night I was murdered."

"Tell me everything," he said, barely recognizing the guttural sound as his voice.

Lina began recounting the details as best she could. As she spoke, Nord felt a long-banked anger begin to coil and burn within him. Red tinged his vision and his body tensed, bracing for attack. She might be speaking of an event that had happened years ago, but to him it was unfolding in the present. Hearing that the one he was sworn to protect had been captured and tortured . . . it was almost more than he could bear.

Worse, the monster that had killed his charge continued to torment her, and there was nothing he could do about it.

Nord seethed. The need to pummel something overtaking reason. He needed to unleash his fury. Now.

"Meet me in the gym." Nord sent the order to Finley along the telepathic link they shared as Guardians. Finley could handle the side effects of his berserker nature. Lina couldn't.

Finley's response was immediate, as Nord expected since his partner had known this was a possibility given his history. *"On my way."*

His anger swelled now that battle was imminent, even as a throb of relief pulsed through the rage. It had been ages since he'd been lost to the bloodlust, and longer still since it had swallowed him completely. His control had been absolute for so long, he hadn't been prepared. His mistake. He should have known Lina's presence changed everything.

He let go of her, noting the wounded expression she wore. Any other time, he could have explained, but as lost as he was, her hurt only fueled his need for blood.

"Nord?" she asked as he pulled away and started for the door.

He paused long enough to look back at her, not sure what she was reading in his expression, but knowing by the slight nod she gave him that she'd reached some sort of understanding.

He'd have to explain eventually. She deserved an explanation, but until he drew blood, he wouldn't be able to give her anything. Turning from her, he made his way to the training room, a storm of fury and vengeance begging to be unleashed.

Finley was waiting for him when he burst into the room. Nord was on him before he could open his mouth. Blood sprayed over Nord's fist as it slammed into the other man's face, the crack of bones making the monster that had taken over howl with pleasure.

Finley wiped his mouth, smearing blood across his face. "What crawled up your ass?"

Nord threw two more punches, both of which Finley dodged, prepared now.

"All right, caveman, we'll talk afterward."

Nord grunted, his only warning before raining down a flurry of blows that were impossible for the human eye to track. Finley's Guardian abilities were the only thing that kept the fight fair. Had he been anyone else, he might have died from the first blow alone.

Time held no meaning as the bottomless wrath coursed through Nord. It wouldn't ease up until he'd defeated his enemy, but sparring with Fin allowed him to dull the edge enough that he'd be able to reassert his control. Already he could feel some of the need abating.

Sweat poured down his face, and his shirt clung to his torso. He'd managed to knock Finley to the floor, but his partner was back on his feet almost immediately.

He spat more blood on the floor. "That all you got, mate?"

Nord knew there was nothing human about the smile he aimed Finley's way. "Best not to taunt me right now, Brother."

"Ah, I don't know about that. You're talking again, which means you're past the worst of it. You're not as scary as you think."

The monster reared its head once more, and Nord threw a punch that broke at least two of Finley's ribs.

His partner dropped to his knees, chest heaving as he cradled his torso with one arm. His smirk was absent when he tilted his head up and said, "All right, point taken."

The submission, intentional or not, was enough to soothe Nord's beast. The haze of red cleared, and the endless rage retreated. Nord held out a hand to help Finley stand.

He eyed it warily before accepting. "Just like that?" he asked.

Nord nodded. "Sometimes."

Finley limped over to the wall where his bottle of water and a towel waited. "And other times?"

Memories of corpse-strewn battlefields and hands covered with blood and viscera filled Nord's mind. Some of that must have shown on his face because Finley pressed his lips together and shook his head.

"Never mind," he said. "I don't want to know."

Nord would have laughed, but nothing was funny about how quickly the bloodlust had taken over. Part of the reason he preferred mental games to physical ones was the unpredictability of his inner beast. Equal parts asset and liability, there was no knowing what it would take to break through the bloodlust's hold. Believed by his people to be a gift from the gods, granted to their warriors as a way to ensure victory in battle, its relentless drive would persist through a body's natural limitations. Add to that his Guardian's strength and immortality, and Nord became an unstoppable force.

He was lucky Finley had been here.

There was no telling what would have happened if he hadn't found an outlet.

Nord touched his lip, wincing slightly at the sting of pain. "You held your own."

Finley guzzled some of his water and laughed. "Is that a compliment?"

He shrugged. "I can't remember the last time someone managed to draw my blood."

Finley pressed his lips together and nodded. "Good. Least I can do is make the fucker that broke my ribs bleed a little."

Nord ran a hand through his sweat-matted hair. "Sorry about that."

Finley waved a hand. "Don't be. I knew what I was getting into when I stepped foot in here."

"Did you?" Nord asked, finding it hard to believe anyone who hadn't seen a berserker in the midst of his frenzy could be remotely prepared for the experience.

"Okay, maybe not entirely, but enough to know injuries were part of the bargain." He made to remove his bloodstained shirt, and paused halfway, breathing hard.

"Are you going to be okay?"

"Feels like they cracked in multiple places. I'd heal it myself, but it's a hard spot to get a good view of."

"Want me to take a look?"

Finley shook his head. "Probably better to leave it to the experts. We've got some healers at the bureau. I'll make a stop before heading into the office this morning. What about you? Need me to take care of that ugly mug?"

"No," he said, his guilt at hurting his friend not allowing him to accept the offer. "I'll deal with it."

He wished there were a way to get through the bloodlust that didn't insist on causing harm, at least to allies. But it was as futile a wish as resenting the air his lungs needed to breathe. It simply was.

"Suit yourself, but clean up at the very least," Finley said as he slowly made his way to the showers at the back of their gym. "You don't want her to see you like this."

Nord nodded, not needing a mirror to know that he was covered in Finley's blood. He'd reveled in each hot splash of it against his skin as he'd fought through the rage.

"Oh," he added, "once you're sorted, let her know that her clearance came through. I'd do it, but she'll have questions if she catches me before I see the healers. I'm guessing you'd rather not have to answer those just yet . . ." he trailed off and gave Nord a half-grin. "Anyway, you can bring her down when you're both ready."

"Fin," Nord called, when his friend was almost out of the main room.

"Yeah?"

"Thank you."

Finley grinned. "Anytime, mate. But just know, it'll be me beating your ass to the ground next time. I was taking it easy on you."

Nord tamped down hard on the primal urge that twisted up, ready to answer the challenge. If Finley noticed, he didn't acknowledge it, giving a parting wave as he exited.

Instead of following Finley to the showers, Nord turned to the punching bag hanging in the corner. The fury that had abated at Finley's submission had started to simmer again at his parting words. Knowing he wasn't nearly in control enough to risk seeing Lina yet, Nord began wailing on the bag.

Four broken bags later, he finally deemed himself ready.

CHAPTER EIGHT

Lina

Lina gave Nord's busted knuckles a curious glance as he held the door open to a nondescript building located about thirty minutes away from the penthouse.

After all but running out on her that morning, he'd come back almost three hours later, freshly showered and covered in a series of nasty bruises. His bottom lip was swollen and split, looking somehow more kissable despite it. His only explanation for his battered state was a muttered, "Sparring practice."

She'd lifted her brows, but otherwise managed to keep the barrage of questions she had from spewing forth.

His relief at that was apparent, which was enough for her.

For now.

She wasn't about to assume she understood what had happened back in the kitchen, but she trusted Nord. He would fill her in when he was ready.

As she moved through the open door, her stomach gave a little flutter when his hand came to rest protectively on her lower back. If not for the force of his hand propelling her forward, Lina would have stopped dead as soon as she stepped inside. The exterior of the building had not, in any way, prepared her for what lay within. Perhaps that was the point.

Two glass elevators flanked either side of a circular reception desk and soared a dizzying distance upward. What had seemed to be two to three floors outside, was easily over twenty—and that was just what she could count. Their footsteps were muffled by a plush burgundy carpet with an elongated silver emblem. It was hard to decipher with Nord's pace, but Lina craned her neck backward and was just able to make out the interlocking B O G that stood for Brotherhood of Guardians hidden within.

People rushed past on either side of them, some talking together in hushed voices, others snapping out harried orders.

"Listen, I don't care what you have to do, don't let that vamp out of your sight. No telling how long it'll be before he surfaces again," one Brother said.

Lina did a double take as he headed straight for the wall.

"Portals," Nord reminded her as they neared the receptionist.

Lina let out a breath she hadn't realized she was holding when the man vanished through the wall. If the framed glyph she'd initially mistaken as a piece of abstract art was any indication, there were six portals in total. One glyph placed just above each, likely to identify them, she guessed.

"Where do they go?" she whispered.

"These six are connected to our international offices."

"Oh," she murmured, somewhat disappointed.

Nord must have caught something in the word because he raised a brow. "Expecting a more exotic answer?"

Heat crept into her cheeks. That was exactly what she'd been expecting, although the reality made far more sense. "Maybe."

His answering smile was gone as quickly as it appeared. "We keep those portals upstairs."

There was no chance for her to reply as the receptionist looked up and gave Nord an appreciative once-over that had Lina bristling.

The woman's smile stretched, obviously pleased with what she was seeing. In a move so smooth it was clearly practiced, she leaned forward with her hands clasped loosely on the desk. It would have been a casual pose, if not for the fact that it caused her breasts to practically spill out of her shirt.

Lina barely resisted rolling her eyes. She'd quickly grown used to women fawning over Nord, it'd happened often enough during their outing the other day; and honestly, she couldn't blame them, but something about the way this woman was undressing him with her eyes had Lina wanting to punch someone. Preferably her.

"Welcome, Mr. Andersson. What can I do for you today?"

Her attention snagged on the less than subtle emphasis of the question and the calculated look in the redhead's eyes. For his part, Nord seemed utterly immune to the woman's obvious come on, but Lina was over it.

Forcing the woman to acknowledge her presence, Lina took an instinctive step into Nord, extinguishing the space between their bodies. His fingers flexed against the silk of her shirt before his hand slid comfortingly around to rest on her hip, anchoring her body to his. She couldn't help the satisfied curl of her lips as the woman finally looked her way.

The receptionist lost her smile, her eyes slithering over Lina, before dismissing her entirely.

Bitch.

"Ms. Jones needs to sign in. We're here to access the archive. Oh, and Susan, can you please inform O'Connor we're here?"

With a face like she'd bitten into a lemon, Susan shoved a clipboard toward Lina and then reached for the phone.

While she was murmuring into the receiver, Lina scrawled her name on the sheet and then looked up at Nord. "Andersson? Why do I get the feeling that's not your real name?"

"Because it isn't, no more than you're really Lina Jones."

"Ah, but see, according to this fancy piece of plastic Finley gave me, that *is* my real name."

His lips twitched. "Fair point."

Her eyebrows puckered. "Why the anonymity?" She dropped her voice and cast her eyes around. "Is it a spy thing?"

Nord stared at her for a second before tipping his head back and laughing. The sound rolled around her, warming her from the inside out.

"No, Lina. It's not a spy thing. I left my birth name behind long ago. When it came time for a new one, I let another pick it out because I couldn't be bothered to care. I've been Nord Andersson ever since, which is basically the equivalent of John Smith for as generic as it is, and that suits me just fine."

There was a story there. One she was desperate to hear, although intuition warned her it was not a happy one. As he'd gone on explaining, his eyes had gone distant and his jaw had tensed, ever so slightly. Lina sighed. Nord had a past she wanted to learn almost as badly as she wanted her own, but she wouldn't dig.

Instead, she kept her tone light. "I'd hardly say Nord is generic."

He turned to face her more fully and raised a brow. "It couldn't be *more* generic."

"How do you figure? How many people named Nord do you think are walking around out there?"

"I was named for the general direction I came from—North. Moreover, it was a term used to describe all people that came from that area. My name essentially means 'man from the North.' Now tell me, how is that not generic?"

"Okay, maybe back in the Dark Ages or something, but not now. You'd have to be almost a thousand years old for that to be true." Laughter was bubbling up, suffusing her voice with mirth, but her words triggered something in Nord and his eyes flashed white-hot. "What?" she asked, worried she'd somehow offended him.

He shook his head, looking pained.

"Nord, what did I say?" she insisted, lifting a hand to rest it on the marble cut of his arm and leaning closer.

A muscle fluttered in his jaw, making her think he was fighting the urge to answer.

"Sometimes I get things mixed up," she rambled, hoping her apology would tip the scales. "Like with the handshake. Everything I know to be true; I've learned by living vicariously through others. Snippets of conversations, television shows, books left open on tables—that's all I have to rely on, and most of it is all jumbled up and usually taken out of context. So if I said something wrong, or offended you somehow, please tell me."

Nord's eyes had closed as she spoke, his expression warm when she finished, and they fluttered back open. "Lina," he murmured, his hand lifting to cup her cheek.

"There you two are," Finley called.

Nord jumped away from her, like they'd been caught doing something they shouldn't. Lina resisted the urge to pull his hand back and return it to her face. She wanted to send Finley's ass back from wherever it came from and recapture the moment that had been lost. But mostly she wanted to slap the satisfied smirk off of Susan's face. The receptionist had caught Nord's hasty retreat from Lina and wasn't bothering to hide her glee.

Lina shot her a look that promised retaliation.

Susan's smile froze and then fell away.

Message received.

"What took you so long?" Finley asked, coming up to press a kiss to Lina's cheek. He winced when he looked at Nord. "We should have one of the healers look at that."

"It's nothing," Nord insisted.

"Regardless, it doesn't reflect well for one of the Brothers to walk around looking like he lost a fight."

Nord gave Finley a dark look. "If I recall correctly, *you* were the one that lost the fight."

Lina found that hard to believe since Nord was the one sporting bruises, but Finley surprised her with his chuckling admission.

"That might be true, but I'm still prettier than you. Aren't I, Lina?"

Both men's eyes turned to her, holding her prisoner in their twin stares. Her face prickled with heat as they waited for her assessment.

"Some girls don't like pretty," she finally answered, causing Nord's eyes to smolder and Finley to act like she physically assaulted him.

He clutched his chest dramatically. "You wound me." Then his arms dropped, and he winked at her. "Give me time, love. I bet I could sway you." His hazel eyes twinkled, and a dimple flashed as he gave her a lazy grin.

Looking at him, she had no doubt he was probably right . . . if her heart wasn't already settled on someone else. Her eyes darted to Nord, who was openly scowling. The harsh angles of his face, combined with his split lip, made the expression far more threatening than it had any right to be.

And seeing it filled Lina with hope.

He may say they can't be together, but he didn't want anyone else to have her either.

She filed that information away to explore later.

"So, where's this award-winning archive you spoke so highly of?" she asked, pointedly changing the subject.

Finley's knowing smirk stretched as he gestured to the elevator on the left. "Right this way, madam." He ushered her forward, Nord trailing closely behind them.

Finley surprised her by hitting the down button. With all the floors above, she hadn't counted on any below. *Just how big is this place?*

The elevator doors slid open smoothly, interrupting her thoughts. The trio stepped inside, and Finley pressed a small black button with a raised A. The doors closed and the elevator plunged downward into darkness, stealing a startled gasp from Lina.

Nord moved in close, his arm brushing against hers comfortingly. She imagined it was his way of reminding her that he was there. That she was safe. He'd done the same thing when they'd ridden the elevator down from the penthouse that morning.

This ride was a relatively short one, but Lina had the feeling they'd traveled deep underground. There was an oppressive weight—like the feeling of the earth pressing in all around them—that was impossible to ignore. Unease skittered beneath her skin and she couldn't shake off the sense of being buried alive.

She was the first one out when the elevator doors opened. The bright lights and wide-open space helped ease some of the tension, and Lina took a shaky breath.

"You all right?" Nord asked.

"I don't think I like confined spaces," she murmured back. "In fact, I'd put them at the bottom of the list next to coffee."

He captured her hand and gave it a warm squeeze. Her chest loosened even more, and she gave him a grateful look.

Finley moved past them and down a hallway to another desk. This one had an older gentleman who was sitting behind it reading a book. Lina wasn't sure he was even aware he had visitors, but he looked up right as they reached him.

"What can I do for you?" he asked.

Finley flashed some sort of pass. "We're escorting our newest researcher, Ms. Jones."

The old man glanced at Lina with a nod. "Which stack?"

Nord and Finley frowned at each other, unprepared for the question.

The man at the desk raised his brows, his attention sharpening as he leveled shrewd eyes on Lina. "You don't know what you're studying?"

"Genealogy," Finley cut in smoothly, answering for her.

"And anything that would catalog significant markings, like tattoos, birthmarks, those kinds of things," she added.

The old man turned thoughtful, his hand rubbing his chin as he nodded. "If it's pictures you're interested in, probably best to start with the census books. They document all registered supernaturals as far back as the eighteen-hundreds. How far you looking to go?"

That was a tough question. Lina had no clue how long she'd been dead. Time blurred, losing all meaning as years faded into one long stretch.

"Uh . . ."

"The last fifty years," Nord cut in, "to start."

The librarian, as Lina was starting to think of him, nodded. "Very well. Give me some time and I'll get a table set up for Ms. Jones." He started to turn, but Finley stopped him.

"Actually, my partner and I have business down here as well."

The librarian lifted his brows, waiting for them to continue. Finley pulled out another form, this one causing the man's eyes to widen as he looked from the document and back up to Fin.

"The vaults?" he asked.

Finley nodded. "We know the way."

The librarian looked equal parts relieved and impressed. He eyed

Finley and Nord with a new measure of respect. "Suit yourselves. If there's nothing else . . ."

"That'll be all."

With a little nod, the older man turned and disappeared through a door on the left.

"What was all that about?" Lina asked.

Finley's face was suspiciously blank as he asked, "What do you mean?"

Lina tried to recreate the librarian's shocked expression and wary voice as he'd asked about the vaults.

Nord suppressed his smile, but his eyes danced with laughter. Finley was less successful, chuckling as he shook his head.

"Just an area that isn't accessed often."

That was probably true, but she'd bet there was far more to it. They were keeping something from her. *Why?*

"We should probably get a move on. It's easy to get lost down there," Finley said, looking purposefully at Nord.

Nord glanced at Lina and the waiting room, clearly not liking the idea of leaving her on her own.

"She'll be fine. The archivist will be right back," Finley said. "The bureau is probably one of the safest places on Earth for our Lina."

Lina mentally congratulated herself. Librarian, archivist . . . she'd been pretty close, although, archivist was a little on the nose if you asked her.

While she was patting herself on the back, Nord's frown deepened.

"Go," she insisted. "I'll be fine."

His eyes searched hers, flitting between her and the elevator in a silent question. He was worried whatever hidden fear had been triggered in the elevator might return.

Her heart melted at the display of concern. "I'll be fine," she repeated. "Promise."

He took a deep breath before nodding slowly. "All right, but stay put until the archivist comes back. And don't talk to anyone."

Lina's brows snapped together, her stomach twisting unhappily at the tone of his voice. She couldn't pinpoint exactly why, but his order chaffed. It seemed to poke at her judgment and ability to take care of herself in a way that she didn't appreciate. She buried the feeling, certain he hadn't meant anything by it outside of wanting her to be as safe as possible.

"Who exactly do you think I'm going to talk to down here?" she asked flippantly, gesturing to the empty room.

"Okay, smart-ass," Nord said, gifting her with a small smile, "just stay put. We'll meet you as soon as we're done."

She gave him a little salute and settled herself into one of the chairs lining the walls. Nord shook his head as he and Finley started off in the opposite direction the archivist had taken. She watched them retreat, appreciating the way Nord's muscles flexed beneath his tailored shirt and pants.

Despite the trappings of civility, there was something about the coiled grace with which he moved that made her think of wild things. He was a predator hiding in plain sight. All the more dangerous because his ability to blend in meant that no one would see him coming until after he'd already struck.

The realization should have frightened her. There was so little she knew about the man she'd tied her fate to, but if anything, it only made her curious to learn more. He might be a predator, but he was *her* predator. All that leashed violence was hers to command.

Lina shivered, the tiny hairs on the back of her neck lifting as hundreds of goosebumps appeared on her arms. It was like her body couldn't decide if it was hot or cold.

Nord paused, turning back to give Lina a final, searching look.

Hot, she decided. *Definitely hot.*

CHAPTER NINE

Lina

As the minutes slipped by, so did Lina's posture. She'd started straight-backed, hands clasped in her lap, legs crossed at the knees. She ended up with her head propped in one hand, the fingers of the other tapping impatiently on the chair's arm, with her legs sprawled out in front of her.

She was convinced the archivist had forgotten all about her. The old bookworm had probably been led astray by some hereto undiscovered tome, with its musty smell and promise of some rare and ancient mystery just waiting to be uncovered. There was no other explanation for how thirty minutes had passed without sign of him. How long did it take to pull out some record books?

A clock ticked overhead, the sound seeming amplified with each new rotation. Lina felt her eye twitch.

"Where is he?" she growled, pulling herself up to start pacing as a restless thrum of energy pushed her to do *something*.

Lina hadn't pegged herself as impatient, especially given her history —what else was there to do as a ghost but wait? And she was perfectly happy to wait for Nord to reveal his secrets. Okay, maybe not *happy* exactly, but willing to give it time. It wasn't like she could offer him any of hers, so it was hardly fair to demand his. However, it seemed that now that answers were within her reach, she'd lost all sign of her chill.

Lina began counting her steps.

One. Two. Three. Four.

It took twenty-six steps from the elevator back to the desk.

Fifty. Fifty-one. Fifty-two.

Her jaw clenched as she pivoted and continued wearing a path in the carpet. She'd just reached two hundred when she gave up waiting and went off in the direction the archivist had taken.

There wasn't far to go, just a short hallway that ended with two towering doors. Not giving herself a chance to think through what she was doing, Lina opened one of the doors and stepped into what could only be the archive.

The room was massive, filled with antique-looking wooden desks and chairs. Rows of bookcases lined the surrounding walls, while dozens of chandeliers provided the perfect amount of ambient light. Nothing too bright or distracting. The entire room seemed decorated with a scholar's comfort in mind.

Lina's eyes scanned the bookcases, searching for a sign of the pepper-haired man. It wasn't hard to find him. Well, technically she noticed the half-dozen books floating through the air as they slid in and out of place on their various shelves first, but the archivist was only a quick glance down.

Angling in his direction, she passed a frazzled-looking woman muttering to herself about the buoyancy of mermaid fins. Lina hurried away as soon as the words 'skinned versus fresh' left her lips.

From there it was only a few more steps until she reached her target. Wanting to get his attention, but afraid her interruption might cause the books still airborne to come crashing down, Lina opted for clearing her throat.

The archivist glanced her way, his outstretched hand easily catching a book as it floated down from a shelf high above him. "Ah, Ms. Jones. Was something wrong with the waiting room?" His slight smile removed the reproach from his words.

Her irritation at the delay dissipated as embarrassment took its place. "No, I'm sorry. Guess I'm just eager to begin."

He nodded. "Being in the archives is a privilege awarded to few. I can understand your eagerness. This was actually the last of the books I was hunting down for you. If you'll follow me, I'll show you to your station."

Lina rubbed suddenly sweaty palms against her denim-clad legs. "Please, lead the way."

The archivist escorted her deeper into the cavernous room, showing her to a table about halfway down the left-most aisle. "Here we are. Please let me know if you need anything else," he said with a small lift of his lips before turning on his heel and heading away.

"Thanks," she called to his retreating back, a little confused by the abrupt departure, but too focused on the pile of tomes in front of her to give it much thought.

Running a hand over the thick brown leather cover of the closest one, Lina gave a final scan of the room, spotting only two other researchers, before pulling the chair with its emerald-green cushions out and sitting down.

Stomach filled with nervous flutters, Lina blew out a breath and opened the first book.

Ninety minutes, and three books later, she knew her search was doomed. Interesting, but doomed. Pages and pages of faces and descriptions filled each book. Almost like a supernatural yearbook with a list of abilities accompanying each photo instead of accomplishments. Thin white lines linked pictures to show familial relationships, with almost microscopic dates to indicate birth or death. In theory, this was exactly what she was looking for. The problem was she was still on the As. It could be years before she stumbled across a familiar face this way.

Overwhelmed, Lina let her book fall closed and her eyes wander. They settled almost immediately on an older gentleman seated about five tables away. She had every intention of continuing her mindless perusal of the room, but there was something that held her attention captive. It wasn't that she recognized him; his mostly bald head with its ring of thin white hair, caterpillar eyebrows, and thin-framed gold glasses were completely foreign. If anything, it was the methodical— bordering on ritualistic—way he seemed to scan each page before jotting down notes in his elegant leather-bound journal. Each movement was so careful, so calculated, it granted them an importance they might have otherwise lacked. He even paused now and then to realign the book's position on the table, smoothing its pages down, before lifting his pen once more and resuming his work.

She was fascinated.

At one point, he pulled out a snow-white handkerchief, removed his spectacles, and began wiping the lenses. It provided Lina with her first unimpeded view of his face, and she felt her heart clench at the unmistakable grief etched in each line. She'd witnessed enough heartbreak in her ghostly lifetime to recognize the symptoms. It was like his facial muscles forgot how to defy gravity and could do little more than sag in their cocoons of flesh. And there was a brokenness about the eyes; like one morning he'd woken up and the world didn't make sense anymore.

His sadness washed over her, distracting her from her own purpose entirely. She was betting he was a recent widow, consumed by loneliness and filling his days with a series of mundane and otherwise meaningless tasks, all in the hopes that doing so would distract him long enough that he'd manage to get through another one. That was the story she created for him, anyway. He could very well be a retired scholar, spending his free time doing what he loved.

Somehow, she doubted the latter.

She sat for five more minutes, half-heartedly trying to talk herself out of what she was thinking about doing. In the end, it didn't matter. She couldn't have stopped herself even if she'd actually wanted to.

Lina pushed back from her desk and stood.

Nord's order echoed in her mind. *"Don't talk to anybody."*

She ignored it. She'd already broken the one to stay put, what was one more?

Besides, he'd said that when she'd been out in the waiting room when anybody could wander by. This was a grieving old man. What was the harm?

Satisfied that her logic was sound, even as another, wiser, part of her knew Nord would wholeheartedly disagree, Lina found herself standing a few steps away from his desk.

"Hello," she greeted softly, not wanting to startle him.

The gentleman looked up, the move initiated by his eyes before the rest of his head slowly followed. Lina fidgeted nervously as rheumy blue eyes stared at her under an umbrella of storm-cloud colored brows. She gathered he was trying to place her, since she had to assume it was uncommon for complete strangers to start up conversations for no reason.

"Hello," he finally replied, his voice surprising her with its resonance and strength.

He appeared almost frail sitting there, there was even a cane propped against the desk, but there was nothing frail about that voice. Lina's curiosity piqued higher.

She hadn't thought through her plan, well, at all. She'd been so caught up in wanting to ease some of that loneliness that she hadn't thought about what to do after coming over to say hello.

"What are you researching?" she asked, hoping that wasn't some kind of invasion of privacy.

Given the slight raise of his bushy eyebrows, it definitely was.

"If you don't mind my asking," she hurriedly added.

There was a slight glimmer in his eyes now that could have been curiosity or amusement.

Words continued pouring out of her mouth and heat stained her cheeks. "You see, I'm supposed to be researching genealogy, but I had no clue just how tedious it was going to be, and you just look so, um . . ." she bit her lip and twisted her hands together, trying to find the right word, "involved with your subject that I figured I must be doing something wrong or that maybe I might need to consider a topic change." She gave him a wide smile, relieved to offer a seemingly reasonable excuse that also bordered on the truth.

The old man lifted gnarled fingers and covered his mouth.

He was laughing at her.

Flames of embarrassment licked up her neck as her eyes squeezed closed. This had strayed so far from how she'd pictured it going, and she had no clue how to get back on track. All she'd wanted to do was ease some of the pain she'd read on his face, which she guessed she'd accomplished. Although not quite as gracefully as she'd hoped. Why was talking to people so complicated? It always looked so easy.

Lina took a steadying breath and braced herself to try again. The cane caught her attention as her eyes fluttered back open. It was a lacquered black, with an L-shaped handle that had smooth grooves for his fingers on one side, and a metallic object on the other. She wanted to ask him for a better look, but she didn't think 'hood ornament' was the appropriate term to use—although it was the only one that came to mind—and she couldn't risk making a bigger ass of herself.

"Pretty," she said instead, pointing at it. "Handmade?" There. Maybe limiting herself to one word at a time would go better than word vomiting all over him.

He dipped his chin in a nod, his eyes still twinkling. "Family heirloom."

Her knees almost gave, so deep was her relief that he'd actually offered an answer. "It's lovely. What is that on the end?"

His free hand lifted to cover the object, protecting it from her view. "A part of the family's crest."

Well, he clearly didn't want her snooping, but at least he was talking.

"I, uh, hope I'm not bothering you," she offered.

His lips twitched beneath his close-cropped whiskers.

She was obviously bothering him, but he was polite enough not to say so. Although, not quite polite enough to deny it.

Lina felt her own lips curl. This entire situation was so completely awkward and not at all what she'd intended. A soft chuckle escaped, and she shook her head. "I'm sorry. I guess I was just looking for a distraction from my research. I'll leave you to it."

She started to turn.

"Wait."

Her eyes darted back to his face.

"What's your name?"

"Lina," she said, offering her hand.

He studied it for a moment before holding out his own. She clasped it, surprised once more by the strength she felt beneath his paper-thin skin. There was more to this man than the mantle of grief that hung heavy upon him.

"Lina, I'm Alistair. Nice to meet you. Would you care to join me?" He gestured to the empty chairs on the other side of his desk.

"Are you sure you wouldn't mind?" she asked, her hand already curling around the backs of one of the chairs.

He shrugged. "I could use the break."

Lina eased herself into the chair opposite him. "Am I allowed to ask what you're studying now?"

Alistair answered by turning the book he'd been reading around for her to see. Lina leaned over and scanned the complicated-looking equation that spanned both pages. She couldn't make heads or tails of the symbols. The words scrawled randomly along the margins didn't even appear to be in a language she recognized.

"Uh, math?" she guessed.

"Dimensional Mathematics," he confirmed with an amused expression.

"Cool," she said, having absolutely no idea what that meant.

"Not as interesting as you were hoping?" he surmised.

"Let's just say my genealogy books are sounding more and more fascinating."

When he laughed, Lina felt herself relaxing fully. Apparently, making an ass out of herself was a great way to break the ice after all.

"So, Lina. Tell me. Why genealogy? What brings you to the bureau's record room?"

"Uh . . ." she hedged, her mind frantically scrambling for a believable cover story. Where was Finley when she needed him? "I'm trying to trace family lineages."

"Oh?" he asked, sounding politely curious.

Yeah, Lina. Why the hell would you be interested in that?

"Yeah," she nodded. "Trying to track the appearance of certain magical abilities and follow them back to their origin to pinpoint the initial source or deviation."

Wait, what? She barely resisted the urge to smother herself with her hands. Lina had no clue what the bullshit she'd just spouted was supposed to mean, but Alistair looked appropriately impressed, so she figured it at least made some kind of sense.

"That's a large undertaking."

She gave a nervous laugh. "You can understand my need for a diversion."

"Indeed. And what have you discovered thus far? Anything interesting in your own family history?"

Lina's eyes narrowed. Was she imagining it, or did he look far more than casually interested all of a sudden? Alistair steepled his hands beneath his chin as he waited for her to answer.

"No, nothing conclusive yet I'm afraid," she answered vaguely.

He nodded, as if he'd assumed as much. "These things take time." He paused, seeming to consider his words before adding, "If I may offer a word of advice?"

"Of course."

"Be careful, Lina."

Mouth suddenly dry, Lina asked, "Careful?"

"Uncovering family secrets is not always exciting as one might think. In fact, it can sometimes be quite dangerous."

Lina had already experienced a myriad of emotions since her impulsive decision to talk to Alistair, but this was the first time a true tendril of unease unfurled.

"What . . . what do you mean?"

The light in the room seemed to flicker, momentarily casting his face in shadow. "Sometimes that which we hope to uncover is better left dead and buried."

The color drained from her face, and her entire body trembled. Sweat-slicked hands clenched the arms of her chair as her heart raced. Then Alistair laughed, and the shadows fled, causing her to question whether she'd simply imagined them in the first place.

Lina let out her own uneven laugh. "Consider me warned."

CHAPTER TEN

Nord

"Fin, come take a look at this," Nord said, holding up a crime scene photo he'd located.

His partner dropped the stack he'd been sorting through and moved around the table to stand beside him.

"You found it," he breathed.

"Don't get too excited. It's hardly definitive proof."

Finley pointed to the close up of the sigil. "It's practically a perfect match for the one we found on that woman."

"*Practically*. All this tells us is that this kind of magic has been used before. And," he tapped the file folder spread out on the table in front of him, "if you read the case notes, it says that they were never able to solve this case. Which means, same sigil or not, we don't have a suspect. So, we're really no closer than we were when we started."

Finley nudged Nord with his shoulder. "That may be, but there's also a witness list. Maybe it's not a smoking gun, but it's a lead. People for us to question."

Nord lifted the list of names Finley referred to, but before he could inspect it, Finley plucked it from his hand, eyes rapidly scanning it.

"There," Finley said, slapping the paper. "Davis Crombie. He's our ticket."

Nord raised a brow.

"Right. I forget that you haven't been around for a while. Crombie is a notorious black-market goods dealer. People, artifacts, weapons, drugs. You name it, he sells it."

"And this helps us how?"

"Well, Crombie worked out a deal with the Brotherhood several years back. He tells us what we want to know when we want to know it, and we keep him out of prison."

Nord's other brow lifted to join its twin. "The Brotherhood is endorsing trafficking?"

Finley grimaced. "Not in so many words. As long as certain lines aren't crossed, we don't interfere."

"And when they are?"

"We put a stop to what we can."

"But Crombie stays free," Nord surmised.

Finley nodded. "Which is why he's our ticket. He can't say no. If he doesn't have the answers we need, he'll find them."

Nord made a low sound in his throat. He was hardly a fan, but he understood the need for a good informant. "Deal or not, Crombie steps out of line, his face meets my fist."

"Understood, mate. Violence isn't off the table if he yanks too hard at his chains."

"Excellent," Nord said, knowing his smile was feral.

Finley shook his head. "Fucking berserkers. One hint of danger and they get a fucking hard-on. You'd think I just invited you to join my sex club."

Nord suppressed a sigh. He should have known Finley would bring that up again after this morning. He'd gotten out of having to explain earlier, but it seemed that his grace period was over.

Trying to avoid the conversation, he asked, "You have a sex club?"

Finley rolled his eyes. "You're missing the point, mate."

Nord bit back his laughter and gave in, knowing Fin wouldn't let it go until Nord gave him some kind of explanation. "We call it the bloodlust for a reason, Brother. If violence isn't an option, sex is a great alternative. Although, that might be too mild a term for it."

"What . . . sex?"

Nord nodded. "The frenzy," he paused, knowing that one who'd never experienced it couldn't possibly understand. "Let's just say, most partners can't handle it. They don't have the stamina."

Finley fell uncharacteristically silent. "So what, you into orgies or something?"

Nord closed his eyes. "Now who's missing the point?"

"So bloodlust . . . that what happened this morning?" he asked, all trace of levity gone.

Nord nodded.

"Lina triggered it?"

He nodded again.

Finley crossed his arms. "How?"

"She had a dream—a memory—from the night she was murdered."

Finley cursed softly. "And your instinct to protect took over," he muttered. "Makes sense. But this morning in the gym, that was enough to satisfy it?"

Nord grunted. "More like it was enough to blunt the edge. I was able to regain control."

His partner gave him a concerned look. "It's been a long time since you lost control," he guessed.

Nord dipped his chin.

"You tell Lina what happened?"

He shook his head.

"Why not?"

"Most women are scared of it . . . the violence," Nord admitted in a low voice. "For good reasons. Without control . . ." A shudder ran down his back.

"Without control?" Finley prompted.

Nord's expression was bleak when it met Finley's. "Men have murdered their lovers and had absolutely no idea until they woke up beside their corpse."

Finley paled. "Fuck."

"Most people remember the berserkers as mindless killing machines, and maybe we were, but they don't take into account the sheer amount of training we undergo at the first sign of the call. We are taught how to channel the rage from an early age. How to suppress it until it's safe to let go. When we step onto a battlefield, it may appear as though we are little more than wild beasts, but in reality, we are probably the most focused men on that field. So a loss of control for someone like me . . . it's practically unheard of."

Nord could tell by Finley's silence that he understood everything Nord hadn't said.

Finally, he asked, "You gonna tell her?"

"Eventually."

Finley slapped Nord on the arm. "I don't envy you, mate. That's some dark shit."

Tension settled heavily in his shoulders. Even if they got over the hurdle of her past, there was still the reality of who—and what—he was. Nord let out a long, resigned breath. "She has enough going on without having to deal with me."

"Doubt she sees it that way. She's crazy about you."

"She barely knows me. It's only been a couple days."

Finley snorted. "We both know that's not how it works. I see how you look at each other when the other isn't watching. This isn't some lust-induced attraction—on either of your parts."

Nord knew he was right, but admitting it didn't help anyone. Instead, he shrugged.

"Suit yourself. Play dumb. It's your life you're fucking up. But think about this. What are you going to do when someone else makes a play? Because they will, mate. She's a beautiful woman. You going to be able to control all that berserker rage then? When someone tries to take what's yours?"

Nord's hands were clenched into fists at his sides, the metal of his rings biting into his flesh while his pulse throbbed like a battle cry in his ears. He couldn't even form words through the immediate anger that scenario provoked.

"Stop," he warned Finley through their link.

"That's what I thought," he said softly.

"Drop it. Now."

"Consider it dropped."

Nord forced himself to breathe.

Finley wisely changed the subject. "In other news, I know where we can find Crombie."

His voice was more of a growl than a question when he asked, "Where?"

"He holds auctions once a month. The next one is," Finley paused as if doing some swift calculations, "twelve days from now."

"Why wait?"

"Because we know exactly when and where he'll be. It'll be easier to approach him there than try to draw him out beforehand. Besides, this gives us time to make arrangements."

Nord blew out another breath, knowing it was a solid plan, but still not liking it. "Fine."

"Oh, one more thing."

"What's that?" he bit out.

"You'll need to wear your tux." Finley flashed his teeth. "It's black tie."

"For fuck's sake."

"Did you buy Lina any dresses while you were shopping?" Finley asked as he started straightening papers and putting them back in their files.

"She's not coming with us."

Finley paused. "She's not?"

"Too dangerous," Nord said.

"No more so than anything else we do."

Nord grunted, not willing to entertain Finley's logic. "It'll be a room full of supernaturals, and she doesn't seem to have access to her power. It's not safe for her."

"Hmm," Finley replied.

"What?"

"Nothing."

Nord narrowed his eyes. "*What?*" he demanded.

"We'll just see what Lina has to say about that."

"She'll listen to reason."

"Right."

"She will."

"Keep telling yourself that, mate."

Nord closed his eyes and swallowed a groan, praying that for once, Finley was wrong. "Just hurry up," he snapped. "We should go check on her."

"Whatever you say, buddy."

Nord slapped Finley on the back of his head with a folder. In return, his partner's laughter filled the room, making it almost impossible for Nord to hide his own smile.

Almost.

————

NORD'S BODY WAS RIGID WHEN THEY WALKED INTO THE MAIN reading room. "Didn't I tell her not to talk to anybody?"

"What was that you said about her willingly staying home?" Finley asked.

"Fuck you."

Finley chuckled.

"Who is that she's talking to?" Nord asked in a soft voice that only a foolish person would mistake as calm.

Finley squinted. "I can't quite make out his face from here."

Nord stalked down the aisle toward his charge. "Lina," he said tersely.

She jumped and spun around; her flushed cheeks an admission of guilt that only irritated him further. "Hey, Nord."

"What did I tell you?"

Her eyebrows immediately snapped together, and her expression went from guilty to annoyed. "I make my own decisions, Nord. I'm not a child."

"Then why are you acting like one?"

As soon as the words left his lips, he regretted them, but Finley had already provoked him, and he couldn't quite seem to maintain his hold on his usual calm. Especially not when it came to her safety. How could he protect her when she willingly put herself in harm's way? Sure, maybe this time it was fine, but what about next time? If she continued to disregard his warnings, eventually she was going to get herself in trouble.

"Oh yeah, this is going well," Finley muttered.

"Excuse me?" Lina hissed, her eyes darkening like the sky before a storm.

The man seated in front of Lina cleared his throat, dragging Nord's attention away from her. At first look, there wasn't anything remarkable about the man, save for his age. Nord, however, knew better than to trust outward appearances. They were too easy to fake and spoke nothing at all of what lay hidden beneath the surface.

Finley let out a surprised gasp. "Mr. Cuska, I didn't realize you were visiting us today."

"O'Connor," the older man said, looking quietly amused as he took in the scene playing out in front of him.

"You know this guy?" Nord asked Finley.

"He's the ex-head of the Mobius Council."

"That wannabe band of mobsters?"

"Those guys are no joke, Nord. They aren't as powerless as you remember."

Nord raised a brow and studied the old man with more interest now that Finley's words confirmed his initial assessment. *"So, what's he doing here? I thought Council members were banned."*

"Existing ones, sure, but Alistair is under our protection. He defected shortly after his brother's assassination. In exchange for information, we provided him with a new identity."

Nord peered more closely, tapping into his power to find the traces of Guardian magic that had modified the man's appearance. *"Interesting."*

As the silent conversation played out between them, Lina twisted in her seat to look at her companion. "How do you know Fin?" she asked.

Alistair's lips tipped up in a secret smile. "Old acquaintances."

"Really?" she asked, clearly intrigued.

"Oh yes, he used to do his best to put my brother and I behind bars."

"What?" she asked, her voice shaking with incredulous laughter.

"It's quite true, I assure you. I was not always the frail old man that sits before you, my dear."

"Lina, it's time to go," Nord said stiffly, placing a hand on her shoulder.

"But—"

"Now, Lina."

"I don't think I'm ready quite yet." She shot daggers at him with her eyes as she spoke, not at all happy that he was issuing more orders.

She couldn't possibly know that her defiance was like waving a flag in front of a bull or pouring gasoline onto an already raging fire. Nord clamped down hard on the tidal wave of protective anger that threatened to spill out. He was on edge, the events of the day leaving him unmoored. He needed to get her home and then take another round or ten with the bag.

"I wasn't asking," he said stiffly.

Lina's frown deepened.

Seeing that she was about to say something that would only make matters worse, Nord ground out, "Please."

Her expression wavered as she studied him. Lina's trust was one thing he was coming to appreciate most about her. She may not always understand what was going on, but she was willing to defer to him and follow his lead. At least, she was when he asked rather than demanded. He'd need to try to remember that.

"All right," she agreed softly.

His body relaxed infinitesimally.

"I'll let the archivist know we're leaving," Finley said quietly.

"Goodbye, Alistair," Lina said as she rose, offering him a wide smile. "Thanks for allowing me to interrupt your studies."

"It was my pleasure, Lina. Perhaps we'll run into each other again soon."

"I'd like that," she said, giving him a little wave.

Nord glared at the older man over her head. There was absolutely no way he would be coming within thirty feet of his charge again. He didn't know the man, but he didn't trust him. Not even if he was a renounced member of Mobius. That pathetic band of criminals could absolutely not be trusted. Renounced or otherwise.

The smile on the old man's face told him he knew what Nord was thinking.

Good.

Nord let some of the violence simmering in his blood rise to the surface as he returned the man's smile.

Alistair didn't so much as blink, but he did give Nord a little nod.

Knowing his intended message had been received, Nord allowed himself to turn and follow Lina out of the room.

Now Alistair knew what he'd be dealing with the next time he came sniffing around Lina. Nord almost welcomed the idea as the need for blood sang in his veins. It was only a crooning lullaby for now, but it wouldn't stay that way for long.

Oh yes. An opponent would be quite welcome.

Especially one he could rip apart with his bare hands.

CHAPTER ELEVEN

Lina

They'd traveled home in silence, Finley opening a portal that delivered them to the penthouse's doorstep.

"Wouldn't it be more efficient to portal into the actual house?" Lina asked.

"Wards," Finley explained. "No one can portal directly in or out."

"Wards?" she repeated, the word unfamiliar.

"The supernatural equivalent of an alarm system, basically. Most supernatural homes and businesses use some combination of layered protection spells or activated runes to keep intruders out and their possessions safe. The more important the building, the stronger the ward."

"Makes sense," Lina said, stepping past him and moving quickly inside. Now that they were home, her irritation roared back to life.

"You going to tell me what that was about back there?" she asked, turning to face Nord with her arms crossed over her chest.

Finley quietly shut the door while Nord glowered at her. His eyes might be the color of arctic frost, but they were filled with fire.

"You disobeyed a direct order, that's what happened."

Lina's mouth fell open. "He was a lonely old man, Nord. Hardly a threat."

Nord took a step forward, his voice colder than she'd ever heard it. "Maybe that's just what he wanted you to think. Appearances are traps, Lina. Just as much as a few carefully offered words. Anything that makes you lower your guard is dangerous."

"I can take care of myself," she insisted, her voice flinty.

"Oh? With what? Your hidden arsenal of weapons? Your expansive knowledge of martial arts and self-defense? Your magic?"

It couldn't have hurt more if he'd slapped her. In one fell swoop, he'd just exposed her greatest vulnerability with all the finesse of a bulldozer. Lina had none of those things, and he knew it. She was a liability, virtually useless, and he'd just thrown it in her face.

Lina stared at Nord, fighting hard to keep her expression neutral and not let him see that his words had been a direct hit. Her chest rose and fell rapidly with the pounding of her heart as silence stretched between them.

"Lina," he said, voice softening as he took another step toward her. "He could have been anyone. It doesn't matter that he looked safe. Remember the shoe store? Magic can always tip the balance."

She flinched as the woman's gruesome death replayed in her mind. Nord was ruthless, not pulling any punches as he tried to prove his point. He was fighting to win so she would have to do the same. She may not have the same skills at her disposal, but she was far from stupid, and she was a very fast learner.

"So, let me make sure I get this straight. You're telling me not to underestimate people?" she asked, her voice deceptively soft.

He looked relieved. "Yes, exactly."

Behind him, Finley winced. He must already know where she was going with this.

Lina's eyes narrowed, and her voice turned hard once more. "Then why do you insist on underestimating me?"

Nord opened and closed his mouth, beyond frustrated that he'd walked right into that one.

"You think I'm just a liability, Nord? Then train me. Teach me how to protect myself. Help me figure out how to access my magic. Because I'm telling you right now, I'm not going to stand on the sidelines of my own life. I refuse. I waited far too long for the opportunity to live it."

Nord looked like he was battling for control of his temper. "Lina, it's not that—"

"I refuse, Nord," she repeated firmly. "You can give me all the orders you want, but I won't listen to a single one. Not one," she insisted, poking him in the chest, "if you can't give me the courtesy of treating me like an equal, or at the very least, like an adult. It's demeaning, and I don't deserve it."

"When I give you an order, it's not to be dismissive or demeaning," he started, "it's to keep you safe. Everything I do has a reason, and that reason is your protection."

"Maybe that's true, but it doesn't change anything. Just because I inherited this body a couple of days ago, without any of the memories that should have come with it, doesn't mean that I am somehow less capable than you. You want to protect me, Nord? Then give me the tools to protect myself."

"Checkmate," Finley murmured, giving her a wide grin from behind Nord's shoulder. Slapping his friend on the arm, he asked, "What was that you were saying earlier?"

"Fuck off, Finley," Nord grumbled.

Finley laughed and gave Lina a little wave. "Seems like you two have some things to discuss. I'll go get started on dinner."

"Do you understand me?" Lina asked Nord, ignoring Finley's interruption. "I agreed to stay with you because I had nowhere else to go, and I wanted to explore what was growing between us, but that doesn't mean that I have to stay. If you can't find it in yourself to give me this, then I'm gone."

Lina's heart was galloping in her chest, and she hugged herself harder, trying to hide the fact that she was shaking. She hadn't known she was going to throw down that ultimatum until the words were already out there, but once they were, she knew she meant every one of them. She might not have anywhere else to go, but she wouldn't waste her second chance with someone who wanted to keep her in a cage.

Nord's jaw clenched, a muscle fluttering in his neck as he stared at her. The silence stretched, tension hanging heavy between them before he finally nodded. "I understand."

Lina felt like she'd been holding her breath. Her relief was immediate, flooding through her body and making her almost lightheaded as it turned her limbs to jelly. While his answer was the one she'd been hoping for, a part of her didn't actually expect him to give in. She knew this was a massive concession on his part. But she also knew they weren't finished. Not yet.

"I mean it, Nord. I won't budge on this." Her voice was softer now, but no less insistent.

Nord sighed heavily and crossed his arms as he leaned against the wall. When his eyes found hers again, the sincerity Lina discovered there shattered any possible wall she might have erected around her heart.

"The need to keep you safe is far too deeply ingrained. I can't promise I'll always succeed, but I will try, Lina. I don't want you to go."

"I don't want to go either," she whispered, meaning the words from the deepest depths of her being.

"Good." One side of his mouth curled up, and Lina basked in the warmth of it. "Does this mean we can go sit down now? The hallway is nice and all, but it's been a long day."

Lina laughed and nodded. "I'd like that."

Nord pushed off the wall, matching his strides to hers so that they walked down the hall to the living room side by side. Each brush of his arm against hers sent little tingles arcing through her.

"What did Finley mean?" she asked as she sat down on the leather sofa and curled her legs up beneath her.

"About making dinner?" Nord joked, taking a seat beside her.

"Nice try, Viking man. He was giving you grief about something you said earlier. What did he mean?"

"Caught that, did you?" he asked with a soft chuckle.

"Ghost perk," she said with a mischievous grin. "I think you'll find that there's very little I don't catch."

"Yeah, I'm starting to pick up on that," he murmured.

Lina thought there was a hint of pride coloring his voice. "So?" she pressed.

Nord rested his arm over the back of the couch and propped his head up with his fist. "We found something while we were investigating earlier. A sigil similar to the one we found on Rachel. Fin thinks we might have a lead—"

"You're just now telling me this?" she sputtered, sitting up straighter.

"I didn't really get a chance before now," he said pointedly.

Lina could feel the heat creeping into her cheeks and settled back down. "Okay, fair point. Tell me now."

"As I was saying," he started again, his lips twisting with amusement when she rolled her eyes, "Fin recognized a name on the witness list. We're going to see what the guy remembers about that night and if he knows anything about who might have cast the spell."

Lina let out a squeal and threw her arms around him. "Nord, that's amazing."

He tensed under her arms before returning the embrace. "It's all tenuous, but it's something."

She pulled back slightly, unfazed. "It's more than we had this morning."

"True," he agreed, the warmth of his breath fanning lightly over her face.

"When are we going to meet him?"

"Well, that's what Finley was talking about. I told him I didn't want you to come with us because it was too dangerous."

Lina frowned, a protest already on her lips.

Nord placed a finger gently against them. "I won't try to stop you if you want to come. As much as I'd rather know you were safe and sound here, you're right. This is your life we're investigating. It should be your choice." He moved his hand when he finished speaking, letting his thumb brush over her cheek, the cool metal of his ring dragging across her heated flesh before he lowered it.

"I want to come," she insisted, trying hard to ignore the way her body responded to the gentle caress.

He nodded, expecting as much. "There's an auction coming up, Fin thinks we'll be able to corner the guy there."

"What kind of auction is dangerous?"

Nord frowned. "The magical kind. This guy deals in all sorts of illegal stuff. The people that will be there wanting to buy it are hardly the cream of society."

Lina took a deep breath, understanding more of Nord's initial reservations. "So we'll be careful. I'll make sure to stick with one of you guys."

Nord squeezed her leg. "I'd really appreciate that."

"See how much easier it is to get what you want when you talk to me?" she teased.

He returned her smile, but his expression sobered almost immediately. He lifted his hand once more to cradle her face. "I'm sorry that my actions made you feel like I doubt you. I hope you know that could not be further from the truth. It's merely that for as long as I can remember I've been told to let my instinct drive my actions. From the time I was a child, I was taught to blindly trust that part of myself—a belief that was reinforced when I joined the Brotherhood. I forget sometimes that does not give me the right to demand blind obedience from others."

She pressed her hand over his. "It's okay. We're figuring this out together."

Flecks of azure began to glow softly in his eyes. "I call it instinct, but it's more complicated than that. It's like the most primal piece of me. The place where everything is broken down to its most basic component, and there's no such thing as shades of gray. There's no such thing as nuance. Enemies are enemies. Threats are threats. And the need to deal with them is absolute." Nord's accent was more pronounced than usual as he added, "It's been a long time since there's been someone in my life that's tested my control over that part of me."

For Lina, the words were practically a declaration of love. This was not a man who made such admissions easily, especially not ones that might reveal weakness. His doing so now demonstrated just how deeply he trusted her.

"Is that what happened this morning?" she asked softly, taking his free hand in hers.

He nodded. "Instinct overrode reason."

"Because you were scared for me?" she guessed.

Nord closed his eyes and rested his forehead against hers. "I'm not sure if scared is the right word. It was more like I was enraged that someone hurt you and the need to retaliate consumed me."

Lina's heart broke at the tortured sound of his voice. She wasn't sure what she could say to console him. She was here, she was alive, and the faceless monster haunting her dreams was buried in her past. Since there was nothing she could say, she did the only thing she could.

She pressed her lips against his.

At first, Nord was frozen. Suspended in that endless moment between one breath and the next. Then he was moving, hauling her body up against his, devouring her with his lips.

She could taste his fear, but it was quickly overshadowed by his need.

Lina struggled to remember how to breathe as the kiss grew more urgent. His tongue slid against hers, claiming her mouth the way she wished he would claim her body. It was like the first seductive step of a wildly erotic dance she never wanted to end.

Finally.

Nord didn't just kiss her with his lips, he worshipped her with his entire body. One hand tangled in her hair, fisting the silken strands and giving a tug that was the perfect punctuation for the nip of his teeth against her bottom lip. His other hand seared her skin as it ran down her side to curl around her back and pull her closer as he rolled his hips up into the vee of her body.

Lina moaned, sensation exploding beneath her skin at the exquisite friction that was exactly right and nowhere near enough. She wanted—needed—more.

She hissed in a breath as Nord repeated the motion, one long fluid slide of his aroused length against her core. The scrape of fabric over her heated skin only added to the sweet agony. While the reminder of the clothes that separated them had Lina recalling, in perfect detail, how Nord looked without a stitch of it on, she desperately wanted to know what it would feel like without anything between them.

"Kærasta," he groaned.

Fire ignited in her veins and Lina tore her mouth from his, trailing kisses over his jaw and down his neck, loving the slight scrape of his beard against her lips almost as much as the erratic flutter of his pulse.

His breath was coming in harsh pants as she traced the throbbing vein along the side of his neck with her tongue. She knew he was as lost as she was when she bit down on the corded muscle and the hand in her hair fisted tighter, not to pull her away, but to hold her in place.

"Guys, dinner's ready," Finley called out, shattering the spell around them.

Nord and Lina went still, bodies pressed together, breathing uneven. Thousands of unspoken words passed between them as they stared into each other's eyes. It was how she sensed the exact moment he returned to himself and began to rebuild the wall he'd spent the last couple of days erecting between them.

Twisting his head away from her, he yelled, "Be right there," before gently pushing Lina off of him.

She fell back, legs feeling like cooked spaghetti as she watched him with hungry eyes. Before he could fully pull away, her hand fisted in his shirt, tugging him back to her. Her lips had barely grazed his when he caught her wrist with both his hands and gently, but forcibly, pushed her away.

"Lina," he whispered, her name sounding like both a warning and a plea.

Her tongue darted out to wet her kiss-swollen lips. "Don't," she begged, her voice husky.

He swallowed, his eyes hooded. She could read the longing there, along with the regret. "You know this can't happen again. Not until we know for sure."

Lina's breath left her in a whoosh. She'd known it was coming, but it still hurt, especially since she could still practically feel the evidence of how badly he wanted her pressing insistently between her legs.

"Just because you swear that's the case, doesn't mean that I agree. Hell, it doesn't even seem like you agree," she said, dropping her eyes pointedly.

Nord stood abruptly, turning away from her. "Lina," he rasped, "you know it's not a matter of whether or not I want you."

"So, what the hell are you waiting for? I'm right here. Take me."

A tremor worked its way down his body at her words, and she

watched as he clenched and unclenched his hands. "You're not playing fair," he whispered.

"I told you I wouldn't."

His shoulders dipped, defeated. "So you did."

For a second, Lina dared to believe that he might just give in. She stood and placed a hand on his shoulder. They stayed there, his back to her, for one drawn-out second before he snuffed out that hope.

"If you insist on pursuing this, then I guess it's up to me to be strong enough to resist," he said, stepping away but adding in a much quieter tone as he did, "for both of us."

Lina watched him go. It would have been easy to be disheartened, but it was hard to feel like she'd lost when she could still taste him on her lips. War's comprised of multiple battles, and she was pretty sure she'd won that one.

If nothing else, she'd confirmed what she'd already guessed. Nord could deny himself all he wanted, but even with his ironclad control he was far from immune to her. She'd just have to take what she learned and adapt her strategy to press her advantage.

Taking a deep breath, Lina started off in the direction Nord had already left, a smile slowly stretching across her face.

What was that expression people always used? All's fair in love and war?

This was a shot at love they were talking about; she wasn't taking any chances.

Nord had no idea just how dirty she would play if it meant she'd win in the end.

CHAPTER TWELVE

Lina

Candles flickered as an unnatural wind blew through the darkness. It wasn't until the sound of footsteps filled the room—too many to belong solely to her tormentor—that she realized a door must have opened.

She tried to cry out, call for help, but something coated in the metallic taste of her blood had been shoved into her mouth.

A low throbbing beat joined the footsteps. Her terrified brain recognized the source of the sound as a drum.

The drumming grew louder. Like it was calling out to . . . something.

Or summoning it.

Her heart began to pound in time to the driving rhythm, although it stuttered when a chorus of deep voices started chanting.

She couldn't make out any words, just whispers and guttural growls that seemed to stretch on in an endless loop, layering over the relentless beat of the drum.

It was a demonic symphony, one that had her fear spiking to dangerous new levels.

Shadows began to stretch and grow as the candles guttered. Some blew out entirely, the curl of smoke giving the darkness a hazy quality.

The unmistakable sound of metal scraping against metal had her eyes darting from side to side. Tears trickled down her cheeks, blurring what little she could make out.

A sob choked her as the wet slide of a tongue began to trace the tear tracks on her face.

"I don't believe I've ever tasted anything as delicious as your fear," the disembodied voice whispered against her ear as the gag was pulled from her mouth. "Go ahead and scream as much as you want, sweetheart. It only makes it better."

Fiery pain ignited as something sharp dug into the skin above her heart. There was a soft gasp as she sucked in a shocked breath, and then her screams joined the unearthly chorus.

"Beautiful," the voice sighed in her ear, twisting the blade, and dragging it lower. "So fucking beautiful."

LINA AWOKE WITH A GASP, TEARS WET ON HER FACE. HER HAND flew to her chest, half-expecting it to come away covered in the sticky warmth of her blood. Her tears flowed a little faster when she found nothing but silvery moonlight washed over her trembling palm.

Legs shaking, she clambered out of bed and over to the mirror hanging over the dresser. Roughly, she yanked on the neck of her borrowed shirt to confirm that she was, in fact, whole.

Slowly, she let go of the fabric, panting like she'd just run a marathon as she stared with wide eyes at her ashen reflection.

"It's just a dream," she whispered, but that only made her shake harder because she already knew the truth.

It wasn't just a dream, or even a nightmare.

Not even close.

At one point in time, she'd actually been bound in the middle of a dark room while someone carved into her with a knife as part of some kind of dark ritual.

The real question was: why?

It was one thing to know you were murdered. It was another thing to learn that you'd been sacrificed.

Somehow that was so much worse.

———

LINA WANDERED INTO THE KITCHEN THE NEXT MORNING, HER movements wooden, her eyes gritty from lack of sleep.

"I was thinking about what you said last night," Nord said as soon as he saw her, "and you're right."

The fog of exhaustion faded as her heart kicked into gear. "Oh?" she asked casually, her core body temperature ratcheting up as she immediately began picturing him grasping her by her hips and pushing her back against the counter.

"I should be teaching you how to protect yourself," he finished, walking over and holding a cup of coffee out to her.

Lina's heart plummeted. Of course, that was the part he was referring to. She blamed yet another sleepless night for her wishful thinking. If anything could send the lingering vestiges of her nightmare away, the thought of Nord's hands on her body was certainly it.

"That sounds great," she forced out, not meeting his eyes as she accepted the cup and shuffled away from him.

She could tell from his careful silence that he'd picked up on her mood. She risked a glance at him from over the rim of her mug to find him studying her intently.

"You had another dream," he stated.

It wasn't exactly a question, but Lina nodded anyway before taking a sip of the steaming liquid.

"Why didn't you come to me?"

She lifted one shoulder in a shrug, feeling the soft cotton slide down her shoulder. Even though she had her own clothes now, Lina still found herself reaching for Nord's T-shirt when it came time to crawl into bed.

"Just because my sleep was interrupted doesn't mean yours needed to be."

He folded his arms over his chest. "Lina—"

She waved a hand at him. "Seriously, I'm fine."

The slight downward twist of his lips told her he wasn't buying it.

"What did you recall this time?"

Fear skittered across her back and Lina shuddered. "I'd rather not relive this one just yet, if it's all the same to you."

Now his brows veed down, mirroring the frown playing on his lips. It was a good thing broody looked sexy on him because the distraction kept her from caving. Just the mention of her nightmare already had her feeling the phantom blade carving into her flesh. She didn't need any other reminders of her death haunting her waking hours.

He must have sensed the reason she was hesitant because he dipped his chin in a nod, although he didn't look happy about it.

"So, what were you thinking on the protection front?" she asked, hoping to change the subject.

"Well, that's up to you," he replied. Picking up his own mug, he joined her at the bar. "What do you want to start with?"

Lina tapped her fingers on her cup as she thought about it. There was really only one answer. "I want to figure out what's going on with my magic."

He nodded as he took a sip, setting his cup down as he said, "I tend to agree. There's got to be something binding it."

"I didn't seem to have any problems at the ball."

"True," Nord agreed, "but there was also an insane amount of magic permeating the entire event. It must have unlocked something in you, even if only temporarily. Either that, or you were simply drawing on the excess of power as a replacement of your own."

"How is that even possible?"

Nord leaned on his elbows, staring out at the skyline as he thought through his answer. "Well, it's hard to say for sure, but it could have been your instincts reacting to the overflow of magic. If you really are cut off from your magic reservoir, or worse, if it's completely drained, then you could have pulled that excess power into yourself and claimed it as your own. Once that dried up, though, it would have left you back where you started."

"Which is to say, magically bankrupt."

Nord's lips twitched up in a small smile. "In a manner of speaking."

Lina blew out a breath, sending an errant piece of hair flying up off of her face. "Well, that's just great."

He nudged her with his shoulder. "Don't be so quick to lose hope."

"You just said I'm the magic equivalent of barren. Excuse me if that doesn't fill me with optimism. How am I supposed to use magic, if I don't have any of my own, after all?"

"Ah, but you're forgetting the part where I also said you could simply be cut off from it. You clearly have a natural aptitude, which tells me you must have been born with your own source. We just have to figure out what's causing the disruption."

"Disruption?"

"In your ability to access your power source. Think of it like a beaver dam, if that helps."

"So I'm barren or I'm dammed. Excellent."

Nord snickered, and Lina gave him a begrudging smile.

"Okay, magic expert, what do you recommend, then?"

"Well, to start, I can use my power to check and see if there's anything going on down below."

"And by 'down below,' you're referring to what exactly?" Lina asked as her eyebrows lifted. She wasn't sure if that was a sexual innuendo of some kind, but it sure sounded like one. Or maybe she just wished it was.

"Below the surface of your physical form and into the fabric of your essence."

Okay, so certainly intimate, but definitely not sexual. *Bummer*.

"And the goal is to see if there's something that's not supposed to be there? Like with the residual magic from the curse placed on Rachel?"

"Exactly."

"And if there is?"

Nord took a deep breath. "I guess that depends on what we find."

"That sounds ominous," she said, pushing her empty coffee cup away from her.

"Some things are easier to fix than others."

"But, if you do find something, you *can* fix it . . . can't you?"

"I'll certainly try," he said, offering her one of his half-smiles.

Instead of reassuring her, it had the opposite effect. Nord didn't seem at all confident, and that was out of character for her Guardian, at least so far as she could tell.

Lina put her feet on her chair and pulled her knees into her chest. If she let it, the weight of everything she didn't know or understand would crush her. Even sitting there, she could feel a heavy knot forming in her chest, making it hard to breathe.

Resting her chin on her knees, she forced herself to take a steadying breath. She couldn't control whether or not she had memories or magic. And really, it didn't matter if she did.

All she'd ever wanted was the chance to live, to experience and appreciate what so many others took for granted. She didn't need magic too. It was just a bonus since she'd already gotten the one thing she craved more than anything else.

Tilting her eyes back to Nord, she mentally amended. *One of the things.*

Letting out another calming breath, Lina reached a decision. She'd just do the same thing she'd been doing since finding herself standing in a dirty alley clutching an invitation in her very real hand. She'd take it one day—one minute—at a time.

"What do you need me to do?"

CHAPTER THIRTEEN

Nord

"Technically, you don't need to do anything."

"So I, what, just sit here and stare at you?"

Nord could feel the smile trying to form, but he didn't want her to think he was laughing at what was clearly a serious question. Her brows were puckered, a small crease forming between them, and her nose was adorably scrunched.

Lina had a way of looking at the world that he found both endearing and refreshing. There was a purity to her that he'd lost so long ago he couldn't begin to remember what it had felt like. She took almost everything and everyone at face value and had no qualms about going after what she wanted. He'd clocked that quality within seconds of spotting her the first time. And while it was true that her impulsiveness set his teeth on edge because it almost always led to potentially dangerous situations—something he'd also noticed on day one—he couldn't help but appreciate her fearlessness. It was a rare combination that spoke of a wisdom he'd come across only a handful of times in his long life.

In his experience, people bound themselves in chains of their own fear. Fear of failure. Fear of judgment. Even fear of success. These self-imposed limitations led to lifetimes of misery and regret, and yet . . . people could not overcome them long enough to simply try.

Lina, however, had already lost everything—her life included. She knew, better than most, that not trying was akin to not living. It had given her a unique perspective of the world and its hurdles. What others saw as a reason to give up, Lina saw as a challenge to be overcome. She would not allow anything to stand in the way of what she wanted, least of all herself.

This was also why she was, without question, the most incredible woman he'd ever met. He couldn't get enough of her.

Which was the bulk of his problem, really.

Seeing her sitting there, looking a bit like a confused puppy, had him wanting to cuddle her. To pull her into his arms, smooth away that little crease with his lips, and tell her everything would be all right. And that would be fine . . . if he could stop himself there.

But it wouldn't stop there.

Once her body was flush against his, reason would flee and soon his hands would be exploring her luscious curves, memorizing the feel of each peak and valley beneath his palms. And then his lips would follow.

Nord blew out a frustrated breath.

Cuddling was the gateway. Lina was the drug. And Nord . . . he was already addicted.

The only way to stay sane was to avoid temptation at all costs.

That meant no touching—outside of what was strictly necessary for her training. No hugging. And absolutely no kissing.

"Perhaps it'll be easier if you close your eyes," he said finally.

She blinked, the tips of her long lashes tangling together before revealing the brilliant blue of her eyes with their sapphire rings that reminded him of his homeland.

"Like this?" she asked, repeating the movement.

It took a second for Nord to realize she was purposely batting her eyes at him.

He chuckled softly, enjoying her playfulness. "Stop trying to distract me."

"Oh, I'm sorry. I didn't realize you found me so *distracting*," she teased.

Distracting. Desirable. Delicious. Take your pick.

"Just close your eyes, Lina," he said, scrubbing a hand over his face and beard.

Lina reached out and gave the end of his beard a little tug. "I like this."

"You should tell Finley that," he said, pleased to hear it despite himself.

"Oh?"

"He hates my beard."

"Hate seems like a strong word," she said with a little laugh, clearly not believing him.

"It's a direct quote," Nord informed her.

"Well," she said after another bout of laughter, "that seems like an extreme reaction for facial hair."

"He hated my hair too. He's the one that made me cut it and do this," Nord said, running a hand over the shaved sides of his head, not sure why he was telling her any of this.

"Really?" she asked, feigning shock with a hint of laughter.

He nodded. "Told me I looked like a barbarian and that no one wore their hair past their shoulders anymore."

Lina's eyes took on a dreamy quality as she tried to picture him pre-haircut. Given the pink staining her cheeks, she was a fan of the image it brought to her mind.

"Well, he has good taste. It looks great all long on the top and short on the sides, but I'm going to have to disagree with him about the long hair thing. The Viking look is totally in right now."

"It is, huh?"

"Mmhmm," she nodded sagely. "Vikings and lumberjacks. Something about them gives off all these uber-masculine vibes that trigger a primal response in a woman's lizard brain."

Nord's shoulders shook with laughter. "And you're an expert on this how?"

"My last roommate liked her Cosmo, okay? She always left them lying around open on whatever page she was reading last."

Nord pressed his lips together, catching himself before he could ask her something stupid like what kind of primal response she was having to him.

Lina shook her head. "Anyway, I think a beard suits you."

Nord leaned a little closer, loving the way her lips parted on a surprised inhale as he did. Apparently, he didn't need to ask any questions. Her body was already supplying him with the answers.

"Lina?" he murmured in a sensual croon. He shouldn't have done it. He was playing with fire and would surely see himself burned, but he just couldn't seem to help himself. Even if he couldn't touch her, Nord still enjoyed being the cause of that heated expression in her eyes.

"Hmm?" she returned, seeming flustered.

He allowed himself one drawn-out moment to bask in the primitive male satisfaction her reaction caused before putting his lips beside her ear and whispering, "Close your damn eyes."

Lina let out a shaky laugh. "Oh. Right. I forgot we were in the middle of something. All this talk of sexy lumberjacks derailed me."

Nord chuckled as he pulled away. "Lumberjacks. Sure."

Her eyes were squeezed shut, but her cheeks flushed a deeper shade of pink. "You know me," she said breezily. "I just lose my mind at the first sign of a man wielding an ax."

"Just does it for you, hm?" he asked, feeling an absurd need to preen for her. If she preferred her men with axes, he'd start walking around with both of his strapped to his back.

He knew her words were meant to be taken as a joke, but the slightly husky hitch in her breathing gave away the fact that she was still thinking about the night he'd come crashing in with his weapon drawn.

Nord tried to ignore the way his body responded to the realization. She'd made no secret of the fact that she wanted him, but it still gave him a bone-deep satisfaction to learn that she was just as profoundly affected by him as he was by her.

"You know it," she said, sounding a little breathless. "And don't get me started on the plaid . . ."

"Whatever floats your boat, sweetheart," he said, a small smile still lingered on his lips as he drew forth his power. "Now, just relax and let me see what I can find."

CHAPTER FOURTEEN

Lina

What Nord found, as it turns out, was nothing. Nada. Zilch.

Not one single, solitary blip.

In fact, after multiple attempts over the course of multiple days, and even asking Finley to double-check, it would seem that Lina was totally and completely normal—at least by primordial essence standards, not that she knew what that meant.

She could not be more frustrated with her diagnosis.

If there was nothing "wrong" with her . . . then what the hell was wrong with her? How could she go from being able to create music out of thin air and send butterflies made out of smoke traipsing through the sky to . . . nothing?

At least if there was evidence of magical tampering, then she'd have an explanation as well as a path for them to follow. Without one, they were left guessing with little in the way of potential solutions.

It wasn't helping her mood any that her research attempts were also dead ends. After daily visits to the archive, Lina had managed to make her way through the archivist's selection up to the "Ce" section but had yet to have anyone jump out at her.

After voicing her frustrations that morning, Nord had promised he'd take her around to some of the supernatural tattoo shops that afternoon to see if anyone recognized her or her ink. The only caveat? She had to sit through another one of his damned meditation sessions.

A blunt finger tapped her hard in the middle of her forehead, interrupting her wandering thoughts. "You aren't concentrating."

Lina peeled one eye open. "Yes, I am."

"No," Nord insisted, "you're not. I can tell."

She opened her other eye, demanding, "How?"

"Well, for one, you stopped timing your breaths. For another, you're scowling at me."

"My eyes were closed. How could I have been scowling *at* you?"

He waved a hand. "Maybe you were just scowling in my general direction. It doesn't matter. The point stands. Your mind was wandering, and to unpleasant places from the looks of it. If you were really focusing, you'd be at peace."

Lina huffed out a breath. "Nord, this is stupid. Meditation isn't going to accomplish anything."

"How do you know when you refuse to try it?"

"I've tried it," she sputtered. "Twice a day, every day, for the last week I've sat here next to you focusing on my chi or whatever the hell you called it."

Nord was fighting hard not to laugh, and it only infuriated her more.

"I mean it, this is a waste of time."

He was sitting in front of her, his knees almost touching hers in their mirrored pretzel position. After studying her for a moment, he gave her arm a quick, comforting squeeze.

"I know it may feel like a waste, trust me, but there's a lot to be said for knowing how to achieve a calm mind."

"So you keep telling me," she groaned.

Lina pressed the heels of her hands into her eyes. She was sure he was probably right, but she didn't like being alone with her thoughts. It made her itchy. Instead of centering herself, she became aware of every odd inch of her body, especially the places she couldn't touch. It felt like a cat's whiskers brushing across her skin.

"If it makes you feel better, I used to have the same problem sitting still. I wanted to run and explore, not sit in a quiet room and contemplate whatever it was my mentors were trying to get me to learn."

"Not really," she admitted with a rueful smile, dropping her hands back into her lap, "but I appreciate the effort."

"Remind me again why we're doing this. Sometimes it helps if you focus on the why."

"Because you're cruel?" she joked.

Nord was not amused.

Sighing, Lina dutifully repeated the mantra he'd been drilling into her since they started this doomed experiment. "Because in theory I should be able to identify and hopefully access the place where my magic lives if I learn how to focus my mind."

Nord was nodding along. "It's all about exercising perfect control over your body; understanding how something as simple as breathing affects every single cell that lives inside you. Once you learn how to be that in tune with yourself, you will be able to focus on each individual element, including your magic."

Lina blinked at him. "It's been seven days, Nord. I'm no closer to keeping my mind free from idle thoughts today than I was when we started."

"I'm sure that's not true. You sat for at least fifteen minutes before fidgeting that time."

"Seven days, Nord."

He muffled a laugh. "Lina, it takes people years to master this stuff. Any progress is great."

"Years? Nord, I don't want to spend years doing the equivalent of bashing my head into a wall. Maybe we just need to face the fact that any magic I once possessed is long gone," she said baldly, admitting something she'd secretly begun to fear was the case ever since her last nightmare.

Lina bit back a frown as a now familiar niggle of doubt wormed its way into the forefront of her mind. The longer they went on without her having any success, the more she was starting to believe it could be true. That the reason she'd been killed in the first place was because someone wanted her power. It'd certainly explain its absence now, and why that monster had gone after her in such a horrific fashion in the first place.

She fought hard to suppress a shudder of revulsion as the memory swam to the surface. So far Nord had refrained from pressing for details, but she knew it was only a matter of time before he started digging. If he caught one whiff of her fear, he'd be on her in a heartbeat.

Lina was trying to avoid that showdown. She didn't want to admit that she'd been some kind of ritual sacrifice. It made her feel dirty— tainted—like she was missing some essential part of herself now. She didn't think she could bear to see the look in his eyes when he found out.

"I don't think that's the case."

She snorted. "Of course, you don't, because you're too stubborn to admit defeat."

He raised a brow, but otherwise ignored her dig. "Let's give it one more shot before we call it for the day. Then we can take a break before it's time for your strength training."

Lina flopped back on the floor. If anything was worse than forced meditation, it was Nord's damn workout regimen. If she'd realized what she'd been in for when she'd asked Satan's second-in-command to help train her, she might have reconsidered the suggestion.

Nord was merciless in his demands, pushing her until she was little more than a limp, soggy noodle curled up on the floor. She'd barely made it through her first rounds of cardio and strength training, and she had absolutely no hope she'd survive what he was referring to as an endurance test.

"When are we going to get to the actual defense part of self-defense training?" she asked, staring up at the ceiling.

"Making sure you have the stamina to outrun or fight an attacker is a vital part of training," he said.

Since it was the same excuse he'd given her every time she'd asked —panted—the question, she mouthed his answer along with him.

"That's what you keep telling me, and I don't disagree, but what about the part where, I dunno, you start teaching me how to use weapons, or break out of holds or something?"

"I'm not putting a weapon in your hands until you learn the basics, and I'd rather hold off a little longer on the actual hand-to-hand part—"

"You're going to have to touch me eventually, you know," she singsonged up to the ceiling. Since their night on the couch, his attempt to avoid any kind of prolonged contact had become painfully clear. Outside of brief, minimalistic touches, he'd kept his hands to himself. Much to her disappointment. She'd tried more than once to force the issue, by walking too close or finding opportunities to invade his space, but he always found a way to stay just out of reach.

Nord ignored her outburst and talked over her, "—until I know I'm not going to break you in two. Believe it or not Lina, getting in shape is step one."

She sat up and glared at him. "I'm in shape."

He gave her a look. "You've got a nice body, that's not the same as being in shape."

Lina opened her mouth to protest, but he cut her off.

"If you were in shape, you'd be able to run longer than three minutes without looking like you were about to collapse."

Her mouth snapped closed. She knew he was right, but she didn't like hearing him say so. Folding her arms across her chest, she blew out a breath. "Whatever."

"It's not going to happen overnight. Any of it," he added purposefully, "so don't be so quick to give up."

"I'm not giving up," she said. "I'm just . . ." she broke off, searching for the word. Finally, she sighed and said, "Impatient, I guess."

"You don't say," he replied blandly, one side of his mouth quirking up.

She kept her narrow-eyed stare for all of a second before chuckling. "I guess you noticed."

"Hard not to."

Lina wrinkled her nose at him.

"Come on. Let's try this one more time. I have an idea that might help you."

The playfulness of their banter had done a lot to help soothe the restless tension growing within her, so it was with significantly less reluctance that Lina agreed. "Fine. Lay it on me, sensei."

"This time when the idle thoughts come, instead of brushing them away, I want you to acknowledge them. Afterward, if it still has you in its hold, focus on why. Is it stemming from anxiety? Stress? Fear? Discomfort? Whatever it is, no matter how insignificant, try to find what triggered the thought, and just keep following that thread until you find the source of the concern."

"Then what?" Lina asked, nibbling on her lower lip as she processed what he was saying.

"And then let it go."

She snorted. "You say that like it's easy."

"I never said it was easy, but you'd be surprised how just acknowl-edging the root of an issue can help alleviate any negative emotions it might cause. Once you are aware of it, you can process it and then, hopefully, move on." He said all of this matter-of-factly. "Just give it a try. Worst case, it doesn't work and you're back where you started. Best case, it does."

Lina was nodding along as he spoke. She wasn't sure she agreed with him since she knew exactly what the source of her fear was, and that hadn't made it any less terrifying. Maybe it was the processing part she hadn't quite moved on to yet.

"Lina? Are you even listening?"

"Follow the source, I got it."

He nodded encouragingly. "Great. Now, take a deep breath . . ."

She did as she was told, letting her eyes fall closed as she breathed out of her nose.

" . . . and begin."

———

LINA USED HER HAND TO WIPE AWAY A VISIBLE SQUARE IN THE FOGGY mirror.

"All right, Lina. Enough is enough," she told her reflection. Ignoring the pieces of hair plastered all over her face and staring directly into her eyes so that her pep talk really landed. She was done messing around.

Needless to say, Nord's newest plan for her to locate her power source hadn't worked any better than the others. The only resolution she'd reached during their final meditation attempt was that it was time to escalate her seduction efforts.

Over the last week, she tried sexy outfits and then abandoned them in favor of running around half-naked when they didn't work. There'd been lots of intentional bending over, for both necessary and completely unnecessary reasons. Such as attempting new yoga positions while he was in the living room. Or intentionally waiting until the exact moment he was looking to pick up the dropped remote . . . when she'd planted it there twenty minutes earlier. She'd almost gotten stuck crawling underneath the coffee table chasing a tube of lipstick that she'd "accidentally" knocked off.

Nothing was working.

So far, all her attempts had gotten her was a serious case of blue ovaries . . . was that a thing? Blue ovaries, or was it lady balls? Ovaries were the equivalent of man balls . . . so that had to be the expression.

Lina rolled her eyes. "Focus," she told herself as her thoughts wandered. "Time to bring out the big guns."

Tightening the towel wrapped around her, she studied herself a bit more critically. The drowned rat look probably wasn't going to help her accomplish the mission she'd recently dubbed: Project Get Lina Laid. Or, alternatively, Mission Orgasmic Haze. She couldn't decide which title she preferred, but as long as the end result involved her eyes going crossed with the force of her climax around that tree trunk she'd spied between Nord's legs, she didn't think it mattered.

She'd found a slew of articles on the internet that had given her more than enough ways to take care of the situation herself, but why settle for a celery stick when you had your eye on the ribeye? Nope. No, thank you. She wanted the real deal, or nothing at all.

But it had been over a week since she'd thrown down the gauntlet, and she was done suffering to prove a point.

Especially since she couldn't seem to get close enough to Nord to kiss him again. She just knew that if she could lock her lips onto his, he'd be helpless to resist her. He'd already proven it. All she needed was to distract him long enough to strike, and then he'd take matters into his own hands.

She was sure of it.

Thus, her plan. Since it was just as important as the overall mission, it even had its own name. Operation Slip and Slide. Finley was off at some kind of business dinner, so it was just the two of them tonight. The perfect time for her to spring her trap.

It shouldn't be too difficult. She'd go out to retrieve the hairbrush she'd so conveniently left in the living room that morning and then just happen to stumble as she walked past, drop her towel, and fall on top of him. There's no way Nord would let her fall on her face, and once his hands were on her naked body, there was no way he'd let her go.

It was fool proof. Dare she say, perfect.

Using a spare towel, she dried her hair as best she could, and then piled it high on top of her head, grabbing a clip to hold it in place. Then she put on a little mascara and some Chapstick so that she looked a bit more put together.

"Not a drowned rat anymore," she said, giving the mirror her best seductive stare before breaking out into excited giggles. "One last thing before it's officially go-time."

She did a little twist to test the towel's holding power, wanting to double check the most important part of her plan. She frowned and then did another. The towel didn't budge.

"That won't work," she muttered.

It needed to fall off without much effort but stay in place until she was ready. Fussing with it a bit more, she did another little shimmy. When it immediately started coming undone, she knew she'd found the right balance.

"Much better. Now you can go claim your Viking."

Eyes bright with her assured victory, Lina spun on her heel and began marching to the living room.

Nord's head was down, eyes skimming some official-looking report Finley must have left for him. Lina fought the urge to spy on him. It was rare that she had the chance to look her fill, and he looked amazing painted in the sunlight shining through the windows.

"I can feel you staring," he called without looking up.

"I didn't know you were in here," she lied, padding further into the room.

He made a non-committal grunt as he turned the page.

Lina narrowed her eyes. The least he could do was look at her while he was talking to her. She moved out from behind the couch and was standing a bit to his right.

"Did you need something?" he asked when she hovered.

"Uh, just left my brush in here."

He nodded absently. "Don't let me stop you. Just finishing up . . ." His eyes finally lifted. "Lina," he said, his voice a warning.

It's now or never.

There were only two steps needed before she'd be directly in front of him. She took one of them, dropped her shoulder a little to initiate the towel slippage. Nord flew up off the couch, his hand fisted in her towel, keeping it closed in his death grip.

Lina gaped at him. He'd moved so fast she didn't realize what had happened until he was right in front of her. It was like he'd known exactly what she'd been planning. All that prep and he'd subverted her brilliant strategy before she'd even really got started. She didn't even have a chance to do her fake stumble. How had she not anticipated him countering her with his freaky Guardian reflexes?

"I . . . uh . . ."

His eyes were hot when they met hers, his lips lifted in a slight smile. "Nice try."

"I . . . I don't know what you're talking about."

"Uh-huh. So, this isn't another one of your seduction schemes?"

"I told you, I needed my brush."

"Since when do you walk around the penthouse in your towel?"

"I didn't think you'd be in here."

He lifted a brow. "When I told you I had some work to do, and I'd be down here if you needed me?"

Shit. He had said that. Lina blew out a frustrated breath. "I still need my brush," she said flatly.

Nord reached over and grabbed it without loosening his hold on her towel and thereby robbing her of a second attempt to salvage her plan.

"There you go," he said, his voice washing over her and causing her body to break out in goosebumps.

Lina took it from him, cursing when he somehow managed to keep her fingers from brushing his.

"Thanks," she muttered, disappointment lacing the word.

He nudged her chin with the tip of a finger. "Better luck next time."

Her eyes narrowed, and he smirked.

"If you really meant that, why don't you let me finish what I started?" she taunted.

He lost his smirk, and a flash of azure sparked in his eyes. "Go get dressed. We'll grab lunch before heading to the tattoo shops."

Lina's shoulders slumped, and she was coming up with all sorts of creative names for her Guardian and his stupid misplaced sense of honor as she stomped away.

"Hey, Lina?" he called just before she left the room.

She glanced back, not bothering to hide the fact that she was sulking.

"Just because I didn't fall for it, doesn't mean I don't enjoy watching you try," he said, eyes drifting over her towel-clad body before returning to her face and giving her a sexy wink. "Looking forward to seeing what you come up with next."

She narrowed her eyes at him, but when she walked out, her head was held high.

Challenge accepted, motherfucker.

CHAPTER FIFTEEN

Lina

"You know, when you say you're going to take a girl to lunch, she expects something a little fancier than street dogs."

"Don't act like you didn't just inhale three of them," Nord said.

Lina grinned. "A gentleman wouldn't have counted."

He chuckled. "Fair enough."

"The point still stands though. I thought there'd at least be sitting involved. Maybe a tablecloth, or heck, physical menus and a waiter to take our order."

"What does that stuff matter so long as the food's good?"

"It doesn't, but if you're going to take a girl on a date—"

Nord held up his hands. "This isn't a date."

"Sure it is. You and me, out in the world together, sharing a meal. How is that anything except a date?"

"Lina," he sighed, exasperation heavy in the word.

"And," she added, giving him a poke in the chest for emphasis, "we're going home together after." She wiggled her eyebrows. "All the best dates end that way."

"Leave it to you to twist something as basic as grabbing lunch into something as complicated as a date."

Her smile widened. "I think it's a gift."

"That's one word for it. Come on, we're here," he said, pulling a beat-up door open.

Lina peered inside. "This is a tattoo shop?"

"It is."

"Where are the," she paused and gestured with her hands, "you know, people?"

"Probably inside. In you go."

She raised her eyebrow at him but crossed the threshold. The slight tingle of magic over her skin told her she'd just crossed some kind of magical barrier. The immediate noise and chaotic atmosphere that greeted her after confirmed it.

A short man with green skin, elongated ears, and piercings over practically every inch of his face lifted his chin in greeting.

Lina assumed he was some kind of goblin.

"Take a wrong turn, sweetheart?" he asked as his yellow eyes traversed her body.

Nord sidled up beside her. "We're here for Donny."

The goblin flicked a hand, gesturing for the two other people in the small room to leave.

"That'd be me," he said, giving Nord a once-over. "I thought your lot didn't step foot in establishments like mine."

"Why's that?" Nord asked, although the disinterest in his voice made it clear he didn't care about the answer.

"Too afraid to be caught getting your hands dirty."

"Lucky for you what I need doesn't require me using my hands at all."

"Is that so?" Donny asked, tilting his chin up. "Why don't you tell me what you're here for then, *Guardian*, so you can hurry up and get the fuck out of my shop."

Lina shifted uncomfortably beside Nord. She'd been warned that Bell Falls' supernatural community wasn't overly fond of the Brotherhood—no one ever appreciated outsiders poking their noses around—but she hadn't expected outright hostility.

Hoping to defuse some of the tension, she stepped forward. "We were hoping you could take a look at my tattoos."

"Why's that? Need one of 'em covered up?"

"No. Actually, I—we—were hoping you might be able to tell me who did them?"

Donny frowned. "I can take a look, but a name will cost ya. I don't give out nothin' for free."

"Totally fair," Lina said before Nord could react. Pulling off her jacket, she showed the goblin her arms.

After carefully inspecting each of her tattoos, Donny stepped back and shook his head.

"It's good work, but I don't recognize it. Most of us have a signature style, ya know? But those look clean. Coulda been done by anyone."

Lina wasn't sure what she'd been expecting, it was only their first stop, but disappointment ate at her anyway. She slid her jacket back on. "Well, thanks for looking."

He gave her a slow nod. "I did what you asked, now if you wouldn't mind . . . " he trailed off and gestured meaningfully to the door. "You're scaring off my paying customers."

As they exited the shop, the unexpected feeling of pins and needles crawled up her neck. It hadn't happened since the last time they'd been out in a crowded place. So was it merely a side effect of being around so many people, or was it something else?

If it'd only been the one time, she could have brushed it off. Hell, she'd practically forgotten all about it, but to have it happen again . . . it didn't seem like the kind of thing she should ignore.

Lina shivered, eyes darting up and down the busy street that had seemed so unassuming only minutes before.

"What's wrong?" Nord asked, immediately noticing the way she was rubbing at her skin.

"Nothing," she said slowly, not ready to worry him unless she had a valid reason. Her eyes scanned the crowd one last time before returning to his face. "Just a weird feeling."

His eyes narrowed. "You sure?"

She nodded. "Yup. Should we head to the next spot?"

He studied her for a long moment before nodding. "Sure. It's just a couple blocks away, you up for walking?"

Lina agreed and fell into step beside him, but she couldn't escape the feeling that she was being watched. Keeping her eyes on the people around them, she scooted a little closer to her Guardian, covering the move by weaving her arm through his.

"People on dates do stuff like this all the time," she said.

Instead of reminding her it wasn't a date, Nord pulled her a little closer. She must not be doing as good of a job masking her apprehension if he was willingly waving his no-touching rule, but she didn't care. Knowing he was close eased some of her anxiety.

The pins and needles feeling only grew stronger as they continued visiting shop after shop. Not only weren't they finding out anything, but Lina was a nervous wreck by the time they left their fifth shop.

"Okay. What the hell is going on?" Nord demanded, pulling her around to face him. "You keep glancing out the window like you're looking for someone."

Lina shoved clammy hands in her pockets and licked her lips, stalling while she tried to figure out what to say. "It's just a feeling I can't shake."

He frowned. "What kind of feeling?"

"Like someone is watching me."

"And you're just mentioning this now?" he asked, head snapping up and eyes already glowing as he used his power to scan the street.

"I didn't want to worry you."

"It's my job to worry about you."

She flinched, the comment stinging although she knew he didn't mean for it to.

"It's probably nothing. Just an overreaction to being around so many people. The same thing happened that day we went shopping."

"What?" he practically roared. "And you never thought to say anything? Lina," he groaned, "what if you *were* being followed?"

"Well . . ." she started miserably, eyes shifting away from his to stare at the brick building behind him. She'd just opened her mouth to say something, when she thought she saw a pair of pale gray eyes peering around the corner of the building. Sucking in a startled breath, she pointed in that direction. "There!"

Nord spun and raced down the street without any further encouragement. Lina followed as best she could, but by the time she turned the corner, Nord was standing in the middle of an alley with his hands on his hips.

Alone.

The alley was a dead end, so there was nowhere anyone should have been able to hide. Plus, with Nord's abilities, he would have spotted any signs of a magical escape.

Lina's shoulders drooped. Her over-anxious imagination must have been seeing things.

He turned to her as she reached him.

"I guess I was wrong," she said, trying to smile.

"Or they just know the area better than we do," he said gently. "Either way, I don't want to risk it. We should head home, it's getting dark."

She nodded, more than ready to get back to the safety of the penthouse. "Sounds good."

The pins and needles feeling started to fade as soon as they began walking, and with each step she felt more and more foolish for overreacting. Risking a glance at Nord from the corner of her eye, she could tell that overreaction or not, he was taking the threat seriously.

Feeling awful that she'd inadvertently ruined the relaxed mood, she tried to at least get him to smile. "All right, fine, you can be right. This wasn't a date."

"What made you change your mind?" he asked as his eyes continued to scan the street.

"If it was a real date, there'd be less stalking and more groping."

His lips twitched, and he reached over to squeeze her hand. "Damn straight."

CHAPTER SIXTEEN

Lina

Finley snickered as Lina blinked up at him in a daze. That was the third time she'd been knocked on her ass in as many minutes.

"Who am I? Where am I? What am I?" she asked in a thready wheeze.

Holding a hand down for her, Finley helped haul her up.

Rubbing her backside, she peered at him. "Aren't you supposed to be at work?"

"Aren't you supposed to be getting better?"

She threw out an elbow, intending on hitting him in the side, but Finley's reflexes were light-years better than hers, and he dodged her clumsy attempt with ease.

"Okay, so I'm not a fighter. What are you gonna do? Throw rotten food at me? Call me names? Kick me out for daring to sully your home with my inferiority? We can't all be ninjas like you two."

Nord and Finley were openly laughing now, although Nord had one hand covering his mouth. His hand did nothing to disguise the merriment shining in his eyes.

"Nothing that dire," Nord promised. "Just some extra training sessions."

Lina groaned. "You're a fucking sadist."

"Weren't you the one begging me to 'move on to the real stuff'?" he quoted.

"Try not to rub it in," she muttered.

The day after their failed tour of the tattoo shops, Nord declared it was time to move on to more advanced training. Lina was certain it had more to do with the fact she thought she was being followed than her skill. It'd only been a couple of days since they started practicing actual maneuvers, but it had become immediately apparent that Lina was not a natural fighter.

There was something almost clumsy about her strikes—a lack of conviction, according to Nord. Her skills at evasion were practically nonexistent, meaning everything she was supposed to dodge landed. And, to Nord's endless amusement, Lina got distracted every time he wrapped himself around her in a hold that she was supposed to be breaking through.

"It's not like I'm not trying," she insisted. *It just feels so damn good having you pressed up against me.*

In her defense, the hour or two they spent training each day was the only time he broke his self-imposed no-touching rule. Lina couldn't help it if her instincts had her wanting to burrow deeper instead of pulling away. The way she saw it, she was just soaking it up while she could. What warm-blooded female wouldn't behave in the exact same way?

"Maybe if we show her what it's supposed to look like?" Finley offered.

Nord nodded. "It might be easier for her if she can see what she's supposed to be doing."

"Oh, you mean I wasn't supposed to end up on my back with you standing over my prone body? Silly me. Here I am thinking I was getting it *right* this whole time."

Finley snorted, but there was a flash of something hot in Nord's eyes. Lina felt an answering flicker in her core. Instead of dampening her attraction, his distance this last week and a half had only made her crave him more. It didn't help matters that she already knew how good it felt to have his hands running over her desire-flushed skin. It made the promise of what could be far too tantalizing.

She was getting desperate . . . and it was making her stupid.

She was starting to obsess about things like the way his throat worked when he'd stop for a drink of water, or the way sweat dripped down his bare chest and back. Worse, she was getting jealous of the droplets that disappeared out of sight. Now that they were practicing holds, she was too busy paying attention to the flex of his arms around her body and the hard press of his legs up against hers. She'd even caught herself closing her eyes and tilting her head closer to his neck just to enjoy the masculine scent of him.

Thus, all the time she spent ass first on the mat.

It was like her mind emptied of every move he'd taught her as soon as he laid a finger on her. Lina knew it wasn't sexual, that he was only doing it because it was a requirement of the task. Moreover, she knew that she was the one who asked for his help and should be focusing on the very important skills he was trying to impart instead of how good it felt to be close to him.

But in this case, knowing something and being able to actually do it were about as unlikely as an anemic dating a vampire.

Dropping her gaze so that she could actually focus, Lina stepped back while Finley unknotted his tie and discarded his button-up. After kicking off his shoes, he moved to the center of the room and faced off with Nord.

Lina looked up and stared at the two half-naked men standing in front of her.

Yup. She was laser-focused now.

Just on all of the wrong things.

She pinched herself, welcoming the sharp sting of pain as the men slid into position.

Nord was the attacker, bear-hugging Finley from behind. Finley's arms were pinned down, just as Lina's had been. In slow motion, Finley began to squat down, sliding out of Nord's hold. Then he shifted his hips to the side, creating a direct path to his attacker's groin. Swinging his arm back, Finley "struck" Nord, causing his hold to break and allowing Finley to step through, the idea from there being he was now free to attack or run.

"Now at full speed," Nord instructed, as they moved back into place.

If she'd blinked, she would have missed it. Finley moved like a flash, dropping and swinging his arm so fast that he was already freed before she'd even processed that they'd begun.

No wonder Nord kept knocking her over, she was moving way too slow. By the time she'd gotten into her squat position, he'd already managed to get his leg through and in front of one of hers. Which meant, even though she'd manage to break his hold by swinging her arm back, she still went flying over his leg. She was giving him the opportunity to trip her without even realizing it.

"Let me try again," she said.

Finley stepped away as she walked back onto the mat and faced away from Nord.

"Ready?" he asked, his breath stirring the fine hairs at the base of her neck.

Ignoring the tingles that raced down her spine, Lina gave a sharp nod. "Ready."

Nord wrapped his arms around her.

Dropping her weight, she swung her hips to the side, threw her arm back, and . . . went flying to the floor.

"Sonofabitch," she cursed as the wind was knocked out of her again. "I don't understand how I'm still doing it wrong. I did exactly what Finley did."

"Finley's had years of practice," Nord told her as he shifted to look down at her. "You okay?"

"I'll live. It's just a case of wounded pride."

"For what it's worth, I really think you would have gotten it that time if you were fighting someone without enhanced abilities."

"Well, if I ever get normal mugged instead of targeted by supernatural assailants, I should be just fine, then," she snapped, pushing herself to a seated position.

Nord chuckled. "We'll get you there, I promise."

She knew he wouldn't give up until she could free herself from any hold and inflict some serious damage, she just hadn't expected it would be quite so hard to get there.

"That's probably enough for one day. Can't have you too bruised for the auction tonight," Finley said, helping her up once more.

Lina was lucky she was still allowed to go to the auction after what happened the other day. Even though she'd promised to tell him immediately if she felt the pins and needles again, it'd still taken Finley to persuade Nord that she'd be perfectly safe with them.

"You are a kind, merciful man," she moaned once she was standing. "Not you," she clarified, pointing at Nord. "You are still a sadist."

His lips twitched up. "You really want to call me names when I'm the one in charge of your training?"

She bit her lip, evaluating her aching body before answering, "Yes."

Nord's smile grew, and his voice was soft with affection when he said, "Go take a shower and get yourself ready. We've only got a couple hours before we need to head out."

Lina's brows drew together in confusion. "I thought the auction didn't start until ten. It's only"—she glanced at the clock on the wall —"three. Why leave so early when we can just portal to the doorstep?"

Fin shook his head. "We aren't portaling, we're driving."

"Driving? Since when do you drive? We're always walking or taking a taxi when we go somewhere," she asked. "Do you even own a car?"

"Of course, I own a car. Several, actually," he answered with a laugh. "Living in the city, taxis are usually just more convenient."

"So then . . . why?" Maybe that was a stupid question, but with an instantaneous means of travel at their disposal, she just didn't see the purpose.

Finley placed a hand on her shoulder like he was about to impart some secret wisdom. "Because cars are fun," he said, looking her straight in the eye, "and because outside of traveling to Brotherhood sanctioned events or properties, we rarely use our portals. The whole point is to blend in, not to draw attention to ourselves."

"Oh," she said.

"It's also about making a statement," Nord added. "Showing up in an expensive car makes an impression."

"I thought he just said we're driving to avoid being noticed."

"Not quite," Finley said. "There's a difference between blending in and avoiding detection. It's all about making people see what we want them to. It's in our best interest tonight if the other guests believe we have money to spend. It gives us a reason to meet with Crombie without raising eyebrows."

Lina rubbed a hand over her face. "This supernatural spy stuff is way more complicated than I realized."

"What did you think we did? Skulk about in the shadows?" Finley asked with a wide grin.

"Pretty much, yeah," Lina said. "Either that or peer over the tops of bushes or maybe have secret message drops in trash cans."

"More like we pay off people who belong in trash cans," Nord said wryly.

Lina laughed.

"I hate to be the bearer of bad news," Finley said, "but you've seen entirely too many bad movies."

"Don't blame me. Blame my roommates. It's not like I got to make a grab for the remote on movie night."

The men laughed and warmth spread through Lina's chest. She hadn't realized how lonely she'd been as an outsider trapped between worlds. It was an empowering experience, being someone's friend. Making people laugh. Having them listen to and acknowledge her feelings. That was the true power of being alive—the connections formed with others.

Every day came with a new experience, a chance to learn what something was like firsthand versus theory. True, not everything was sunshine and roses, but there were far more good experiences to be had than bad ones. Even with her nightmares.

Nord held a water bottle out to her, and she reached for it, wincing when her muscles screamed in protest.

"Shower. Now," Nord ordered, missing nothing.

Lina nodded, more than happy to go stand under a hot stream of water until the pain in her muscles evaporated. "On it," she said, taking a quick sip of her water before heading toward the door, pausing as an idea came to her. "Hey," she said, turning around, "does this mean one of you will teach me how to drive?"

"Absolutely," Finley said at the same time Nord replied, "No way in hell."

Lina beamed at Finley.

"Why can't she learn how to drive?" Finley asked with a laugh.

"I told her I wasn't giving her a weapon until she learned the basics."

"But it's a car, not a weapon," Lina protested.

"The average car is almost three thousand pounds of metal that can explode. It's a weapon."

"Sorry, love. Guy's got a point."

Lina gaped at them before smiling wickedly. "Fine. Guess I'll just have to teach myself. I'm sure you won't mind, what with all those extra cars you have."

"Lina . . ." Finley started as she walked out of the room. "Lina, wait. Don't you dare touch one of my cars. Lina . . . Lina!"

She snickered all the way to her room. She had no intention of attempting such a thing on her own. She wasn't completely brainless. But it wouldn't hurt them to worry about it for a while. She may not be able to take them out on the mat, but it was still a form of payback.

A win was a win.

"Suckers," she whispered, still smiling as she stepped under the spray of steamy water.

CHAPTER SEVENTEEN

Lina

Lina inspected the massive red and purple bruise mottling her upper thigh and sighed. "At least it's not one of my arms," she muttered, leaving the bathroom and heading to her closet.

The sight of a gift box lying on top of her bed stopped her short. The box was a glossy black and tied with a mauve bow. She crossed the room and ran her fingers along the satin ribbon, spotting something nestled in the center. Plucking up the square piece of stationary, she flipped it over to find bold, slanted writing that must have been Nord's. It looked far too bossy to be anyone else's.

Lina's smile grew as she read his message.

The first of many weapons.

Curiosity beyond piqued, Lina untied the bow and lifted off the top of the box, a soft gasp escaping as she discovered the lace and bead masterpiece lying contained within.

Since evening gowns hadn't made it on the "things to buy" list when they'd gone shopping last week, she'd assumed she'd be wearing the same dress she'd worn to the ball. Seeing Nord's gift now, she realized how underdressed she would have been.

Carefully picking up the gown, she moved to the mirror and held it up against her body. From neck to wrist and all the way to the floor, she'd be covered in intricately woven black lace accented in hundreds of tiny beads that cast off all the colors of an oil slick as they caught the light.

Dropping her robe, Lina stepped into the gown, putting it up and sliding her arms into the sleeves. Her breath caught and held when she caught the first glimpse of herself in the mirror.

The dress was deceptively conservative, with its strategically placed bands of layered lace around the chest and hips. It hugged her curves until mid-thigh where it started to fall in a bell-shaped train. The sheerest part of the gown was the sleeves, as they were only a single layer of the lace from shoulder to wrist. Next was the bodice, which only had two layers. The second of which created a plunging V effect as it crossed over her breasts before blending into the skirt. If not for the band around her chest, she would have seemed almost naked. The skirt of the gown appeared almost opaque, but that was merely an illusion caused by the way the fabric draped over itself. Every time she'd step forward, the flash of her skin would be unmistakable. A siren's lure to distract and tempt her prey.

Elegant.

Stunning.

And if it allowed her to draw in their target, potentially lethal.

She could understand now why Nord referred to it as a weapon.

There was only one problem. Lina couldn't reach around to zip up the back of it.

She stood in the center of the room, contorting her body to try to reach the zipper at the base of her spine, but the constriction of the lace made it impossible. She went so far as to peel her arms out and try to start zipping up, but then she couldn't get her arms back in.

By the time a brisk knock sounded on the door, she'd managed to get her arms back into the dress but was no closer to inching the zipper up.

"Lina, everything okay?" Nord called.

She bit her lip, slanting her eyes toward the door. A part of her really didn't want to have to admit she was struggling to figure out a zipper, while the other welcomed the idea of assistance.

"Uh . . . yeah?"

"Why does that sound like a question?" came back the amused response.

"Because it is?"

"I'm coming in," he said one second before the door cracked open.

Lina was facing away from him but could see him clearly in the mirror in front of her as he pushed the door all the way open, revealing him leaning against the doorframe. She would have laughed at the multitude of expressions crossing his face if she hadn't been busy fighting against her own reaction to him.

Surprise.

Approval.

Desire.

It was all there, burning in those eyes the color of frost. If she searched her own, she knew she'd find a twin flame alight there.

Nord was wearing a black tuxedo, expertly tailored for his muscular frame. Its silky lapels were the perfect accent for his black shirt and bow tie. His hair was slightly darker than usual, likely due to the product he'd used to hold it in a more polished version of his regular style. She even caught a flash of a thick silver wrist band peeking out from beneath his sleeves.

Despite the formal attire, there was an unmistakable aura of power radiating off of him. *He looks like an expensive rebel*, she decided.

His eyes followed the length of her body before taking a return journey back up. Their gazes clashed in the mirror; a wordless conversation exchanged between them as Nord straightened to his full height.

Lina's lips parted on a soundless breath as he moved into her room with the same animalistic grace she always appreciated. With each step that brought him closer to her, her heart beat faster, anticipation making her tingle.

His eyes never once strayed from hers until he came to stand directly behind her. Then they dropped once more. Wordlessly, he took the zipper and began sliding it up. His knuckle dragged against her spine, the heat his slight touch created reminding her of a match igniting. Shivers raced up and down her skin, and she could feel color blooming in her cheeks.

The only sound in the room was the soft clicking of the metal teeth and her shallow breaths. Although, Lina wouldn't have been surprised if Nord could hear the frantic beating of her heart. It was pounding in her ears like a war drum.

Liquid heat began spiraling through her as his hands moved higher. She kept her eyes glued to his face as the backs of his fingers brushed over the silk fabric of her bra. If she hadn't been looking for it, she would have missed the flare of his nostrils and wild pulsing of the vein in his neck.

As he finally reached the base of her neck, he used one hand to push away the few strands of hair that had fallen out of her makeshift updo away, the cool feel of his rings sending goosebumps racing across her shoulders and down her arms.

Finally, it was done, both of his hands coming to rest on her shoulders as he looked at her face once more.

"Stunning," he whispered, his accent making his voice thick and the word sound wonderfully foreign.

"Thank you for the gift," she managed. "I'm glad I took the time to watch those videos so that I could do it justice."

It took him a moment to understand that she was referring to the hair and makeup tutorials she'd clicked through during breakfast.

"You don't need any of it," he assured her, his eyes hooded, but doing nothing to conceal the smoldering heat there. "They are merely the trappings; you are the true work of art."

Tiny bubbles of happiness burst inside her chest and her mouth opened and closed, unsure of how to respond. One part of her wanted to return the compliment. To tell him how devastatingly sexy he looked. The other wanted to beg him to peel the dress off of her and take her to bed. On second thought, screw the bed. The floor would work just fine.

She might have given in to the temptation if he hadn't distracted her by running his fingers down her arms. Her breath stuttered, and she idly wondered if it was possible to orgasm from the feeling of fingertips over skin alone. She was pretty sure she was about to find out.

Then he dropped his hands and took a measured step away from her.

"Ready?" he asked.

"I still need to put my shoes on," she whispered, cheeks still flushed with color as her heart—or maybe it was another body part—silently begged him to come back.

"Allow me."

Lina's mouth went dry as he lifted the strappy black heels and knelt down in front of her. She stopped breathing when he began to drag her dress up and reach for her leg.

If she thought the slight brush of a finger over her back was hot, the feeling of his warm hands sliding up her ankles and calves was a far more brutal form of torture. She couldn't even clamp her thighs together to try to alleviate the desperate ache building between them as he lifted first one of her feet, and then the other, to slide her heels into place.

Thankfully, she had his shoulders to hold onto, because her knees felt like they were one finger-flick away from buckling.

Releasing her, Nord stood. She still wasn't as tall as him in her five-inch heels, but her eyes were now in-line with his mouth. With each rapid heartbeat came the whispered command.

Kiss me.

Kiss me.

Kiss me.

She was already leaning forward, her hands still clenched on his shoulders, her chin tilted up, and her lips slightly parted. Her eyes were just starting to fall closed, as she breathed in the spicy scent of whatever soap he used.

"We should go."

With three words, he shattered the spell that had woven itself around them.

"Right," she managed, letting her arms fall to her sides. "Lead the way."

Nord surprised her by holding his arm out. It wasn't the act of chivalry in general, but more that it was a move that invited touch when he seemed to be trying to reestablish some physical distance.

Trying not to overthink it, Lina slid her arm through his as they made their way out of her room and down the hall. Finley was waiting for them, frowning slightly as he read something on his phone, before pressing his lips together and putting the phone in his jacket pocket.

"Something wrong?" she asked as they reached him.

Finley looked up, blinked, and then blinked again.

"Lina, you look fantastic," he said, moving to place a kiss on her cheek.

Nord's arm tensed beneath her hand, and Lina bit back a smile.

"Thank you," she said. "So do you."

Instead of black, Finley had gone with a royal blue tux with the same black silk lapels as Nord. It was stylish and sophisticated, and he looked absolutely sinful with his tousled hair and sparkling hazel eyes.

"Everyone have what they need?" he asked, hitting a button on the wall she'd always assumed was a light switch. A hidden panel slid open, revealing a variety of keys. Selecting one of the rings, he pressed the button again, and the panel closed.

Nord and Lina nodded, so Finley opened the front door and ushered them past a massive marble fireplace to a door Lina hadn't noticed because it was perfectly camouflaged as part of the wall.

"Where's this go?" she asked.

Finley stopped, and then shot Nord a dark look. "You let me go on and on about Lina stealing one of the cars, and she doesn't even know how to get to the garage?"

"You deserved it."

Lina snickered as Nord winked at her.

Finley shook his head. "I'll repay you for that."

"You can certainly try," Nord taunted.

Finley sighed as he gestured for Lina to cross the threshold into what she'd come to realize was a hidden elevator.

As she went to take a step, it felt like she was moving through an electric force field. Every hair along her body stood on end, and she shivered at the intensity of the uncomfortable prickle.

"Sorry," Nord murmured. "I forgot to warn you about the warding.

It's a fair bit stronger than the ones around the penthouse, and it can be a little uncomfortable passing through the first few times."

"No kidding." Lina blinked open her eyes. "Why is your elevator warded?"

"Because cars aren't the only thing down there," Finley said with a tight smile, moving in behind her.

"All right, then," she said with a little nod, still mildly disorientated.

Nord shifted at her side, and Lina caught a flash out of the corner of her eye that was there and gone. Like he wasn't the only person standing beside her. She turned her head, blinking rapidly to clear her vision.

Her Guardian gave her a concerned look. "You okay? I know you aren't overly fond of elevators."

Lina forced a smile. "I'm fine, just shaking off the aftereffects of your ward."

He nodded but took her hand and gave it a firm squeeze. For all that he may try to keep his distance, he never missed an opportunity to offer comfort or assistance. A fact for which she was vastly grateful. She appreciated his concern, glad that his steady presence was there to counteract the discomfort that came upon her as soon as the door closed.

There were only two buttons in the cube, so she assumed it was a direct connection from the penthouse to the private garage below. The trip was a quick one, over almost as quickly as it began. Lina was the first to shuffle out, her eyes growing wide at the row upon row of vehicles stretching out in every direction.

"You call this a couple cars?" she managed, before startled laughter bubbled up.

Finley's dimples flashed as he clicked a button on the key fob in his hand and tilted his head. "Come on."

Lina didn't know enough about cars to be able to tell any of them apart, but she could appreciate the pristine condition they were in and knew that Finley's collection must be worth a fortune.

"If you ever wanted to run a small country, I'm pretty sure you could use your cars for seed money."

Finley looked aghast. "Sell my cars? Are you mad?"

"Just saying."

He came to a stop beside a sleek black car, leaning over to whisper loudly, "You just go on and pretend you never heard a word that mean lady said, sweet girl. You know I'd never sell you."

Lina's eyes darted to Nord. "It's just a car, isn't it? It's not like a robot or Transformer or something?"

"Yup," Nord confirmed with a smirk. "Just a car."

"How dare you," Finley hissed, standing quickly. "This is a McLaren F1—hardly *just* a car."

"Can we even all fit in there?" Lina asked suspiciously.

Scoffing, Finley slid his fingers beneath a panel that jutted out slightly from the side of the car, pressing up and opening the door. There was no handle, like with a normal car, and instead of pulling out along its hinge, the door swiveled up. It sort of reminded Lina of a dog perking its ear, but she didn't think Finley would appreciate the comparison.

"Are you sure that's a car and not like . . . a rocket ship?"

Finley grinned. "It's fast enough, but alas, the only flying she does is on the streets."

Impressed despite herself, Lina peered into the car, noticing that the driver's seat was in the middle and it was flanked on either side by two passenger seats. Not only could all three of them fit; it seemed like they'd all have ample legroom as well.

She ran her hand over the supple leather before backing up. "So, which one of us is driving?" she asked with a mischievous smile.

Nord laughed when Finley clutched the keys tighter.

"Ha ha," he deadpanned, climbing into the driver's seat. "Nice try."

Nord helped Lina get settled before closing the door and moving around to the other side. Once they were all in, Finley gunned the engine, beaming like a child on Christmas morning.

"Okay, sweet girl, time to fly."

CHAPTER EIGHTEEN

Lina

"Remember the game plan," Nord cautioned as Finley handed the car keys to a stunned-looking valet.

Lina discreetly watched him stroke the top of Fin's "sweet girl" before climbing in and pulling the door closed with a look of reverent awe. When her eyes returned to the Guardians, they were both looking at her expectantly.

"What?" she blurted. "Why are you looking at me like I'm the one who's going to fuck things up?"

Finley smirked as Nord replied, "Never hurts to cover our bases."

She glared at him. "What's so complicated about sticking close and only talking to someone if you introduce me to them first?"

"Your penchant for not following the rules, perhaps?" Finley offered.

Lina didn't dignify that with a comment, keeping her eyes glued to Nord.

"Right," Nord said, speaking in a low murmur as they neared the entrance. "If we introduce you, it means we know the person and consider them safe. If we don't, they're not to be trusted. Do not, under any circumstances, go off on your own. I've said it before, but it bears repeating: this is not a gathering of the supernatural community's finest. While there will be a handful of guests here for business reasons, the majority of the people you'll see tonight are some of the most unsavory, foul creatures to ever walk the face of this earth."

A little shiver of apprehension worked its way down her body. "Got it."

The trio fell silent, slipping into their roles of bored socialites seconds before reaching a roped off door beneath a green and silver striped awning. Lina could just make out the words "The District" painted in black.

A doorman moved into the center of the entry, his arms folded across his beefy chest as he inspected them with beady black eyes. He was on the shorter side, maybe only an inch taller than Lina at most, but it did nothing to diminish the aura of violence radiating from him. Next to Nord, whose height and bulk gave the impression of muscles created by a lifetime of hard labor, the doorman's body appeared manufactured. Like he'd been injected with steroids and growth hormones until his skin could literally not contain anymore.

With his barrel chest, thick arms, and short stature, he reminded her of a gorilla. Since there wasn't a name tag in sight, and he didn't seem like the type to offer a name, Lina dubbed him King Kong, or Kiko for short.

"Invitation," Kiko grunted.

Lina's eyes darted to Finley, who was reaching into his jacket to produce the three bronze medallions that would enable them to join in tonight's festivities.

As she watched, that odd wavering at the edge of her vision she'd experienced in the elevator returned. This time coming from where Kiko was standing on her left. She blinked, trying to clear the haziness, but it persisted until she finally snapped her eyes back to the doorway.

There was nothing there but Kiko, who met her stare head-on, his expression carved in the same stoic mask as before.

Lina's lips dipped in a frown. The wavering was gone, but in its place a dull throb had taken up residence in her temples.

Stupid ward.

Finley flashed the medallions, but that wasn't good enough for Kiko, who held out his hand and curled his fingers in a "hand 'em over" motion. Fin complied but rolled his eyes and sighed loudly, as if he was thoroughly put out by the request.

Kiko held them up, one at a time, peering closely at the surface like he was checking for counterfeits. Lina was half-expecting him to put one in his mouth and bite down, but he didn't. After examining each, he placed all three in his pocket and unhooked the velvet rope.

"Go on." He gestured to the stairs behind him with his shaved head.

Finley took the lead, while Nord placed his hand on her back, wordlessly telling her to go next.

"Try not to get too bored out here, Kiko," she murmured as she brushed passed.

The doorman's eyebrows lifted in surprise.

Shit.

She'd gotten so comfortable with her little nickname that it slipped out.

"Uh, I mean, thanks," she rushed, hustling up the stairs.

She was halfway when Nord leaned over to whisper in her ear. "You didn't even make it two minutes without breaking the rules."

If she'd had a mirror, she knew her cheeks would be crimson. "Surely social niceties don't count as talking."

"You gave him a pet name," Nord pointed out. "I think that extends a bit beyond niceties. How did you come up with that, by the way?"

"He reminded me a bit of King Kong," she muttered under her breath as they neared the top of the narrow staircase.

Nord's bark of laughter created a cocoon around her. "Not too far off, actually," he said in a low voice. "He's half stone giant," he continued, falling silent as they reached the landing.

"What's the other half?" she asked, thinking it odd that anything part giant could be so short.

"Orc, I think."

Lina hummed, her attention shifting as she reached the top of the stairs. A green and silver carpet runner led the way to a coat check, where a woman in a cigarette girl outfit stood to the side holding a tray of drinks.

"Champagne?" she offered.

"No thanks," Finley answered smoothly, giving her his signature dimpled grin to take the sting out of his refusal.

The girl, who looked no older than eighteen, blushed and dipped her violet eyes. "If you don't have anything you wish to check with us, you can head on in."

Finley nodded and strode toward the door a little further down the corridor. It opened as he neared the threshold, although opened isn't quite the right word. The door shimmered and then vanished entirely, revealing a room filled with smoke and debauchery in its place.

Every sense was assaulted at once, the purpose unmistakable. This was a den of sin, and all were expected to partake. Why would they be here otherwise?

The main room was a study in opulence. One large square room, it continued the green and silver décor from outside. Two of the walls were lined with hidden alcoves, shadowed silhouettes the only indication of someone's presence within. Directly across from the entrance, spanning the entire length of the wall, was a bar mostly obscured by guests. Jade-colored lights illuminated the bottles lining the shelves behind the half-circle made of silvery granite snaking with shimmering obsidian and flecks of emerald. In place of any kind of dance floor was a sunken area in the center of the room. There was a massive chandelier hanging in the middle with a circle of black leather couches surrounding a half dozen cocktail tables below.

It was impossible to not become intoxicated by the sights and sounds, especially when Nord began ushering her further inside, and she started to take notice of the other details.

The music was something low and sultry, the beat heavy and slow, bringing to mind all sorts of bedroom games. The air was perfumed with a combination of vanilla and tobacco, the sweet and earthy combination of feminine and masculine scents twining together in perfect balance. Drinks were flowing both at a bar and on trays being discreetly offered by men and women in similar attire to the woman in the hall.

But the true focal points were the four aerial dancers spaced throughout the room, whose mostly naked bodies were swathed in green fabric as they spun and twirled in the air.

Lina watched in rapt fascination as one of the male performers completed a series of spins that brought him within an inch of the floor. He must have heard her breathless gasp as he came to a perfect stop because he looked up and caught her eye, winking before grasping two fistfuls of silk and climbing back up.

"Faerie," Nord whispered, his voice sending electric tingles coursing through her.

"I thought faeries had wings?" she asked.

"They do."

Lina's eyes roved the performer who was currently balancing between the two pieces of fabric by his ankles, his legs stretched out in a split that made her wince. "I don't see any."

"Glamour. Everyone here is using it to some degree. It's part of what makes them so dangerous. Most won't know what kind of threat they're dealing with until it's too late."

Lina pressed her lips together and gave a little nod to indicate she'd received his warning.

Finley was a few steps ahead, chatting with one of the servers. The woman hurried away as Nord and Lina reached him.

"Hope you don't mind. I took the liberty of ordering us all drinks."

"Do you really think it safe to accept anything they offer here?" Nord asked.

"Who said anything about drinking them? Appearances, remember?"

While they waited for their drinks, Lina let her eyes travel across the room, trying to guess what kind of supernatural each guest was based on their outfits alone.

The woman closest to her was wearing a glittering red and gold number that immediately brought the flicker of flames to mind. Some kind of elemental, perhaps? The man she was speaking to was harder to pinpoint. He was slender where many others bulged with muscle, his hair a deep auburn, his eyes copper. Fox shifter, maybe? There was something about the alert intensity of his expression that gave her a sense of cunning.

The waitress' return interrupted her game. Lina accepted her cocktail with a soft, "Thanks."

Lifting the drink up to her lips, using the move to disguise her question, she asked, "Where's our host?"

Nord wasn't looking at her as he replied, "I was wondering the same."

"Most likely back there," Finley murmured, tipping his head to the far corner where two of Kiko's siblings stood.

"So, we just stand here and wait, hoping he decides to mingle? That's stupid."

Nord's brows flew up. "You have a better suggestion?"

Lina bit down on her lip as an idea began to take shape in her mind. "Why yes, I believe I do," she said, slamming her drink back.

"Lina," Nord hissed. "What did we *just* say?"

She placed a hand on his chest. "Look, you gave me a weapon. Let me use it. You two are right here, if anything makes your super senses tingle, you'll be able to intervene before anything gets out of hand."

Finley snorted. "It took her, what, less than five minutes to completely disregard the plan?" he muttered. "Is that a new record?"

"I knew bringing her was a bad idea," Nord groaned, a deep line forming between his brows.

Lina knew she had them between a rock and a hard place. They couldn't afford to cause a scene here. Not without raising all the wrong kind of attention. Sure, Nord could haul her ass out to keep her from doing anything, but he wouldn't risk leaving Fin alone.

"I'm just going to go to the bar and get another drink. Nothing crazy, all right?"

A muscle pulsed in Nord's jaw. "Not alone."

"Listen, I can't have you scaring everyone away. If the whole point is to get information, we're going to have to talk to somebody."

"Me, not you," he insisted, his face carved from stone.

"Don't you trust me?" she asked.

It was one of those questions that only had one answer, and they both knew it. He couldn't admit he didn't trust her without causing irreparable damage.

"You're not really giving me reason to right now," he finally said.

"Then why give me this dress if you didn't want me to use it. I'm the bait, right? So, let me go catch our fish."

Nord's nostrils flared, the flecks of azure ringing his pupil starting to glow. "You were the lure, not the bait."

"Same difference in the end."

As their hushed conversation went on, the room continued to fill, making it impossible to continue the argument without risk of being overheard.

It was Finley who made the decision for them. Since he was technically the leader of their op, Nord's protests fell on deaf ears.

"I don't like it any more than you do," he started, "but no one currently at the bar poses significant risk. If that changes, one of us will go and get her. She'll be in sight the entire time."

Nord glowered and the high-ball glass in his hand started to crack under the pressure of his grip.

"I'll touch my hair if someone makes me uncomfortable, okay?" Lina offered.

"Go before I change my mind," he growled.

Even though she was getting her way, Lina was smart enough to know this wasn't a victory. Nord was pissed, and she'd pay for it later. If she was being honest, she was looking forward to it, especially with how things ended the last time they fought. And, if she was being *really* honest, the reminder of that night may have been part of what prompted her to go against their plan in the first place. Not that she'd ever admit it.

She'd deal with the consequences—pleasant or otherwise—when she had to. For now, it was time to put her spy skills to the test.

Assuming, of course, that she had any to begin with.

Giving the men one final look, Lina made her way to the bar, making a point to make her movements unhurried. She let her eyes wander, offering small, close-lipped smiles she hoped passed for mysterious to anyone that made eye contact. So far there were no aghast looks of recognition, although there were more than a few leers.

Lina ignored them, spying a free spot at the bar. When she was only a few steps away, that odd blurring just outside the farthest edges of her vision started up again, this time coming from both sides. The sensation was disorientating, and she faltered, wobbling slightly on her heels and drawing the attention of a woman around her age who was leaning against the bar sipping a crimson-colored cocktail.

Lina blinked rapidly, trying to repel the fog, and between one rapid eyelid flutter and the next, the woman's face appeared to transform. It happened far too quickly for Lina to absorb any details, and by the time her eyes were open and focused once more, the effect was gone. She stared at the stranger for a couple seconds longer, just in case it happened again, which was probably what prompted the woman to speak to her.

"I have that effect on people." She smirked, lifting her glass in a mock toast.

Lina laughed, the unexpected joke alleviating any unease as she closed the distance between them. "I can see why," she said with a genuine smile. And she could. The woman was gorgeous. Even in a sea full of beautiful and glamorous people, she stood out.

Pale, ivory skin contrasted sharply with jet black hair that fell well past her waist, even though she wore it up in a sleek ponytail. Her wide, almond-shaped eyes were lined with kohl, their unique color mesmerizing. Not quite purple, not quite red, it was a color which oscillated in-between and seemed to ripple like an endless pool as she studied Lina.

Her dress was a deep scarlet—a perfect match to the lipstick painting her lips—with a plunging neckline, and a slit that went all the way up to the top of her thigh, revealing a shapely leg encased in black fishnets. To complete her ensemble, she wore a frontlet that draped across her forehead, its clusters of rubies and onyx glittering against her skin.

Clearly, this was a woman who also recognized her clothing was a weapon.

"I'm Lina."

The woman's smile stretched. "Quinn. Looks like you need a drink, Lina." Without waiting for an answer, she flagged the nearest bartender down. "We'll take two more of these," she said, waving her glass at him. As he turned away to prep their drinks, Quinn glanced back at Lina. "So, what brings you here?"

"The auction," Lina replied.

Quinn laughed. "Well, obviously. But is there something in particular you're hoping to take home with you?"

Seeing her opening, Lina leaned forward and dropped her voice like she was about to reveal a secret. "Well, actually . . ." she trailed off, her eyes drifting to where Nord and Finley were standing, pretending not to be looking their way.

"Oh, I see," Quinn murmured, both eyebrows raised as she took stock of Lina's companions. "It's a different kind of hunt altogether."

"Those two?" Lina laughed. "No, I have my eye on a different prize entirely."

"Really? So, they're fair game?" Quinn asked, her eyes taking on a calculating gleam.

Something hot and uncomfortable slithered around in Lina's stomach. Resting her hand lightly on Quinn's arm, she gave the other woman a sympathetic pout. "Unfortunately, those two only have eyes for each other. Bummer, right? Why do you think I'm on the prowl?" She forced a laugh, hoping Quinn would accept her assessment and find a new target of her own.

"Oh, that is too bad," she said, giving a sultry pout of her own.

When those wine-colored eyes shifted back to Lina, she couldn't help but notice the twinkle of amusement shining in them. If she was onto her, Quinn was too polite to call her out on it.

The bartender returned, setting the two drinks down and moving away.

"Not very chatty, is he?" Lina commented, watching him retreat while taking an idle sip. The cinnamon and cherry flavor exploded on her tongue, and her eyes widened in delight. "This is delicious."

Quinn gave her a mysterious smile. "I had a feeling you'd like it."

"What's it called?"

"Blood fever."

Lina nervously set the drink down.

"Named for the drink's color and sweet heat, not a hidden ingredient," Quinn assured her, correctly guessing the reason for her sudden change of heart.

"Am I that transparent?" Lina asked, feeling the heat creep into her face.

"Delightfully so. It's refreshing. I think you and I are going to be great friends."

For a second, Lina forgot that she was on a mission. That she was either supposed to be gathering information about their mark, or with a few not-so-subtly dropped hints, she piqued his curiosity enough that he'd come out to her. In that suspended moment, she was just a twenty-something-year-old woman grabbing drinks with her friend. It was so wholly unexpected that Lina's answering smile was radiant.

"I think I'm looking forward to it."

Quinn winked at her. "So, if not those two, who are you hunting?" Her eyes swept the room as if trying to scope out Lina's prey.

This was the opening she'd been waiting for, but now that it was here, she wasn't sure how to approach it. Should she be blunt? Coy? This was the part of the whole social skills thing she'd yet to master. Usually, she didn't mind blundering her way through, but if she made a misstep now, she risked ruining the entire mission.

Needing to buy some more time, Lina opted for a one-shouldered shrug and took another sip of her drink. Warmth spread out through her limbs, warning her it was far stronger than she'd realized. Wanting to keep a steady head, she set her drink back down.

Fuck it. She'd come this far on instinct and sheer nerve alone. It seemed to serve her well, up to this point. Why stop now?

"Well, actually. I'm quite intrigued by our host."

Quinn's eyes flared with interest. "My, that would be a delicious scandal. He's notoriously hard to catch. You think you're up for the task?"

Lina gave what she hoped was a confident smile. "I think I have something he wants."

"Really?" Quinn whispered, her eyes darting to a place just over Lina's shoulder. "Well, now's your chance to find out. He's coming this way."

CHAPTER NINETEEN

Lina

Lina tried not to make it obvious as she glanced over her shoulder, but all pretense was lost as the man they'd been waiting for strode across the room.

There was no mistaking him, even though she'd only had the barest sketch of a description from Finley, who'd never personally met the black-market auctioneer. But, unless Finley was a master illusionist like Nord, she didn't think he'd have done the man justice even if he had.

Davis Crombie moved with a dark grace that had the voice of reason in her head screaming at her to run. He was of an average height, with a dancer's build, all lean, sinewy muscles. His black hair hung past his cheekbones, offering only the briefest glimpse of stormy-gray eyes fringed with thick black lashes. What she could make out of his face was sharp, angular lines. His long perfectly straight nose over his full, pouty lips.

"Careful, doll. I think you're drooling."

Quinn's laughter-tinged voice made her face flame, and Lina spun back around.

"I mean . . . I'd heard stories, but . . . I was not prepared."

"Few are when they meet the fae princeling the first time. You picked a hell of a man to land, dearest."

Lina was having second, third, and fourth thoughts about her plan. But then . . . that was nothing new. Life was fleeting; there wasn't time enough for regrets. She might fail, but she had to try.

"You seem to know a thing or two about the man. Any suggestions on getting an audience?"

Quinn pursed her lips. "He's a collector of pretty, expensive things. It stands to reason all you need do is catch his eye."

Luck must be on her side then because that was about what she'd been hoping for.

"Shouldn't be too difficult, right?" Lina asked with a nervous laugh.

"Here," Quinn said, switching places with her. "This way he has a better chance of spotting you."

This time when Lina let her eyes wander to their host, she let them linger, not bothering to disguise her interest. He was just as handsome upon a second inspection, although there was something terrifying about the cold, dispassionate expression he wore. One of his body-guards leaned over to whisper something in his ear. Crombie's face did not change, but Lina could have sworn she heard the distant clap of thunder when he shook his head.

She shivered.

The slight movement caught his attention. Suddenly, Lina found herself pinned by a pair of unyielding gray eyes.

To her right, Lina could see Nord and Finley moving in. She wasn't surprised they were trying to intercept him. If she'd realized exactly what kind of man they were dealing with, she might not have been so gung-ho about going off on her own. There was intimidating, and then there was Crombie. It was hard to fully comprehend that kind of intensity without experiencing it firsthand.

But then if he really did deal in the trading of supernatural beings and not just objects . . . he'd have to be a bit of a monster.

Unfortunately for all of them, this monster only had eyes for her.

Lina watched as Finley opened his mouth.

Crombie dismissed him with no more than the flick of his hand. With a whispered order, his three bodyguards shifted back as he switched direction to head straight for her.

Lina hoped the panicked-rabbit feeling that had taken hold wasn't broadcasted on her face. Not knowing what else to do, she picked up her drink and took a healthy gulp.

Quinn let out a snort of surprise before doing the same. "I'll drink in solidarity. You might as well finish that. I'm willing to bet you're going to need it."

"You're probably right," Lina managed, her throat growing tight with nerves.

She could just make out Nord and Finley's faces, both lined with worry, as Crombie reached her. The magnetic force of presence she'd sensed from halfway across the room magnified tenfold now that she was the center of its focus.

Lina took Quinn's advice and finished her drink. She hoped her death grip on the glass at least hid the tremor in her hands, knowing it did nothing to help reinforce the air of confidence she'd intended to portray.

"Would you like another?" Crombie asked, his voice a sensual caress that was at complete odds with the hard cast of his face.

"I probably shouldn't," she answered honestly.

For some reason, that seemed to amuse him. "I find that making any decision based on whether I should or should *not* do something is an absolute waste of time." Snapping his fingers, he managed to request another round without saying a word or even acknowledging the bartender that rushed to follow the silent order.

Lina swallowed as he leaned closer, his gray eyes sparkling with a playful challenge she didn't anticipate could stem from one with such a dangerous aura.

"The only factor that should ever be taken into consideration is how much you'll enjoy yourself."

She knew her cheeks were flushed, she could feel the warmth crawling across her skin, but she didn't know whether to blame the drink or the man.

"I do believe I've shocked you," he whispered in genuine surprise as one of his long fingers reached out to brush her cheek. Instead of Nord's fiery touch, which always seared her with its heat, this felt like a cube of ice being dragged across her skin. "How can a temptress be such an innocent?"

Come on, Lina. You can do this. Don't just stand here. Nord and Fin are counting on you. Do what you came over here to do.

"I'm hardly innocent," she said, willing herself to hold his gaze.

"Is that so?" Crombie's lips twitched as his head tilted ever so slightly to the side, sending inky strands of hair falling over his forehead. His eyes were locked onto hers, staring so intently it was as if he were attempting to suss out her secrets by sight alone. The silence hung between them, and his lips curled into a predatory smile. "I'm not sure I believe that, Miss . . ."

"Jones," she supplied. "But you can call me Lina."

"Lina," he repeated, taking one of her hands and holding it up to his lips. "But I do love a riddle," he added, his lips moving against her flesh before he pressed a lingering kiss to the back of her hand.

"I fear you'll be disappointed," she rasped in a throaty voice she didn't recognize.

He continued to study her, his eyes slowly dropping to her mouth. "No . . . for the first time in a long while, I don't believe I will."

Before she could rebuff yet another skillfully delivered line, Lina's vision blurred. Unlike the last few times, this was not a simple flickering at the edge of her periphery. It was a full-scale assault, making the entire room dip and sway like a ship at sea. Sharp pain began to prick behind her eyes as faces began to swim in and out of focus.

She swallowed back a scream as men with fangs and demonic-looking wings replaced the classically handsome faces of the bartenders. And they weren't the only ones that had changed. There were women with serpentine features and forked tongues standing at the bar. Goblin-like creatures replaced a couple sitting on one of the couches. Crombie's understated, suit-clad bodyguards were now towering figures with mottled gray skin and black, pupilless eyes.

Cool beads of sweat began to drip down her back as her brain struggled to process what she was seeing. Crombie's icy fingers circled her upper arm, and Lina gave a violent flinch before recognition set in. He still looked exactly the same. That, along with the firm touch anchoring her, helped the room snap back into focus.

"Lina?"

"These drinks are a lot stronger than I'm used to. The alcohol must have gone straight to my head," she said, trying to laugh the episode off.

"Perhaps some water, then," Crombie murmured, his eyes narrowing shrewdly. Lina doubted he was buying her excuse, but he seemed willing to go along with it.

Knowing that Nord and Finley wouldn't have missed the incident from where they were standing, she risked a glance at them. Her Guardian's eyes were trained on her, a vein pulsing visibly in his forehead. His eyes were swirling with power, his teeth bared in a feral snarl. He looked seconds away from snapping entirely. The only thing that seemed to be keeping him in place was Finley's hand clamped on the back of his neck and whatever words he was furiously whispering in his ear.

Lina made a gesture with her hand, trying to tell them she was fine, and they should stay put. Nord gave a single shake of his head. Lina repeated the movement, more forcefully this time. Nord shrugged Finley off and crossed his arms. His message was clear. One more slip like that and he was pulling her out, appearances be damned.

Clearing her throat, Lina took a thankful sip of the water that had been set by her elbow.

"So now that I've completely embarrassed myself, it's your turn," Lina said, trying her best at a coy smile although her heart was still racing.

"You want me to embarrass myself?" Crombie asked, mirroring her posture and leaning against the bar.

"It's only fair."

Claiming the drink he'd ordered for her, he took a sip, never breaking eye contact as he swallowed and set the glass back down. "Just one problem."

"What's that?"

"You have to give a shit about what other people think to be embarrassed."

From anyone else, she might have expected a sexy smirk or some other hint that it was a crock of BS, but he spoke with such matter-of-fact simplicity that she knew he was being completely honest. Crombie truly didn't care.

The blunt honesty did nothing to diminish the apprehension coursing through her veins. If anything, the admission only reinforced the need to proceed with caution.

"Must be nice," she said, meaning it.

He lifted one shoulder in a careless shrug. "It has its perks."

"Such as?"

"I'm more interested in learning about you."

"There's not much to tell," she said, internally snickering at the irony of the comment. She was telling the truth, but he'd think she was just playing games. It was time to use his interest in her to their benefit. She just needed to figure out how to steer the conversation in that direction.

Crombie's fingers were brushing a few fallen strands of hair over her still flushed skin before she so much as tracked the movement. After tucking them behind her ear, he extended the caress, fingers lingering on her jaw as he leaned closer.

"Allow me to be the judge of that."

Scrambling for a way to place them back on even footing, Lina rested a hand against his chest and leaned back. "Now why should I spill my secrets if you refuse to do the same?"

"Who said I refused?" he asked, one side of his mouth curving up.

Now they were getting somewhere.

Lina raised a brow. "Are we really going to play the verbal equivalent of 'you show me yours; I'll show you mine'?"

"You tell me." For a man who was supposed to be running this event, Crombie seemed like he had nothing but time on his hands.

Lina knew if she could get Crombie alone, Nord and Finley would follow, and then they'd be able to proceed with their interrogation without any of the other guests becoming any the wiser. Flutters of excitement exploded in her belly as she realized she might just pull this off after all.

"Here? In front of all these people?" she asked, fiddling with her water glass.

His eyes flared with interest. "That's easily remedied."

Lina suppressed a whoop of victory. Not wanting to appear too eager, she drained her water, and then very deliberately reached for the mostly full cocktail Crombie had claimed as his own. Eyes never leaving his, she finished that drink as well and set the heavy crystal glass back on the bar.

Her lips parted, ready to tell him to lead the way, when her mind fractured.

With a wordless gasp, she pitched forward, no longer able to remain upright as white-hot pain lanced through her skull.

CHAPTER TWENTY

Nord

"If he doesn't stop fucking touching her, I'm going to rip his arm off and beat him with it," Nord growled under his breath.

"Now, now. Is that any way to make friends?" Finley chided in an entirely too amused voice.

Nord speared him with a look promising a slow and painful death. "Who needs friends?"

His partner's eyes glittered with something just as dark and dangerous as what he knew to be in his own. "Careful, Guardian. That sounds a lot like a threat."

"I don't do threats."

"Neither do I."

Nord huffed out an angry breath and looked back at Lina. He hated everything about this. The fucking clothes. The damned bottom-feeders circling them like a bunch of bloodthirsty sharks. And, more than anything, the fact that the woman he was supposed to protect was standing over there being manhandled by King Bottom-Feeder himself.

"Why are we standing here playing fucking games?" he asked for the dozenth time. "The asshole's right there. Let's grab him, get the information we need, and get the fuck out of here."

"What part of undercover don't you understand?"

Nord's chest vibrated like a beast rattling the bars of its cage. "This is bullshit."

"She's perfectly safe," Finley replied, his tone a bit gentler. "We're right here. Nothing is going to happen to her."

The words did nothing to soothe Nord's temper. If anything, it only stoked the flames of his rage higher. He knew better than most how quickly danger could strike. That death could claim its next victim in less time than it takes to draw a breath.

More often than not, he was death's instrument in those scenarios.

The only reason he'd gone along with Lina's plan in the first place was because he saw how desperately she wanted to play more than just a supporting role in uncovering the truth about her past.

Each day that passed without her reclaiming her magic, or making progress with her research at the bureau, ate away at her. He knew that she felt like she was failing. Add to that the toll her nightmares took, and it was like watching a ghost being recreated before his eyes. Little by little these perceived failures chipped away at her vibrancy, her hunger for being alive. Even her attempts to ambush him into taking her to bed had dwindled. He'd taken to provoking her just to see a flicker of her natural fire rekindle. He couldn't bear to watch any more of the woman he'd met at The Monster Ball disappear.

So he caved.

Now, he was stuck fighting against every instinct he had not to storm over to the bar and beat the man bloody who dared to touch her.

Tension knotted his muscles and pulsed in his veins. He could feel the spasm of a muscle ticking in his jaw, and if he ground his teeth together any harder, there wouldn't be anything but gums left.

"Easy, mate."

"So help me, Finley, if you tell me to calm down one more time, I will rip your fucking jaw off."

It wouldn't be the first time.

Finley wisely kept his mouth shut.

"I'm giving her five more minutes, then we're going in. I don't care if we're undercover or not. If I have to watch him eye fuck her any longer then that, I might start murdering people."

"Understood."

Something in his chest loosened enough that Nord was able to draw in a full breath. At least the end of this fucked-up charade was in sight.

It was the worst possible time to let his guard drop.

He watched as Lina finished both her drink and the bottom-feeder's. Then, without warning, her face drained of color and her eyes rolled back in her head.

The monster within slipped free of its chains, that primal rage overtaking every trace of humanity that he'd clung to.

The world sharpened, a red haze coating his vision.

Nord's last coherent thought was that at least the motherfucker put his hands out to catch her.

It would be the last thing he ever did.

"Shit. Fuck, Nord," Finley growled, reaching out for him and grasping his forearm.

Nord broke his hand without hesitation and kept prowling forward.

One of Crombie's men noticed him. He reached for a weapon, and Nord sprang forward, slamming his fist into and then through the man's throat. There was a gasp, and then a wet gurgle. His fingers opened and closed around bone, yanking sharply and pulling what had once been the man's spine out of the gaping hole.

Hot streams of blood sprayed his face, and the muted sounds of screaming reached his ears.

Nord grinned savagely, welcoming the bloodlust. Embracing the violence surging through him.

It was like coming home.

This is who he was.

What he had always been destined to be.

Without faltering, the berserker looked up, staring straight into the eyes of his next victim.

And then he struck.

CHAPTER TWENTY-ONE

Lina

Pain held her in chains more binding than steel. There was nothing but the sense of being ripped apart at the seams. Agony clawed at her throat. Tears that felt like acid left trails of fire down her cheeks. Muscles spasmed and quaked as if the very cells that made her were imploding. She was coming undone.

It hurt to move. To breathe. To simply exist.

She welcomed the end. She just wanted it to stop. All of it.

Anything to put her out of her misery.

Swirling gray was replaced by blinding white and her eyes flew open, her body obeying a command that was issued without her consent.

It felt like shards of glass were being slowly shoved into her eyes. If she were capable of touching her face, she knew her fingers would come away smeared with blood. She shouldn't be able to see through the pain, to process and catalog the images that pushed their way to the surface. But she could.

Perfectly.

She was noticing details at a level she'd never experienced before. Her face was pressed against the solid wall of a chest, and she could count every fiber in the fabric. She could make out the rush of blood through veins over the steady beat of a heart. Her fingers dug into the muscular arms that cradled her and knew by the way they flexed with the touch how much force would be required to pierce the flesh.

It was too much to process. Her eyelids were heavy, the weight of them slowly dragging the swollen flesh down in an attempt to cut out the light. Instead of bringing relief, the action only served to bury the imaginary shards of glass deeper. Her eyes flew back open. It helped alleviate the feeling, but only just.

She must have stopped shaking, because the world shifted. She was standing once more, although two hands still grasped her arms, keeping her upright.

The owner of those hands gripped hard, and she flinched in protest. Her eyes shifted up, noting the way his lips were shaping her name. She stumbled out of his grasp, not sure how she managed to control her limbs long enough to break his hold.

She attempted a step forward, and it was like trying to walk down the stairs only to find that the steps were not where she thought they were. Her arms lifted to her sides to help her catch her balance, but the abrupt move was uncomfortable. Her skin no longer felt like it fit right. There was too much it was trying to contain.

Something had broken free.

A low, rumbling growl caught her attention. Even through the fog of chaos she recognized the source.

Her head snapped up, eyes snagging on her Guardian's gore-splattered tux. He was bowed over a body, his blond head stained red. As she watched, he looked up slowly, his wild eyes finding her. His teeth were bared in a bloody grin, and he straightened, his latest target falling lifelessly to his feet.

Time didn't seem to be functioning properly. Around them, people were only just starting to notice the dead bodies on the floor. She counted at least three. But while they seemed stuck moving in slow motion, her Guardian was in fast forward. He struck with preternatural grace and speed. Already his hands were wrapped around the head of his next victim.

She should have been horrified as he loosed a ferocious battle cry and snapped the man's neck with such brutal force that he tore through the flesh. But Lina didn't feel afraid. She was confused.

She barely noticed that the dead man—who'd partially shifted into his bear form—sagged. Or that as he dropped to the floor, his head flopped back, held onto the rest of the body by only a thin sliver of fur-covered skin.

She barely noticed because she was too busy staring at the man responsible for ripping the other guests apart limb from limb.

The man who'd proclaimed himself her Guardian.

Who had kissed her with such tender passion that she could still feel the ghost of his lips moving over hers.

The man, who right now, was wearing someone else's face.

It wasn't quite a mask, more like his features were shifting and slithering beneath the surface. When they settled, it was only for seconds at a time. First, he looked like an old man, his weathered face scarred, his eyes glittering like a night sky. Even his beard seemed to lengthen, the blond strands liberally peppered with gray. When she blinked, his facial hair vanished entirely. This time he was young again, but thick swirling tattoos were inked across his bald head and down the left side of his face, his eyes glowing, but not with the azure light she'd grown accustomed to. Both of his frost-colored orbs were now a burning crimson, the same hue as the blood that covered him.

Her breath froze in her lungs.

Nord barely looked human.

And then he changed once more, and Lina realized her mistake. He wasn't human at all.

He was a savage. A beast born to bathe in bloodshed and revel in death.

And he was terrifying.

Blue snaking runes the color of the darkest ocean slid across bone-white skin. All that was left of his eyes were two never-ending black pits. Instead of a nose, there were only two skull-like holes. And those lips, the same ones whose phantom kisses she cherished as she laid awake at night, were chapped and bleeding beneath the row of Xs stitching them closed.

She was little more than a statue, barely daring to draw in a breath as she watched this creature stalk toward her wearing her Guardian's tux.

Sudden heat blossomed deep within her chest. At first, she thought it was her lungs begging for oxygen, but the heat expanded, exploding outward like a supernova and filling her entire body with its searing warmth. She was soon choking on it, the taste of ash heavy in her mouth as she gasped and panted for air. It felt like she was drowning, if it were possible to drown without being anywhere near a body of water.

Her vision began to blur once more, although not with any kind of gray fog. This time it was different. Now it was tendrils of darkness, robbing her of her sight entirely.

She could hear the sound of her erratic heart pumping furiously, the swoosh of blood sounding like a roar in her head. Her nails dug into her chest, some of them breaking as she scratched and tore at the bodice of her dress in her fight for air.

I'm going to die.

The realization pierced through to the fragment within that wasn't yet consumed by the flameless fire burning her from the inside out.

No. Not again.

I refuse to die again.

As she dropped to her knees, Lina's head fell back, and her mouth opened on a soundless scream borne of desperation.

It was almost as if the unfamiliar heat had been waiting for her to do just that. It paused, no longer expanding outward from her chest, but instead pulling itself back together. The reversal was instantaneous, like a rubber band stretched too far, it snapped back together and then shot out of her body.

She was locked into place as white-gold light burst out, not only from her wide-open mouth, but also her eyes, ears, and the tips of her fingers.

Tingles of electric energy arced over and through her as the beam continued to pour out. There was nothing she could do to stop it. She ceased to be in that moment. The energy—the power—owning her absolutely. Lina was merely the vessel, a slave to the whims of whatever had taken control of her body.

All around her, glass shattered, sending colorful shards raining down from every direction, and then . . . glorious silence.

CHAPTER TWENTY-TWO

Nord

As the body fell with a wet thump to the ground, Nord's attention shifted, his prey finally within range. Even with the acrid smell of death heavy in his nose, he could identify the night and whisky scent of the monster masquerading as a man.

The bottom-feeder who dared hurt the one who belonged to him.

The fool didn't even realize he'd signed his death warrant, but he would. Nord grinned, welcoming the chance to deliver the message.

Sheep never realized that there was a wolf among them until it was too late. Unfortunately for this sheep, he thought he was the wolf. Worse, he believed he was the only hunter here. Monsters always did. They never thought something worse than them could exist in the world, hiding in plain sight.

The beast within roared, eager to watch that cocksure confidence fade from his prey's eyes as he learned otherwise.

Nord looked up from his last kill, expecting to see the one he hunted standing before him. The only one whose death would quench his insatiable thirst for blood. Instead, his prey was momentarily forgotten as he found himself ensnared by a pair of glowing golden eyes and a room frozen in time.

No one was moving, save for himself and the woman in front of him, and she wasn't moving as much as sucking in air. She stared back at him, her face expressionless behind the magic swirling in her eyes. Something in the brilliant depths called to him, reaching past the blinding rage straight to the heart of him.

Recognition flickered. A thread of a thought. A name.

Lina.

The shock of it, of finding Lina's eyes glowing like a fucking goddess, was enough to force the beast back. Only by an inch, but that inch was all it took.

For the first time in his entire existence, Nord was able to stave off the bloodlust by sheer force of will.

And it was because of her.

Since she was also the reason he was now prone to losing control in the first place, maybe that shouldn't have come as such a surprise, but it shocked him to the fucking core. He'd known when he found her that she was meant for him, that the course of his fate would be irrevocably altered, but he hadn't realized what it truly meant to be owned by another. How his life was no longer his own.

Nord blinked as Lina's eyes seemed to glow even brighter, lit from within by her very own power source.

He didn't know why the other guests were frozen, nor did he care. Right now, the only thing that mattered was reaching her. He needed to touch her and ensure that she was truly safe.

Prowling forward, he easily stepped over the corpse at his feet without looking. Before he made it halfway, Lina let out a barely audible hiss and clutched her chest. Despite the desperate need to get to her, he hadn't managed another step before she was dropping to her knees, her head thrown back as invisible wind whipped around her. The luminescence that before had only shone in her eyes was now surging beneath her skin and exploding outward. Beams of light jutted out from her body, but his eyes were locked on the agonized expression on her face.

"Lina!" he roared, the beast within rattling its chains as it fought to break free once more.

Glass shattered, and he knew that some of the blood dripping down his face and hands was now his own, but he didn't register the pain.

His sole focus was getting to her before whatever was flowing out of her tore her apart. Then he heard something that turned his blood to ice, and Nord feared he was too late. It was a sound usually reserved for battlefields and hospital beds. A soft, ragged wheeze that almost exclusively preceded the soul leaving the body.

It was the soundtrack of the dying.

CHAPTER TWENTY-THREE

Lina

Lina slumped forward onto her hands and knees, hair spilling down around her face as it slipped free of its pins, palms grinding into jagged shards of broken chandelier and stemware.

Perhaps she should have felt empty with whatever she'd just exorcised, but she felt . . . full.

Whole in a way she hadn't realized was even possible.

The room was shockingly still. *Shouldn't people be screaming?* But there was nothing. The only sound she could make out was the ragged pull of her breath. Then the crunch of glass and a tortured whisper.

"Lina?"

Body still trembling with dozens of tiny aftershocks, she could do little more than lift her eyes.

Nord towered above her, looking every inch her Viking warrior even with his face blanched of color beneath the dark spray of blood. He lifted a hand, and she flinched. Rejection flickered in his eyes but was swiftly replaced with relief.

"Don't," she rasped, voice raw. "Please."

It wasn't that she was afraid of him. No matter what face he wore,

she didn't think she'd ever truly been afraid. Initially shocked? Absolutely. But long-term fear? Never. Not of him.

Not even knowing he could quite literally rip a man's head from his
body using only his bare hands.

It was the thought of being touched right now—the possibility of
any additional sensation while her skin was still zinging with little
sparks—that was too much. She was overstimulated at the most
intense possible level.

"What . . ." she paused to lick her lips, her mouth and throat still
feeling charred, "happened?"

Moving slowly as if trying not to startle her, Nord crouched down
so that he was almost level with her face. "I was hoping you could
tell me."

She blamed her sluggishness on the fact that she'd just been the
victim of some kind of magical attack. It was the only explanation she
was able to supply for what had just happened.

"Allow me to fill in the blanks," offered a voice too seductive to be
labeled as polite.

Crombie.

Nord bared his teeth in answer, his crystalline eyes darkening as his
muscular frame practically turned to stone.

Knowing that she couldn't continue this conversation on her hands
and knees, even though the thought of moving made her want to
whimper, she pushed herself back and used a chair that had fallen over
to help her get back to her feet.

Nord looked personally insulted that she'd chosen a piece of furniture over his assistance, but she could barely stand the scrape of her
dress over her skin let alone what his touch did to her.

"It was a surge," Crombie said once she was upright.

"Excuse me?"

His eyes narrowed. "A surge," he repeated, eyes shifting between
her and Nord when it was obvious she still wasn't following him. "Your
magic," he added, speaking slowly as if talking to a small child. "The
thing that happens when you pull too much at one time . . ." He trailed
off, shaking his head like she was the one not making any sense.

And then his words clicked. *Her* magic. That's what had detonated inside of her.

It was back.

CHAPTER TWENTY-FOUR

Lina

"**B**ut how?" she croaked, eyes darting to her Guardian. Nord gave her a slow head shake, as at a loss for an explanation as she was. "I thought *he* slipped something into your drink."

Crombie's eyes narrowed further as he threw Nord a dark look. Anyone else would have shrunk away from the simmering anger in those silvery depths, but Nord returned the glare with one of his own. Eventually, Crombie turned his attention back to Lina. "Are you telling me you're not the one that called on your power?"

Lina's eyes were wide as she shook her head, not sure what else, if anything, to reveal.

"How about you tell me why you're the only other person in this room moving right now?" Nord snarled.

With each full breath, Lina was feeling stronger and more clear-headed, but even so, it took longer than she cared to admit to follow Nord's question. Once her brain caught up, Lina's head snapped to the side, and she started scanning the immobile party guests with horrified fascination. She'd picked up on the eerie silence but hadn't actually pieced together what it meant.

"Did I . . . did I do this?" she asked, gesturing to the human statues all around them.

Crombie laughed. "Don't be stupid. I did."

"You? Why?" she asked.

"Isn't it obvious?" he asked, raising a brow.

"Would she have asked the question if it were?" Nord countered, shifting so that he was standing just slightly in front of her.

Crombie sighed. "Your posturing is annoying. And unnecessary. If I wanted to harm her, you and I both know there's nothing you could do to stop me."

Nord's voice was glacial as he replied, "Don't be so sure."

"Not even you are immune to the laws of time."

Nord's jaw clenched, and she could just make out the grating sound of his teeth grinding together. Placing a gentle hand on his arm, she asked Crombie, "Are they okay?"

"Perfectly."

"So, you what? Just stopped time?"

"Precisely. Couldn't exactly have everyone catching wind of what was happening. It would ruin my reputation."

"I thought you didn't care what people think," Lina said.

Crombie laughed. "I don't give two shits what people think about me personally, but I'm a businessman. People have certain expectations when they come to my events. If I can't keep people safe, they aren't going to fork over their money. I'm not about to risk my empire because your boyfriend doesn't know how to control himself."

Nord snarled, but Lina squeezed his arm, hard. "If you stopped time, how is this possible then?" she asked, circling her finger around at the three of them.

Crombie looked bored as he crossed his arms and leaned his back against the bar. "I already told you, I love a riddle. I was curious to see how this was going to play out. It was fairly obvious that you were surging, but I couldn't figure out why. What I didn't expect was your surge to trigger him." Crombie's eyes flicked to Nord. "I can't remember the last time I came across a berserker in a full-blown lust. Nor one who was able to regain control with such an insignificant body count." His eyes dropped to the bodies on the floor and he looked thoroughly put out. "While educational to witness, I can't say I'm pleased about what you did to my men. It'll be a pain in the ass to replace them."

"I was going for you," Nord growled.

Crombie's eyes darkened, and his lips lifted into a cruel smile. "Seems like you missed."

"Do you really want to taunt the man that just did *that* using only his hands?"

"Sweetheart, you haven't seen what I can do yet." Dropping his voice, Crombie added, "And I won't even have to get my hands dirty."

Oh shit. Lina swallowed, her mind working overtime to try to find a way to diffuse the situation.

Nord's fists were clenched at his sides, but he wasn't rising to the bait. Yet.

"You still haven't answered my question," Lina pointed out.

Crombie shrugged. "Technically, we're in a pocket."

Lina blinked, sure she'd misheard him. "A what?"

He blew out a breath. "A pocket of time. Sort of like another realm, but it exists on the same physical plane. It belongs to me; I can pull people into and out of it at will."

"I don't understand a single thing coming out of your mouth right now."

Crombie sighed. "Think of it as another room in a house and I'm the only one with the key to unlock the door."

Her brows bunched together. It kind of made sense.

He gestured to the people around them. "While we're in my room, they are paused. Once we return to their room, time will pick up where it left off."

"Won't they have questions about what happened?"

"Why would they?"

Lina gave him a look and pointed to the floor.

"What?" He glanced down. "That? You don't get where I'm at without learning how to hide a body. It's easy enough to restore the rest."

Right. Magic.

The reminder that her power had returned had her itching to test out what she could do, but her brain still felt a bit like scrambled eggs, and Crombie's explanations weren't helping. It probably wasn't the best time to start playing with something she didn't fully understand.

"Now that I've answered your questions, maybe you could explain something to me."

She lifted a brow, instantly wary. "All right," she agreed slowly, her fingers spasming where they dug into Nord's arm.

"You're clearly spoken for, so what was with the flirting? And before you tell me you're looking for a third, I should warn you, I don't share. You might be able to convince me to let him watch, though . . . maybe he'll learn a thing or two."

Lina couldn't help it. As soon as he planted the idea in her mind, it wouldn't let her go. She knew her cheeks were crimson, but the thought of being sandwiched between the two men was doing funny things to her insides.

Nord, on the other hand, sounded as if he'd just swallowed a fistful of gravel. "As if she'd be interested in a prissy fuck like you warming her bed."

"Oh, I don't know." Crombie taunted. "She seems quite enamored with the idea. Maybe you're not giving her what she needs."

You don't know the half of it.

Lina cleared her throat, not caring to be reminded of her untouched status. There was still a job to do.

"Actually, you're right. I—we—were hoping to get you alone, but not . . . not for that."

His lips twitched. "Pity."

The ass. He was purposely baiting Nord. Was he trying to get himself killed? Her Guardian was practically vibrating with fury. She wasn't sure how much longer he could cling to his control before snapping, but she guessed it wouldn't take much to throw him over the edge.

"Do you want to set him off again?" she hissed in exasperation, pushing herself in front of Nord. Lina didn't miss the flicker of amusement in Crombie's eyes at her protective maneuver. They both knew that the only thing her move accomplished was ensuring she was in the splash zone if body parts started flying.

"Maybe."

Lina snorted. "You're insane."

Crombie adjusted the cuffs of his shirt and shrugged. "Quite possibly. Tell me what you want from me, Lina, and we'll see if I'm able to indulge you. I have guests to return to."

Now that the time was at hand, Lina was at a loss about where to start. This was supposed to be Finley's gig, she hadn't even seen the sigil they were supposed to be asking about.

"Maybe we should, um, unfreeze Fin so he can join us?" Lina suggested, glancing to the place where her friend stood cradling his hand against his chest, his face twisted in an angry scowl.

Crombie rolled his eyes, but Finley stumbled forward, his expression comically shifting from anger to confusion to dark recognition faster than she could blink.

"What the hell kind of game are you playing?" he sneered, eyes flaring brightly as he used his power to reset the broken bones in his hand before stalking toward their little group.

"Who me?" Crombie asked, far too innocently.

Finley narrowed his eyes until they were barely more than hazel slits. "You know the law. Temporal rifts are considered offensive magic. It's a banishable offense to use offensive magic against a member of the Brotherhood. Not even our little agreement will keep your ass safe if I choose to report this."

"Oh please. You should be thanking me. I did you a favor." Crombie's voice turned sly. "Unless you want it to get out that one of your dogs has slipped his leash. Can't imagine how people will react when they learn that the Brotherhood doesn't follow its own rules . . ."

Lina glanced between the three men uneasily, the air around them had gone from tense to oppressive. They were one dirty look away from trading blows, and that would get them exactly nowhere. Once again, it looked like it was up to her to save the day. She would have laughed at the thought, but she was too busy banking on the hope that whatever instinctual voice was whispering in her ear wasn't about to doom them all.

"Put your dicks away," she snapped. "No one has time for a pissing contest."

She wasn't exactly sure what a pissing contest was, but she'd over-heard the phrase a couple of times and was pretty sure it applied to the alpha-male posturing she was currently witnessing. And if it didn't, the waspish tone of her voice and unimpressed look plastered on her face would carry the bulk of her meaning, anyway.

Crombie was the first to break out of the staring contest, his lips tilting up in a small smirk. "Our little viper is showing off her fangs."

Something about the comment sent warning bells off in her head. Of all the fang-related animals he could have chosen, why a snake? Had he seen her tattoo, or was it something else . . .

Lina's hand curled protectively around the symbol obscured beneath a thin layer of lace. There was no way Crombie could have made out the details. She'd checked herself before they left, and unless someone knew exactly what to look for, the shapes on her arm were just blurs of ink.

Just who, exactly, was this fae prince?

The hair on the back of her neck stood on end, and for the first time, Lina ignored the inner voice demanding an explanation and listened instead to the one insisting on caution. If Crombie was playing a game, she didn't want him to figure out she was onto it.

Lina bared her teeth in imitation of the feral grin she'd seen Nord wear often. "The most effective weapons are the ones you never see coming."

There. That sounded appropriately threat-like. It wasn't exactly on the same level as the ones Nord delivered with deadly ease, but at least her voice was steady. Hopefully he was buying into the confidence she was trying so hard to project.

"How well I know it," Crombie murmured, his eyes sharpening with interest.

Fuck. It worked too well. The last thing she wanted was him paying closer attention.

Conversations were already difficult for her to navigate on a good day, but this was a damn minefield. She was all too aware of what one wrong step could do.

She forced herself to stand perfectly still while Crombie let his eyes trail over her a moment longer. A low rumbling sound was emanating from Nord's chest and Lina discreetly pressed her body into his, hoping it would calm him.

Finally, Crombie shifted his attention back to Finley. "So, what do you want, Guardian?"

"Information."

"You're going to have to be a bit more specific," Crombie replied.

"I would love to wipe that smug-ass grin off your face. Just give me a fucking reason, Tinkerbelle," Finley snarled.

Lina's brows flew up. She was used to displays of temper from Nord, but it was wholly unexpected coming from the usually laid-back Finley. Apparently, he was just better at keeping his inner badass under wraps.

"Dibs," Nord grunted.

Three sets of eyes shifted back to him.

"Excuse me?" Crombie said, sounding bored.

The flecks ringing Nord's pupils began to shine. His voice was glacial as he replied in little more than a whisper, "If anyone gets the honor of putting you in the ground, it'll be me."

He looked entirely too excited by the prospect.

Lina couldn't help the little shiver that worked its way down her body. But fear wasn't the cause of those tingles. Not even close. What did it say about her that the danger he was exuding only made her want him more?

"I'd love to see you try, Berserker," Crombie purred, not remotely affected by the threat.

Nord's rumbling turned into a full-fledged growl, but Crombie didn't even blink. The man was carved from ice. Nothing affected him.

"For fuck's sake," Lina sighed, pulling a napkin off the counter and shoving it at Finley. "Show him the sigil and let's get out of here. You guys are exhausting."

"What and miss the big event? You can't come all this way and leave before the auction."

"No offense, Crombie, but I'm not interested in a bunch of stolen artifacts or the self-important assholes who want to possess them as much as they want everyone else to watch them wave their money around like it means something."

"So, what are you interested in?" he asked in that seductive croon.

Lina's reply was instant. "All I want are answers, and maybe a shower. No," she corrected, holding up a finger, "*definitely* a shower."

She wasn't the one coated in blood, but she felt filthy by association.

Mischief sparked in the back of Crombie's stormy eyes, and she knew he was about to say something that was going to set one or both of the Guardians off. Before the words could fall from his lips, Finley slapped the napkin with a sketch of the sigil against Crombie's chest.

"There," he grunted, pocketing a pen. "Tell us what you know about the owner of that."

Crombie shot Finley an annoyed look as he peeled the napkin away and glanced down at it. If she hadn't been staring so closely, searching for a reaction, she would have missed it. His eyes widened, ever so slightly, but his voice was the same cultured drawl when he handed the napkin back to Fin.

"Sorry, can't help you."

Nord pressed a hand against Crombie's chest, shoving him back against the bar. "Can't or won't?"

"Won't," Crombie hissed, the distant sound of thunder reaching Lina's ears once more.

"Not an option," Finley said, crossing his arms. "We know you were there. Start talking."

"I'm not painting a target on my back. Threaten me all you want, but I'd rather take my chances pissing off your precious Brotherhood than them."

"Them who?" Finley demanded.

Crombie snarled, his eyes darkening until they were practically black.

Nord's hand fisted in Crombie's shirt, and he gave the fae prince another shove. "Answer him."

"Fuck you," Crombie spat. "You want answers, ask her."

"Me?" Lina asked, unable to fight the slight quaver in her voice.

"No," Crombie said, jutting his chin out. "Her."

Lina looked over her shoulder where Quinn was frozen, mid-sip, her focus trained on the spot she and Crombie had been standing.

"Is that . . ." Finley trailed off, his eyes taking on the unfocused quality of someone sorting through information in their mind.

"The Satori heir," Crombie intoned, nodding.

"It can't be."

"She most certainly is."

"But she's been missing for well over a decade," Finley breathed, sounding almost awed by Crombie's announcement. "All the heirs have." Then his eyes refocused on Crombie and he asked, "How can you be sure? The heirs' identities are so closely guarded that even the Brotherhood doesn't know who half of them are."

"Quinn's done some jobs for me, and in our line of work, that requires a certain amount of transparency and mutually assured destruction. Besides, there are only so many memory weavers in existence, it was no huge leap to connect her back to her family." Crombie shrugged, annoyance pulling his lips down as his shirt resisted the movement. "Do you mind?" he snarled at Nord.

"Yes," Nord replied, but released him anyway.

Lina's eyes were bouncing between the men, trying to follow the conversation.

"What's Quinn got to do with the sigil?" she finally asked when no one else seemed inclined to keep speaking.

"Maybe nothing," Crombie said, smoothing out the wrinkles in his shirt and sighing when it proved fruitless. "But if anyone here will speak freely about the going-ons of the Mobius Council, she's going to be your best bet. Now, I've already said more than I should. If you're too thick-headed to pick up the pieces from here, then I'm of no use to you, anyway."

Satori heir?

Mobius Council?

Memory weaver?

It sounded like Crombie was giving them answers, but all they did was raise more questions.

Her eyes darted to Nord, curious to see if he was as lost as she was, but given the hard set of his jaw and the dark glower he was leveling at Quinn, she was guessing that she was the only one in the dark.

"I trust we're done here," Crombie said.

Finley gave a tight nod.

"Good, then clean up your mess so that I may resume my festivities."

"It goes without saying that you will not repeat a word of this to anyone," Finley said.

Crombie smirked. "If it goes without saying, why mention it?"

"Because I trust you less than the rats crawling in your walls," Nord replied, his eyes sparking with power once more.

Crombie smiled, but his eyes were shooting daggers. "As always, your secret is safe with me."

"Good," Finley interjected. "We'll know where to find you if we learn otherwise."

"Why must our meetings always be so tedious? I wish I could say I looked forward to these little interludes, but as usual, the Brotherhood is more trouble than it's worth." Crombie paused and raised a brow. "Are you planning on questioning the girl here?"

Finley and Nord exchanged a glance, and then Finley shook his head. "No, although we may need to utilize her services," Finley added, his eyes scanning the crowd and identifying a few patrons who clearly had taken note of Nord's rampage.

Crombie's lips dipped in a frown. "Get to work with the cleanup. I'll take care of her," he sighed, rubbing at his temples.

"I don't take orders from you," Nord growled.

Crombie dropped his hand and went rigid, his face twisting in the first sign of genuine anger. When she saw what he'd been hiding behind his carefully crafted mask, Lina's spine went ramrod straight and her heart started to race. When was she going to learn that just because someone appeared human, didn't mean that they were?

Crombie pushed away from the bar and squared off with Nord. Her Guardian had almost a full foot on the fae prince, not to mention a good fifty pounds of solid muscle, but Lina knew better than to underestimate anyone with that much violence simmering in their unearthly eyes.

It had only taken one look to know that Crombie was a beautiful monster, but now she was truly afraid. He was a creature of the night. Smoke and shadow. Sin and seduction. Any who found themselves tangled in his web would thank him for the privilege of being there, even as he swallowed them whole.

Here she thought she was the one using beauty as a weapon when this whole time he'd been playing the same game but with a mastery she could never hope to emulate. She was so far outmatched, it was obvious to her now that this whole time he'd been the one playing her, not the other way around.

"Maybe I can help," she offered, swallowing hard when Crombie's eyes snapped to her.

His nostrils flared, as if he could smell her fear. Instead of reveling in it, as she'd expected, it seemed to soothe whatever had shaken loose within him. Crombie blinked, his face a placid mask once more.

"I have no doubt that you can."

Without another glance at either of the Guardians, he brushed past Nord and moved to stand in front of Quinn. Grasping her by the elbow, he leaned close and whispered something in her ear.

Quinn gave a slow blink, like she'd just awakened from an unexpected nap. Her eyes found Lina's before taking in the aftermath of Nord's rage. If she was horrified, she concealed it well.

She gave Crombie a tight nod and stepped back.

"I'll assume our usual arrangement will be satisfactory?" he asked.

Quinn shook her head. "This one's on the house."

From where she was standing, Lina couldn't make out his face, but she sensed his surprise.

"Very well," he said smoothly. "But don't think you can try to collect later."

Quinn's eyes lingered on Lina for a moment as she replied, "I won't." Then she turned and started moving around the room, easily identifying which guests required her unique gifts.

Finley had already started working on putting the room to rights, using his Guardian powers to reassemble the chandelier and various pieces of broken furniture. That left Lina and Nord to deal with the bodies.

"Um," Lina started, her tongue darting out to wet her lips, "I'm not sure where to start. This seems a lot more complicated than making a butterfly take flight."

"Let's try something small," Nord said, sounding calm now that it was just the two of them.

Lina bit her bottom lip and nodded. "Okay."

Looking around for something, Nord finally held out his arm. "Try to make the blood disappear."

In her limited experience with magic thus far, she'd only managed to animate things or make them appear. Disappearing was new territory.

Her brows furrowed, and her eyes lifted to his. "How?"

"Picture what you want to happen, and then will it into being."

Lina rolled her eyes. He made this shit sound so easy.

"Just try it, Kærasta."

The soft rasp of his voice distracted her enough that she was obeying before she realized it. Lina closed her eyes and pictured Nord leaning against her doorframe and staring hungrily at her in her dress.

"Very good," he murmured. "Now focus on the details."

Lina tried, squeezing her eyes even harder as she pictured the clean lines of his hands and pale gold of his hair, but it was starting to feel like she was staring into rippling water. Her head started to throb, and her body shook with exertion.

"That's enough. Open your eyes," Nord demanded, his hands grasping her forearms.

The disorientation was instant. Lina's eyes opened, and she swayed. "What was that?"

Nord was definitely cleaner, but his beard and face were still tinged pink and pieces of his tux were darker than the others.

"Why did you stop me? I didn't finish."

"You were pushing yourself too hard. The magic started to fizzle. Your power is back, and it's substantial, but the surge must have left your internal reservoir quite low. Don't worry. We'll practice, but that's enough for tonight."

Lina nodded, feeling a bit like a useless child as she watched the others finish repairing the room. It was hard not to be disappointed in herself. Sure, her power was back—sort of—but she was the only one standing around not doing anything.

"Don't be discouraged," Finley said, coming to stand by her side as he dealt with the final body. "It takes people years to manage what you are able to do with minimal effort. This is temporary. Give your body a couple of days to recharge and you'll see."

She gave him a small smile. "Thanks, Fin."

He nudged her with his shoulder. "Anytime. Good work tonight."

She rolled her eyes, but her smile grew. "Not too bad for my first mission, huh?"

"I wouldn't go that far," he teased, as Nord joined them.

"Better than yours," Nord countered.

"As if I need a reminder." Finley made a face. "We should go. It'll raise more eyebrows if the others see us leave before the auction kicks off, and I'd rather not risk anyone realizing their memories were tampered with."

Lina frowned, her eyes following Quinn as she made her way around the room. "What exactly does a memory weaver do, anyway?"

Nord shook his head, letting her know this wasn't the place for questions. "Come on, let's go home," he said gently, tugging her wrist. "We've gotten what we came for."

She nodded eagerly, more than ready to get away from this place. "Should we say goodbye?"

"Already taken care of," Finley said, moving toward the door.

Lina wove her arm through Nord's, and they followed after him, although at a slightly slower pace.

The night had seemed like such an adventure when it began, but now exhaustion nipped at her, and all she wanted was to stand beneath the hot spray of water before curling up in Nord's shirt and falling over in bed. Preferably his, but that was about as likely as Nord offering Crombie an apology for his bad behavior.

The thought made her smile.

Finley was already halfway down the stairs by the time they crossed the room. Lina hesitated at the door, feeling a pair of eyes on her. She craned her neck back, surprised to find that it was Quinn, and not Crombie, watching her intently. Lifting the drink in her hand, Quinn gave Lina a silent toast, before draining her glass.

A shiver of apprehension worked its way down her spine as Lina spun back around, hurrying to catch up with the others. She'd just made it to the top of the stairs when the haunting strains of music and the low murmur of voices resumed.

"Everything okay?" Nord asked when she accidentally bumped into him.

"Fine," she said, forcing a smile.

He must have realized she was distracted—he was way too attuned to her not to—but he didn't push, for which she was thankful.

Her mind was already occupied, trying to seek out any hidden meaning she might have overlooked during her conversation with Quinn. As she revisited their time together, a tight knot formed in the pit of her stomach. They may have only spoken briefly at the bar, and hadn't exchanged another since, but Lina understood the Satori heir's parting message perfectly.

They'd be seeing each other again.

Sooner rather than later.

CHAPTER TWENTY-FIVE

Nord

"Well, that was a shit show," Finley said, tossing his jacket on the sofa.

Nord glared at him. "You were the one egging her on."

"Who said anything about Lina? I was talking about you," Finley replied as he flopped down on top of his jacket.

"What did I do?"

Finley's forearm was covering his eyes, and he lifted it slightly to stare at Nord. "You're joking, right?"

"I did what I felt was necessary," he said, crossing his arms.

"Breaking my hand was necessary?"

"You got in the way."

"And those other guys?"

"So did they."

Finley blew out a breath and shook his head. "You must have balls the size of Texas, mate. I'd love to see you give that explanation to the Director." He groaned a little and added, "But I meant what I said. That shit can't happen again. You can't just go off like that when we're on a job. I can't trust you if you're going to be a constant liability."

"I thought she'd been hurt," Nord said. It was hardly an excuse as far as excuses went, but for him, it said everything. He'd toe any line, follow any rule, right up until something happened to Lina. Her safety was his hard limit, the one thing he would not—could not—tolerate being jeopardized. "We never should have let her go off on her own like that."

"She was hardly alone; we were right there."

"Not close enough."

Finley sighed. "We had no way of knowing she was going to surge. Up until tonight she'd shown no sign of regaining her power. What do you think set her off, anyway?"

Nord had been wondering the same thing himself. He shrugged. "I don't know, but I'm guessing it had something to do with passing through our ward. I noticed she had a couple of odd moments tonight, the first occurring almost immediately after we went through it."

Finley frowned and sat up. "The one to the garage?"

Nord nodded.

"Why would the warding affect her?"

"No clue, but it's ancient and arcane magic. It's probably the most powerful thing she's come into contact with since she was brought back."

Finley's frown deepened, and he scrubbed a hand down his face. Nord could make out a few muffled curses and then, without warning, Finley's head snapped up. "She must have set off the defense mechanism."

"What?"

"The ward. It's spelled to prevent anything it deems a threat from gaining access to our vault. Something within her must have triggered the spell. Maybe whatever was preventing her from accessing her magic was responsible?" Finley shrugged, his eyes shining as the words continued to come out in a rush, "I'm not sure, it's just a guess, but it's the only thing that makes any sense. Lina clearly doesn't mean the two of us any harm, but perhaps the ward sensed something lying dormant within her and attacked it. You said it yourself, it's ancient magic."

"So why now and not when we were at the bureau?" Nord asked. "Surely their warding is just as strong, if not more so, than ours?"

"Maybe because of the work she's been doing with you? Perhaps all that meditation and seeking out her power source weakened the barrier enough for the ward's magic to grab hold?" Finley shook his head. "I can't say for certain; this isn't my area of expertise."

Nord shrugged. It sounded feasible, but at best they were grasping at straws. "I guess the how doesn't really matter."

"She's going to want answers."

"So, we give her your explanation. As far as we know, that's exactly what happened."

Finley slumped back down. "Those aren't the only answers she's going to want. She heard what Crombie said. Are you prepared to fill in the blanks for her?"

"Why wouldn't I be?" Nord asked, his eyes narrowing.

"Because I hardly know what to make of it myself. So far, we've been able to conduct our investigation under the radar, but if the Mobius Council or the lost heirs are involved . . ." Finley trailed off. "I'm not going to be able to keep that a secret for long. All those records are encrypted. Even if I did have that level of clearance, they're going to be flagged. People will be alerted the second we start digging."

"Well then I guess it's a good thing you have access to something they can't encrypt. Your defector."

Finley blinked up at him. "Alistair has been interrogated at great length about what he knows of the heirs. Why would he suddenly start revealing new information now?"

"Things have changed. One of the heirs seems to have returned. Maybe he can positively identify her?"

Finley was shaking his head. "Quinn Satori and Emerson Alinari are the only two heirs we've ever successfully identified. Even if Alistair confirmed it, we wouldn't learn anything new. Not unless he was suddenly willing to give us the names of the other three."

Nord gave him a dark grin. "Maybe you should let me do the interrogating."

"Not happening. You're a fucking loose cannon. At the rate you're going, you'd be as likely to kill the geezer as you would be to get any usable intel. Plus, you're still technically on probation. They wouldn't let you anywhere near Alistair in an official capacity."

"We'll do it unofficially."

"Did you listen to anything I just said?"

"I caught the gist."

Finley chucked a pillow at him. "This isn't a fucking joke."

Nord caught it easily. "Do I look like I'm joking? I heard you. You think my rage is a liability, but so long as Lina doesn't step foot in that room, I'm not at risk of lusting out."

Finley smirked. "I feel like this would be a great time for a boner joke."

Nord nailed Finley with the pillow. His partner wasn't smiling anymore when it fell into his lap.

"Fucker."

"Maybe if you had better hand-eye coordination, you would have caught it."

"I hate you."

Nord grinned.

"You're an insufferable ass."

He waved a hand for Finley to continue with his barrage of insults.

"I didn't do anything to deserve being paired with you. You might be the worst form of karmic punishment that's ever been meted out."

"You've got one thing right; you definitely don't deserve me."

"Oh, just fuck off already," Finley growled. "I'm still dealing with the last migraine you caused. Could you at least try not to set off another one?"

Nord laughed. "I'll leave you alone, but tomorrow I'm going to have a little chat with Alistair. With or without you."

Finley scowled at him. "The hell you will. You're not going within twenty feet of him without me."

"So, come babysit me, then, if it will make you feel better. Either way, it's happening. If you weren't planning the same thing, you wouldn't have let that Satori girl out of your sight. We both know it."

Finley sighed. "I already told you why we had to walk away."

And he had, via their telepathic link while they'd been dealing with Crombie. Nord gave Finley a small nod.

"Look, I know you aren't happy about it, but we can't risk tipping off the rest of the Council if she's still in touch with them. Besides, any member of the Council is off-limits without permission of the Director. All jokes aside, you know I'm in this with you. One hundred percent, whatever you need, no questions asked. But we aren't prepared for the kind of shit storm that will rain down on us if we come at the Mobius Council without a fucking army at our backs. Until we know for sure how—or even if—they're involved, we lie low."

Even though some of the tension drained away at the reminder of Fin's loyalty, Nord couldn't resist taunting him. "Not even one question, huh?" Nord asked, giving his friend a shit-eating grin.

"I'm about two more smart-ass remarks away from slitting your throat in your sleep."

"Aw, Fin. I love you too, Brother."

"One," Finley warned, although he was smiling.

"You're no fun."

"Don't you have a woman to pretend you don't want? What the fuck are you still doing in here talking to me?"

Nord scowled, his body reacting immediately to the reminder of Lina in her curve-hugging dress.

"That's what I thought," Finley said, moving the throw pillow from his lap to the couch and getting comfortable.

Nord made a show of leaving the room, although he paused and called out, "Hey, Fin?"

"Yeah?"

"You ever come into my room in the middle of the night, and it's not a fucking emergency, I'll rip your throat out with my teeth."

He didn't bother waiting for a response, Finley's immediate pallor was more than satisfying enough on its own.

Perhaps he should feel bad about how easy it was to put that hint of fear in his friend's eyes, but it was important that Finley remembered what he was dealing with. They might be friends, and Nord had no intention of ever inflicting true harm, but friends or not, Finley couldn't afford to drop his guard. When the bloodlust took over, being a friend didn't count for much.

The reminder was probably unnecessary after what happened tonight, but it couldn't hurt to reiterate it either. And he wasn't about to apologize or be made to feel guilty about what had gone down. That ship had long since sailed.

Nord could no more deny the violence flowing through his blood than he could the need to draw breath. It was a part of him. One that had been latent for centuries, but now that it was back . . . well, he couldn't say he was disappointed.

Who better to protect his ward than a berserker?

With a last nod, Nord turned and made his way to the bathroom, some of his satisfaction at getting the last word dwindling as he braced himself for yet another cold shower. They had become an unfortunate daily—and more often than not, twice daily—occurrence since Lina showed up. It wasn't just the violent urges she'd ushered back into his life, but also their twin need. Lust. And it was only growing worse. Lately it seemed that trying to drown himself in the icy spray was barely enough to help stave off the sexual hunger that always seemed to be burning just beneath the surface.

He groaned as memories flooded his mind. Helping Lina get dressed had been the sweetest form of torture. It had been hard enough to resist tugging the dress down her body instead of settling for the feel of his fingers brushing against her spine as he zipped it up.

And then there were the shoes.

He was so thankful the skirt had covered his face and hands while he'd knelt at her feet. He'd been trembling as he'd focused on strapping those heels on. It had taken everything he had not to give in to the desire to slide his hands up her calves, spread open her thighs, and bury his face in her sweet heat.

Nord tried to remember why he was fighting so hard to resist what he desperately wanted. What Lina was more than willing to give.

Right. Her lack of memories.

He sighed, slamming his bedroom door open and heading straight for the shower.

If she is taken, you can always just kill the asshole and be done with it. Problem solved.

Nord wished he were strong enough to dismiss the idea outright. If he were half as honorable as he claimed to be, the idea wouldn't hold any appeal at all. The real issue was that it did.

He wanted to claim her with his body, the same way he did with his vow of protection. He needed to make her his, and he was running out of reasons why waiting to see if she got her memory back was the right course of action.

"Fuck," he groaned, not even bothering to undress as he turned the water on full blast and stepped in, shoes and all.

This battle against himself was proving to be the one that would defeat him.

And for the first time he could ever remember, losing didn't seem so bad.

In fact, it was all he could think about.

CHAPTER TWENTY-SIX

Lina

Lina slid down deeper into the sudsy tub, knowing that it was well past time to get out. She'd taken a shower, but even after she felt clean once more, she wasn't ready to leave the therapeutic spray of the hot water or the feel of its heat seeping into her tired muscles. Instead, she'd pinned her wet hair up high on her head and filled the Viking-sized bathtub and submerged herself in a pool of bubbles.

That had been over an hour ago.

Her bath was starting to cool, but there was still enough warmth in the lavender-and-almond-scented water for her to be content.

Eyes closed, she trailed the tips of her fingers along the surface, creating little ripples that splashed against the porcelain. The sound was as soothing as the bath itself, and her mind started to wander.

"Enjoying yourself?"

Lina's eyes flew open, her heart stuttering as she startled, and her head dipped beneath the thin layer of bubbles. She'd been so deep in her trance she'd never even heard the door open.

"I was," she sputtered once she was above the water again. It took her a little longer to wipe away the film of bubbles now covering her face. Once she could see again, she shot a glare over her shoulder, but any actual irritation she might have felt at the interruption died a swift and fiery death.

Standing in the doorway, wearing only a pair of low-slung sweat-pants and still glistening from his own shower, was Nord. Lina's mouth went dry, and her eyes devoured the display of ink-covered muscles.

Sweet mother of god, he should charge admission to this show.

Nord tried to hide his smile by running his fingers over his mouth and beard, but there was no hiding the laughter shining in his eyes. "Sorry, didn't mean to scare you. I knocked, but there was no answer. I just wanted to make sure you were doing okay after everything that happened tonight."

"And you took my lack of a response as an invitation to just waltz right in?" she asked with an arched brow. "What if I was sleeping?"

Thank you, whoever is out there listening, that I wasn't sleeping. I owe you one.

"What if you were passed out? I couldn't be sure."

"And when you saw the light on in the bathroom and realized I wasn't sleeping?"

Nord lifted a shoulder and smirked. "What if you'd fallen asleep in the tub and accidentally drowned?"

"Uh-huh. More like you wanted to sneak a peek."

Nord crossed his arms, causing the muscles in his arms and chest to bunch and flex. Lina just prayed she wasn't drooling. "I remained a respectful distance away."

It was true. From the door, he probably only saw the top of her head and tips of her toes. Everything else had been safely beneath the bubbles. Although . . . there were a lot less suds now that she'd floundered around than there had been.

Feeling bold, Lina playfully narrowed her eyes and slowly turned her body around to face him. "Why? If you're going to go to all the trouble of sneaking up on me, why not try to get an eyeful?"

She let off a silent whoop as his throat bobbed, and his eyes dropped to the water.

"What's the problem? Afraid you'll see something you like?"

Nord's eyes were smoldering when they lifted to hers. "You know that's never been the issue."

"So, what are you waiting for? An invitation? Fine, consider yourself invited."

Lina knew she couldn't afford to exhibit even the barest hint of doubt. It would only give him a reason to hesitate, and she'd lose him before they ever started. Bracing her hand on the edge of the tub, she pushed herself up, the sound of her racing heart all but drowning out the splash of water. She lifted her chin and stared straight at him, daring him not to look.

If this didn't force him to act, nothing would.

"Lin—" The word was cut off as he sucked in a breath.

She watched his lips fall open, noting the rapid rise and fall of his chest. It was strangely erotic. Not the part where she was completely naked standing in front of someone still wearing clothes—that was expected—but watching him react to her nudity. If anything, watching him, watching her, was the catalyst to her own response.

There was a new heaviness in her breasts, a hollowness low in her belly, and an ache in her core.

A shudder racked his large frame and his eyes dropped once more. Unable to help herself, her own eyes dipped, her breath catching at the growing evidence of his arousal. She squeezed her thighs together, suddenly hating those fucking sweats. They were snug, tented, and doing nothing to hide the swelling shape of him. But they didn't reveal nearly enough. She wanted all of him.

Every.

Fucking.

Inch.

As his gaze raked over her body, she felt it like a physical caress, her nipples budding into two stiff peaks, her breath coming in shallow pants. It wasn't enough. Nothing but his hands on—or in—her would satisfy her need.

She burned for him.

After weeks of wanting him to finish what they started the night they first met, her desperation had only grown. Lina was starting to think that nothing would ever sate her desire completely. She also wasn't sure she wanted it to.

This was what people wished for, right? To experience this kind of soul-shattering need for someone else instead of settling for some underwhelming jackhammering beneath the sheets? One look at Nord, and Lina knew without a doubt that if he gave in, there would be nothing underwhelming about it.

Her name was torn from his throat, sounding more like a ragged groan than an actual word as he ripped her from her musings and closed the distance between them.

When his fingers dug into her hips, she was ready. Throwing her arms around his neck, she wrapped her legs around his waist, and her lips were already parted when his mouth slammed down on hers.

Finally.

It had been over a week since he'd kissed her, and she'd been slowly coming undone ever since.

He'd ignored every advance, seemingly immune. But she'd known it was an act. That if she just kept at him, he'd eventually cave.

No one could deny themselves forever.

She'd been banking on it.

A distant part of her registered that they were moving, but she was too wholly focused on the feel of his tongue sliding against hers to pay much attention to the scenery. He tasted like smoke and honey, and she was immediately addicted, craving more even as his lips assaulted hers.

Then she was airborne, flying backward and bouncing a little as he tossed her onto the mattress. Her legs were flung open, her breath shallow, but there was nothing unwilling in any fiber of her body.

Anyone else might have felt uncertain, being the subject of someone's scrutiny while they were on such an intimate display, but Lina reveled in it. She didn't care if he could track the evidence of her desire dripping down her thigh. As long as he backed up those hot looks by touching her, there wasn't much in this world she did care about.

"*Allra kvenna fegrst,*" he whispered, the words guttural and so thickly accented she could barely make them out.

"What does that mean?" she managed.

"Most beautiful woman," he repeated with a wolfish grin.

His words warmed her already feverish flesh. "Stop talking and get over here. Now."

"Your wish is my command."

"Yes," she groaned as his hands ran up the sides of her legs. "Just don't stop. I want all of you."

"I don't think I could stop if I wanted to."

"It's about time."

Nord laughed, but it was a hoarse, humorless sound. "Do you have any idea what you do to me?"

Lina didn't stop and think. She just gave in to instinct and let her hand shift to cup his hard length. "I have an idea."

Nord leaned over her, his teeth clamping down on the lobe of her ear as he growled, "That's just the beginning."

As he pulled back, his frost-colored eyes peered deep into hers, and she smiled. "Good. It would be beyond disappointing if that was all you had to offer."

Nord's lips twisted up as his fingers tightened in her hair. "Kærasta, if you manage to fucking walk when I'm done with you, I'll be impressed."

"I hope you can back up those promises, Viking, because I've been waiting a long time to understand what all the fuss was about."

Nord leaned down, his lips back at her ear as he breathed, "But you've never known anyone like me."

The words, delivered in his carnal whisper, had her arching up to press her body against his.

"Prove it," she demanded.

"Spread 'em," Nord growled, biting down hard on the muscle that joined her neck and shoulder as his hands grasped her thighs and pushed them further apart.

Lina shuddered as liquid heat surged through her in response. She could not be more ready for him to make good on his words.

Nord stood back, his face flushed, his eyes hooded as he studied her.

She fought against the urge to squirm, letting him look his fill. If their positions were reversed, she'd want the same. Then his eyes caught hers, and he gave her a wicked grin. Brushing his fingers up and down her sides, he stoked the flames of her desire even higher. Ribs, to belly, to hips and then back up. Always skimming, never touching her in the places she desperately desired. Finally, he slid his hands down, shifting from her ribs to her hips, and then lower, his knuckles scraping along her inner thighs.

"I need to know how you taste," he rasped, slowly dropping to his knees, his eyes never leaving hers.

Coherent thought was impossible after that. Lina couldn't stop sending prayers up to whatever deity was listening. *Yes. Thank you. Oh, yes, please.*

Her back arched up off the bed, and she let out a long wanton moan as he licked along her seam. Pressing a large palm into her abdomen, Nord pushed Lina back down onto the soft sheets.

"Relax," he breathed, the vibration of his voice sending answering tingles racing along her body.

"Yeah, okay. Whatever you say," she gasped as he drove his tongue into her opening. The answering cry that came out of her wasn't remotely human. And Lina didn't give a fuck. All she wanted was for him to keep going, because if he stopped now, she might actually die. Again. But the loss of him might be worse than what came before.

She still only had fragments from the night she died, but if she had to guess, Nord stopping what he'd begun would be an even worse form of torture. She'd rather be flayed alive than have to live another moment without knowing what it felt like for him to fill her completely.

As he continued to fuck her with his tongue, lights exploded behind her eyes, and she was lost to the sensation, aware only of the throbbing ache between her legs and how each lap of his tongue sent her spiraling higher.

It felt like she existed in frequency, no longer comprised of human flesh, but of vibration. As he licked, and nipped, and sucked, she was aware only of the throbbing heat between her legs.

"Please," she begged, not even sure what she was asking him for.

That's when he slid two thick fingers inside of her.

Lina shot off the bed again. "Yes," she groaned, as he shifted his relentless attention, biting down and flicking his tongue against her swollen center.

The sounds coming out of her were nothing like the artificial shrieks she'd heard from the women in the videos one of her room-mates preferred. It was then she realized those women had no idea what actual pleasure felt like, because this was like being torn apart and put back together all at the same time. It was so extreme that it hurt, but it was also so absolutely incredible that she knew she wouldn't be above begging to experience it again.

Her thighs were shaking, her throat burning, and the only thing she cared about was that the man fucking her with his fingers never stopped. And then he curved them, pressing in on some special button that had her moving restlessly against his digits.

It felt like she was chasing something, like lightning was coursing through her veins and a storm was on the horizon.

She'd witnessed more than her fair share of people having sex, but nothing prepared her for the reality.

Nothing.

There was no way she could have anticipated the way Nord worked her body like it was some kind of instrument made solely for pleasure. If she'd known what she'd been missing, there was no way she would have lasted this long.

As his teeth brushed against her, she moaned, desperate for more. "D-d-don't," she managed.

His lips vibrated as he spoke, but she couldn't even process words at this point. She was lost to the sea of sensations. Need and pleasure coiling until she was screaming when she finally came undone.

Her inner muscles clamped down hard on his fingers, her hips lifting up off the bed and pushing against his mouth.

Nord, thankfully, never stopped his tender assault. His lips and tongue worked tirelessly, seeing her through the storm to the blissful peace waiting for her on the other side.

If she could have formed words, she would have thanked him, but as it stood, it was nearly impossible to draw in a full breath, let alone force out anything resembling conversation.

She wasn't Lina, former ghost, current magic user, and human woman. She was something else. A creature wholly slave to the sensations he was wringing out of her. And at the moment, she didn't want to be anything more.

Once her body calmed, Nord finally pulled away, shifting so that his face hovered just above hers.

"Hi," he whispered, his eyes glowing with masculine satisfaction.

"Hi," she breathed.

"Enjoying yourself?"

"Fuck off."

"I don't think you mean that."

"Probably not," she agreed, her eyes rolling back in her head as she curled into him, tucking her face into his shoulder. "Is this the part where we shake hands?"

Nord barked out a laugh and swatted her playfully on the ass. "That's another sporting custom for you."

"Spanking?" she asked, squirming slightly.

"It's used for motivation or to signify a job well done."

"Shouldn't I be spanking you then?"

His laughter turned husky. "Your moans were thanks enough."

She hummed contentedly as Nord cuddled her, his lips lifting into a smile where they were pressed against her shoulder.

The aftershocks of his ministrations were still working their way through her body, and she wished she had energy enough for a second round—or to at least return the favor—but her climax was already decimating the slight reserve she still had.

The night's events, the return of her magic, not to mention the force of her first actual orgasm in recent history, were enough to send her consciousness retreating.

"I—"

It was the last sound she managed before her eyes closed and she was able to focus only on the heavy feel of her muscles as she curled and pressed into him.

"Shhh," he whispered again, his warm hand rubbing up and down her back, arousing even as he soothed.

A part of her wanted to protest. To beg for more even as she begged for him to stop. It was almost too much, this desperate, relentless need.

The other part, the one that recognized just how out of her depth she actually was, remained silent. It sensed what was coming, and it welcomed it with open arms and spread legs.

She drifted off between one breath and the next, so thoroughly sated that she couldn't even be bothered by the fact as she floated into oblivion.

Nord shifted slightly, his face barely a breath above her own as he whispered, "Lina?"

She tried to move her lips, but silence was her only answer.

There was a soft chuckle, a sound like velvet and gravel. Were she capable of any form of coherent thought, she would have asked to record it so she could listen to it on repeat later. In her current state, all she could do was enjoy the sound as she relaxed against his hard body.

"Sleep now, Kærasta. I'll be here when you wake."

Lina wanted to tell him she just needed a minute. She knew that there was more she'd yet to experience. Not just her chance to return the favor, but a second release waiting for her just out of reach. Even so, she gave in to his gentle demand.

That voice owned her.

She lived for it.

It could order her to cease being, and she would willingly give in.

Maybe the realization should have terrified her, but instead she felt more invigorated than she'd ever been. Not even being returned to her body had filled her with the same sense of soul-deep excitement.

This was what it meant to live. To be loved and belong to another.

And make no mistake, she belonged to him.

Just as he belonged to her.

Tonight was merely the beginning.

And god, it had been worth the wait.

———

THE WEIGHT PRESSING AGAINST HER CHEST GREW UNBEARABLE. When she tried to shift her arms to pry it off, she realized that they were pinned down on either side of her body. Her lungs were burning, the need for air overwhelming her.

Her mouth opened to suck in the oxygen she so desperately needed, but instead it felt as though a musty cloth was pressed against her nose and mouth.

Where am I?

She couldn't tell if her eyes were opened or closed. Everything was black. The pain radiating through her body was unimaginable. It was like burning from the inside out. Each failed attempt to breathe, each minute twitch of her arms, caused an answering ripple of agony to detonate inside of her.

It was almost impossible to focus through the pain, but something deep within her took over. With a burst of hidden strength, she managed to dislodge her arms, although they didn't move far. She tried to sit up, but it felt like she was being held in place by something soft and damp . . . dirt?

Her nails scraped against a wall of mud as she wriggled her arms further away from her body. As she did, clumps of soil rained down, filling the space created by her limbs.

She struggled hard but couldn't seem to do more than move her arms. It was like trying to swim through sludge. She was surrounded on all sides by a never-ending sea of dirt.

She'd been buried alive.

Her lungs screamed for air. Frantic puffs of breath only pulled the covering on her face deeper into her mouth. A distant part of her warned that she needed to calm down, to think logically, but the need to survive wasn't ruled by logic. It was primal.

She managed to pull her arms back in, her hands making their way to her face. A brush of fingers over her mouth confirmed that a sack of some kind had been tied over her head. As she clawed at the fabric, trying to seek out whatever was holding it in place, she realized it was futile.

Even if she managed to get the cloth off of her head, there was no pocket of air for her to breathe in.

The realization only made her struggle more. She couldn't give up. Not yet.

If she could just draw in a breath, she could find her way to the surface.

One of her nails snagged and ripped as she finally managed to tear open a small hole near her lips. She was met with the scent of damp earth, and as her lungs seized, clumps of dirt fell through the hole she'd created and into her mouth.

She started to choke. She tossed her head from side to side, frantically trying to dislodge the clump of soil, but it only caused more of the dirt above her to slide into the opening in the fabric.

More dirt filled her mouth, sealing off any possibility of precious air.

No.

Not like this.

I can't die like this.

LINA SCREAMED, KICKING AND THRASHING WILDLY AT THE HEAVY weight holding her in place.

"Lina?"

She was gasping for breath, her mind not yet comprehending that she was safe in bed, not buried in some shallow grave. All she wanted was to get free.

Screaming like a wild animal, she threw her head back, barely feeling the sharp crack of pain.

Nord grunted, but didn't release her.

"Let go of me." She couldn't bear the feeling of anything pressing against her right now. Instead of comforting her, she felt trapped, and that was far too similar to her dream.

"Lina—"

"Let me go!"

"Li—"

"GET YOUR FUCKING HANDS OFF OF ME!" she sobbed, her voice breaking.

Nord dropped her like she'd burned him, and Lina immediately shoved away from him to curl on her side.

It had felt so real.

The dirt falling into her mouth.

Her nails breaking as they tore through the cloth.

Suffocating as the last of the air left her body.

She could feel Nord behind her, hovering, uncertain what to do. She felt foolish, reacting so viscerally to a dream. But then . . . it was more than a dream.

It was another memory.

Up until now she'd believed she'd died during the ritual, but it would seem that she hadn't gotten off that easily. It wasn't enough she'd lived through her skin being carved from her chest until the pain rendered her unconscious. She'd been lucky enough to come to just in time to die all over again.

Lina continued to suck in breath after breath, her body shaking as she regained her composure.

"I'm sorry," she whispered, her eyes squeezing shut as salty tears dripped down her cheeks. "I didn't . . . I didn't mean—"

"You don't owe me an apology."

"It was just so real," she croaked.

"Can you tell me what you saw?" he asked gently.

Lina shook her head. "Not . . . not yet."

His warm hand ran over her spine, and Lina shuddered, but relaxed into his touch.

"How often does this happen?"

"You mean the nightmares?"

"Yes," he answered, tucking a piece of sweat-damp hair behind her ear.

"Every night," she whispered.

She sensed him stiffen, and his voice was a little harder when he finally spoke again. "How come you've never come to me? Or at least mentioned it outside of those few times?"

"I didn't want to bother you. It's not like there's anything you can do about it, anyway. It's the past, right? Over and done with."

Nord laid down, curling his body around hers, although he didn't wrap his arm around her this time, seeming to understand that the added weight would send her spiraling.

"I could have done this," he whispered, his fingers tracing soothing circles on her back. "I could have listened while you purged the poison from your mind. I could have told you that you were safe. That you had nothing to be afraid of."

Lina hiccupped as a stray tear joined the others on her pillow. For the first time, Lina understood the danger she was putting them in, searching for answers. "If they realize I'm alive, they'll come for me," she whispered.

Nord stilled, his voice deepening. "Who will come for you?"

"Whoever . . ." she paused and licked her lips, "whoever killed me. They went to great lengths to ensure that I was dead and that I wouldn't be found. If they find out that I'm . . . that I'm back, they'll come to finish the job."

Nord resumed the gentle play of his fingers along her back, so she was startled when she heard the hard edge in his voice. "Let them come. I welcome the chance to repay their courtesy on your behalf. With interest."

Lina managed to take a full breath, her heart returning to a somewhat normal pace as she let the magic of his promise weave itself around her. She'd seen what he could do. She knew that those were not empty words. The knowledge soothed a broken part of her soul, freeing her from the last of the nightmare's chains.

"Thank you."

"You never need to thank me for that." He pressed a kiss to her temple. "Try to rest. I will keep watch while you sleep."

She almost laughed at the thought of falling back to sleep, but her eyes were heavy, and his body was warm. "I'm not sure I can."

"Just try," he murmured. "You have nothing to fear. I am here."

Lina gave a little nod, focusing on the sound of his voice as he continued to talk softly to her both in English and his mother tongue, the way that his breath fanned the side of her face, and the feel of his hand's slow and deliberate strokes along her spine.

Eventually sleep reclaimed her, and this time there were no dreams, only Nord.

Only peace.

CHAPTER TWENTY-SEVEN

Nord

Nord leaned against the counter, staring into his untouched cup of coffee, mulling over the unexpected events of the night before. He'd kept his promise to Lina, not leaving her side until she'd woken.

To be fair, it had been no hardship. Feeling the steady beat of her heart against his palm, listening to the soft hitch of her breath—had calmed something inside of him. These last couple of weeks he'd felt unmoored, like a ship drifting without an anchor. Giving in to his desire for her—while incredibly selfish—had made him feel whole once more.

At least, it had until he'd been forced to stand by helplessly while she'd battled the phantoms from her past. Sitting there, unable to touch her, forced to watch her come undone. It shredded him. He'd never felt a bigger failure. Even now, hours later, he could still hear the echoes of her screams ringing in his ears.

Thankfully, she hadn't woken again, but he wasn't convinced that her rest had been remotely peaceful. If anything, it was more likely that her body had simply shut down, needing sleep to replenish itself after her magic surge. It infuriated him that for all of his gifts, sleep free from nightmares was the one thing he couldn't give her.

Leaving her side this morning had been nearly impossible. She'd looked so fragile curled up next to him, dusky shadows heavy beneath the dark fringe of her lashes. It'd taken her slamming the door in his face for him to finally convince himself to make his way to the kitchen. Even then, he'd still lingered a few extra moments outside of her room, telling himself it was to only ensure that she really was all right, and not because he was acting like some kind of lovesick puppy.

"If you're trying to muster up the courage to declare your undying love to your favorite morning beverage, might I make a suggestion?" Finley asked, setting down a plate laden with food as he sat down at the bar.

"Only if you want my fist down your throat."

"So that's a no to the advice, then?"

Nord sighed and drank deep. "Is it too much to ask that you hold off on crawling up my ass until I at least finish my first cup of coffee?"

"How am I supposed to do that when you're staring at it longingly instead of drinking it?"

"I was not—"

"Oh? What's with the star-crossed lover look on your face, then? Could it possibly have something to do with the lovely Lina?"

Nord growled, which did nothing except deepen Finley's smirk. As much as he wanted to punch the smug look off of his partner's face, he needed his help. It pained him to admit it, but when it came to Lina, he'd sacrifice his ego every time.

"Actually, it does."

Finley's brows flew up. "I . . . I was not expecting you to admit that."

"She had another nightmare."

"Same as before?" Finley asked, immediately all business.

"No . . . I don't think so. She didn't want to talk about it, but it was bad. She was screaming, and wouldn't let me touch her. Whatever those fuckers did to her . . ." Nord trailed off, knowing he didn't have the words.

"We'll find them," Finley promised, coming over to place his hand on Nord's shoulder.

"Killing them won't be enough," Nord said, his voice taking on a guttural rasp.

"I know," he said softly. "But we'll make it count."

Nord's eyes closed, and he breathed deep, fighting hard for control. The beast was eager to take over. He had been ever since he caught the scent of Lina's fear. The only thing keeping him leashed was knowing there was no target for his rage.

Once there was . . . well, then all bets were off.

Nord's grip on his mug tightened, and the ceramic shattered, sending lukewarm liquid flying.

Finley eyed the mess with a dispassionate gaze and reached behind him for a dishtowel. Nord was already scooping up broken shards into the palm of his hand.

"Does she know who's responsible yet?"

Nord shook his head.

Finley was silent for a moment before asking, "Do you think you can convince her to share the details? Maybe there's something she remembers that might help us piece it together?"

Nord stood and dropped the broken cup into the trash. He could have repaired it, but Finley had ten others, and he wasn't feeling particularly careful right now. Tapping into his magic might backfire spectacularly.

"If she wanted to tell me, she would have."

"Can you make her?" Finley asked, dropping the wet towel into the sink.

Nord's eyes narrowed. "Can I, or will I?"

"What's the difference?"

"Are you asking me what I think you are?"

Finley shrugged.

Eyes shifting to the door, Nord switched to their telepathic link. *"Do you really think I'd willingly invade her privacy and sift through her memories without consent?"*

"If it's our only choice . . ."

"No. Absolutely not. That is the kind of invasion that people never forgive. I won't do that to her."

"But if it's the only way—"

"I said no."

"You aren't the only one with the ability—"

Nord had his hand fisted in Finley's shirt and was holding him up off the floor until they were eye level. "Try it and I'll gut you."

Finley held his stare for a tense moment before dipping his chin. "Fine."

Nord dropped him.

"I just meant that it might be helpful," Finley muttered, smoothing out his shirt.

"What would be helpful?" Lina asked.

Nord leveled him with a glare. *"Not a fucking word."*

Finley rolled his eyes. "The Brotherhood has an informant that is familiar with the Mobius Council. I want to interrogate him."

Lina's eyes shot to Nord. "And you don't?"

"I don't trust him," Nord replied as his eyes devoured her face, seeking out any hint of the shadows from the night before and finding none. As for his answer, it was the truth, although it was misleading. Nothing would stop him from speaking with Alistair.

Plucking a piece of bacon off of Finley's plate, she took her usual seat at the bar. "Not that you asked for my opinion, but if there's a chance this guy will provide us with real answers, shouldn't we take the risk?"

"Yeah, Nord. Shouldn't we take the risk?" Finley teased.

"Stop it, or you'll face the same fate as your mug."

"Is it a trait of all berserkers to be deranged fearmongers first thing in the morning, or is that just another Nord special?"

Nord glared at Finley. *"You really want to find out?"*

"Nope."

"Then shut the fuck up."

Finley's eyes sparkled as he sipped his coffee.

"I didn't say we weren't going to interrogate him, just that I didn't trust him."

"To tell the truth or with something else?" Lina asked shrewdly.

"Both," Nord admitted.

Lina chewed on her lip as she considered his answer. "It's probably not ideal for me to go with you, then, huh?"

"When has that ever stopped you?" Finley asked.

Lina grinned. "Fair point. It's just, if you're worried this guy might give the Council a heads-up that we're onto them or whatever, his recognizing me might be dangerous. More so than usual, anyway. So maybe I should sit this one out?"

Relief swelled in Nord's chest. He'd wanted to ask her to leave this one to them, but she never seemed to take it well when he did. Plus, once she realized Alistair was who they were going to see, she wasn't going to see the danger anymore. Technically, Alistair could have already tipped off the Council, but he hadn't had a reason to suspect anything up to this point, so it seemed unlikely. Especially if he was as loyal to the Brotherhood as Finley insisted.

Furthermore, if he had tipped the Council off, they weren't exactly known for sitting idly by. They'd have already come for Lina if they were the ones behind her death and knew she was back.

"Actually, that's not a bad idea," Finley murmured. "We'll need to swing by the bureau beforehand so that I can confirm his address. Want to come with so you can continue your research?"

Lina made a face. "Goodie."

He chuckled. "I just thought you might appreciate not being cooped up here all day by yourself."

"And you think I'll have more fun being cooped up in the archive?"

Finley grimaced. "Okay, so neither is overly appealing."

Lina gave him a warm smile. "No, you were right. It will keep my mind busy, and maybe this way you guys won't be the only ones coming home with new info."

"Excellent. Then you eat some breakfast, I'm going to finish getting ready," Finley said, pushing his plate toward her.

"But what about you?"

"I've already eaten," he lied with a grin, before stepping away. Giving Nord a little salute, Finley left the room, leaving them alone.

Nord knew he was staring, but he wasn't sure how to break the silence. He wanted to ask how she was feeling or if she needed anything, but he also didn't want to sound needy. It never used to be this difficult talking to the women he'd bedded, but then, he'd never cared this much before.

"I can feel you looking at me," Lina said.

"Are we going to talk about what happened last night?" he blurted.

Lina glanced up from her plate, a piece of bacon hanging from her lips. Her cheeks were tinged pink, clueing him in to the direction her thoughts had taken, although her eyes were wary.

"Which part?" she asked. "A few notable things occurred last night."

Nord's lips twitched up. "Any of them."

"Well, up until the part where I woke up screaming bloody murder, I was pretty pleased with the direction the night had taken."

"Me too," he admitted, his voice warming.

Lina's flush deepened. "Well, that's good to hear. I know how against it you've been. Can I ask what changed?" Her eyes dipped back to her plate, and Nord knew she was trying to act like his answer didn't matter.

"I was tired of fighting myself."

He could see her lips curve up as she gave a little hum. "Is that the real reason you came to check on me?"

"It's possible."

"You don't know for sure?" she asked, her gaze returning to his.

"It's not the reason I gave myself at the time, but it's probably at the heart of it."

Lina's smile turned flirtatious. "I'd hoped to return the favor, but you, uh, wore me out."

"I'm looking forward to wearing you out again."

He enjoyed the way her pupils flared, and her breath left her in a little gust. "I'm free right now . . ."

It was tempting, but Finley would be back soon, and they weren't at the point in their relationship where Nord was ready to rush anything. It was too new, and she was someone he wanted to savor. Especially while they were still going through their firsts.

He sighed and pushed away from the counter to cross the distance separating them. "You don't know how badly I want to take you up on that offer," he whispered against her lips before stealing a bacon-flavored kiss.

"Not fair," she said as he pulled away.

"Life rarely is."

"Neither is death," she quipped.

The reminder of her nightmare, intended or not, helped Nord refocus on their immediate task. "How 'bout we both get our work done as quickly as possible so that we can come back here and finish what we started?"

"I'd love that."

He ran his nose along hers and gave her another, lingering kiss. "It's a date."

Nord allowed himself a second to memorize the way she looked in that exact moment, knowing it was one he'd return to frequently. Her face was tilted up toward his, her lips slightly parted, skin flushed. She'd been stunning all dressed up for the auction, but he preferred her like this. Her hair carelessly thrown up, wearing one of his T-shirts and a pair of skin-tight leggings. It was sexy without pretense. Something only the people—the man—closest to her would ever see, which was yet another reminder that she was his.

"Finish up and go get dressed. We'll skip today's training session and give you another day or two to recover before we dive into exploring your magic."

"The orgasm wasn't *that* good . . ."

"Liar," he whispered, stealing a final kiss.

Lina opened her eyes and held up two fingers an inch apart. "Maybe just a little."

He laughed, enjoying the lighthearted moment. After last night, he needed it. It was a way of ensuring she really was okay.

"Eat. Dress. Work. And then . . ."

"And then?" she asked, eyes shining.

"Then we can play."

CHAPTER TWENTY-EIGHT

Lina

Lina's usual table was already set up and waiting for her when she arrived in the archive. There was something about Nord and Finley waving goodbye from the door that made her feel a bit like a child being dropped off at school. Although, instead of parents, she had two hot bodyguards reminding her to behave and not to talk to strangers. Well, one of them was her bodyguard. The other was more like a drunk uncle that was endlessly entertaining and loved to break the rules when no one else was looking.

She laughed out loud at the thought, though her smile immediately faltered at the pile of heavy tomes she'd yet to get through. Sighing, Lina pulled her notebook, phone, and some pens out of her bag, spreading them out in front of her. Once those were all in place, she opened the spiral-bound book to a fresh page after double-checking where she'd left off last time. Identifying the correct tome, she slid it toward her and lazily flipped through the pages until she found the right one.

A dozen unblinking faces greeted her, the small lines of text identifying who each of them were blurring until they were little more than fuzzy gray underlines.

Three pages later, she wasn't even pretending to read the words.

Instead she sat there with her chin propped in one hand, doodling in her notebook while her mind wandered.

There was no clear train of thought, just flickers of images she'd yet to fully process.

The auction calamity.

The return of her power.

The ripples of light and shadow over the hard planes of Nord's body as he stood between her legs.

The taste of damp earth as she choked on it.

"Penny for your thoughts?"

Lina blinked, snapping back to the present as she glanced up at Alistair's quietly amused expression. Giving an embarrassed chuckle, she replied, "They aren't worth that much."

"I don't know about that. You looked pretty wrapped up in them."

She waved a hand dismissively. "Just the usual things."

He canted his head, hands folded together over the top of his cane while his eyes swept across her face. "It's never polite to tell a lady she looks less than perfect, but I'm going to go out on a limb and guess that you can handle a little honesty."

Lina grimaced. "That bad, huh?"

His smile was kind when he replied, "Just seems like you could do with a bit more sleep."

She shuddered. Sleep was the last thing she wanted. If there was a way to avoid ever sleeping again, she'd do it no questions asked. Anything to circumvent more of those bloodcurdling dreams.

Alistair's thick eyebrows furrowed. "Ah, I see. Not just a late night, but trouble sleeping."

Lina let out a startled laugh. "Are you a mind reader, or am I really just that transparent?"

"You have a very expressive face," he replied.

So do you, she thought, noting the same aura of grief clinging to him as she had seen before. She found herself wanting to ask him why he was so sad, but even she, clueless in almost every aspect of social inter-action, knew that wasn't an appropriate question to ask someone she barely knew.

He shifted, wincing slightly, and Lina immediately felt like an ass. She'd just sat there and let an old man with a cane stand around.

"If you're not busy, I'd love for you to sit and join me," she offered.

"You sure I won't be interrupting your work?"

Lina shook her head. "Definitely not."

He slowly lowered himself into the chair across from her and let out a deep sigh. "I've got the company, now I'm just missing my nightly bourbon."

Her eyes darted to her phone screen. "It's ten-thirty in the morning."

Alistair lifted a shoulder. "When you get to be my age, it's always happy hour."

Lina raised both hands, her fingers splayed. "Don't get me wrong, I wasn't judging."

He raised his brow. "Then why check the time?"

"I was worried I'd lost track of it," she said immediately.

His face cut into a wide grin, the wrinkles feathering his eyes and mouth creasing deeply as he laughed. "I like you."

"Right back 'atcha. Actually . . ." she murmured, an idea taking shape. "I may be able to do something about that drink."

"You got some kind of secret bar hidden under your research desk?" he asked.

Lina shook her head, lips pressed together to contain her laughter.

"Good, because I was going to lodge a complaint. I've been coming here for the last seventeen years, and I've never been offered a desk with a pocket bar," he muttered.

"Shh, I need to concentrate," she admonished lightly.

Alistair mimed zipping his lips.

Lina chuckled silently as she let her eyes fall closed. There was no telling if this was going to work, but remembering Nord's advice, Lina pictured what she wanted, willing it into existence. After several heart-beats, there was the tinkle of ice against glass. Barely containing an excited whoop, she opened her eyes to find Alistair staring at her intently.

"Nice trick," he said, reaching out to sniff the amber liquid in one of the crystal high-ball glasses that now sat between them. Taking a sip, his eyes closed, and he let out a satisfied hum.

"Taste okay?" she asked.

"Oh yes."

Lina grinned, lifting the other glass. "Well then, cheers."

They clinked glasses, and both took a sip. Lina immediately sputtered.

Alistair chuckled, "Not to your liking?"

She glared at him. "You told me it tasted good."

His brows lifted. "It does. If you like bourbon."

She set the glass down and pushed it away with her finger. "More like gasoline and smoke."

"Are you really going to make an old man drink alone?"

"Oh, that's a low blow, mister."

He winked. "Best thing about being old, you know all the tricks."

Lina rolled her eyes and picked up her drink once more. "I'm starting to think you're a troublemaker."

"Oh, without a doubt," he agreed.

Lina tossed her drink back, downing it in one. Setting the empty glass down, she made a disgusted face.

"That's not exactly what I meant," he said slowly.

She wrinkled her nose at him. "It was the only way it was going down."

Shrugging, he followed suit. "In that case, Sláinte."

When he set his empty glass back on the desk, she asked, "What language was that?"

"Gaelic."

"I didn't realize you were Ir . . ." she trailed off, realizing it was a weird comment even as she started to say it.

He shook his head, not seeming the least put out. "I'm not Irish. I just like collecting odd bits of knowledge and language." He tapped his temple. "It's a veritable smorgasbord of information up here."

Lina smirked. "I'm starting to see that."

He steepled his fingers in front of him and leaned forward on the desk. "So, Lina, now that we've both had our dose of liquid courage, how about you tell me why you can't seem to sleep."

"Care to be more specific?" she asked, trying hard to keep her voice casual as her spine stiffened. For an old guy, he sure was observant. It was too easy to drop her guard with him. Unfortunately, she was already feeling a warm buzz from the alcohol, and her thoughts had taken on a hazy-around-the-edges quality. This was not the time for her to get into a game of wits.

He waved a hand in the air significantly. "People don't have trouble sleeping for no reason. What ails you? Maybe this brain of mine can offer some pearls of wisdom."

"From what? Your illustrious career as a psychologist?" she teased.

"Live awhile and you learn we all have our own brand of wisdom to offer. It's up to those around us to accept it."

Lina pursed her lips. "You backed me right into a corner with that one."

He winked. "I know. Now tell me. What seems to be the problem?"

"Well, doc," she started, "it seems I have a memory problem. As in, I have none." Her eyes widened slightly as the words left her lips. She hadn't intended to tell him so much of the truth, but what was the harm in admitting she had amnesia? That wasn't exactly classified information.

"Now that is interesting. I'm assuming you mean retrograde amnesia since you seem to recall meeting me well enough?"

"I'm not sure on the exact terminology, but if that means I lost the whole burrito, then yeah. That's what I've got," she said, folding her hands in front of her.

"I think you mean enchilada."

Her stomach growled, and she muttered, "Now I want a burrito. I wish there were a secret restaurant under my desk."

Alistair laughed. "That would be convenient. And retrograde just means you cannot recall your past memories, but do not have any issue creating new ones."

Lina shrugged, her limbs feeling loose and her nose slightly tingly. She rubbed at it and said, "That sounds about right. I just woke up one day, no memory of who I was or how I'd gotten there."

Okay, so that wasn't quite the whole story, but it was close enough. No need to go and tell him she was a full-on living dead girl. Even in the supernatural world, she was pretty sure that kind of thing tended to raise red flags.

His hand scrubbed at his mouth. "And the memory loss, do you have a specific reason why you believe that is the culprit for your inability to sleep?"

"I have dreams," she whispered as another shudder racked her body.

"What kind of dreams?" he asked, his playful tone replaced with concern.

Lina swallowed and gave him a half-smile that she knew he'd see straight through. "The kind that keep you awake at night, terrified of going back to sleep."

Alistair frowned. "And you think they might be related to your past," he correctly guessed.

"Memories like that . . . most would give anything to forget them."

Something in her voice must have given him pause, because he studied her for a second before stating, "Most people . . . but not you."

"Not me," Lina agreed solemnly.

"Lina, it's probably not my place, but if your dreams are as terrible as you have led me to believe, why do you want your memories back?"

"I need to remember who I am."

He studied her. "This is important to you."

She snorted. "I would think it would be important to anyone."

Alistair leaned back in his chair, his gaze growing distant. "You seem to have landed on your feet. I think a lot of people would gladly give up who they were for a chance to live an entirely different life, free of the burden of their past."

"Would you?" she asked softly.

He didn't speak for a long moment, and she worried she'd over-stepped. His gaze didn't quite meet hers when he finally said, "There's a lot about my past I wish I could forget, but then I would also lose the very best pieces of me. So, no. I do not wish to forget them. Instead, I choose to endure."

I choose to endure.

It was on the tip of her tongue to ask the question, to find out what the source of his anguish was, but she hesitated, and the chance was lost.

"If you're serious about wanting to have your memories returned, I know someone who might be able to help you."

Blood rushed in Lina's ears, and her heart stuttered in her chest. "You do?"

He nodded. "I could see if they're available . . ."

Words were tumbling over each other in her haste to get them out. "Yes, I mean, of course"—she was leaning forward, both hands gripping the table as she spoke—"that would be incredible. If it's not any trouble."

Alistair gave her one of his soft smiles. "No trouble at all. I have a few favors owed to me. It's well past time I collect."

"You'd use them on me?" she asked, surprise bringing her brows together.

"I cannot think of a worthier cause."

"But you hardly know me. And I don't have much—well, any —money."

"Repayment isn't necessary."

The furrow between her brows deepened. "I can't accept that kind of help without doing something in return."

"Consider it a gift, or if it helps, a thank you for the drink and company."

Lina pursed her lips. "That seems like a hell of a thank you gift."

Alistair shrugged. "Kindness should never be predicated on repayment or reserved solely for those with whom we have long histories. If it is within your means to help another, isn't it selfish to withhold your assistance?"

"Perhaps, but—"

Alistair cut her off with a smile. "I have been selfish for far too long, dear Lina. Allow an old man his chance to remedy that while he still can."

She narrowed her eyes in mock frustration before blowing out a breath. "I'd be a fool to turn down the help. So as long as you don't mind, I'm not going to stop you."

"Good, then it seems we've reached an accord. I'll set something up for say . . . this evening? Are you familiar with the Tempest Lounge?"

Lina blinked at him. "The fact that you think I'd be familiar with anything is amusing given our conversation."

Alistair's face blanked, and then his head tipped back, and he laughed, deep heaving guffaws. She watched, her own smile stretching at his mirth. After a few moments, he wiped at his eyes with a hand-kerchief he'd pulled from his coat pocket. "Ah, you make me feel young again. May I?" he asked, gesturing toward her notebook.

She pushed it across the desk, her pen tumbling across the surface of the sketch-filled pages as she did.

He quickly jotted down the address and a number. "We'll meet there at seven. Call me if you have any trouble or need to reschedule."

Excitement coursed through her as she accepted the notebook. "Thank you, Alistair. So much."

"Don't thank me just yet. We don't know if it'll work."

"Still . . . just the possibility. It means a lot to me."

This time, when he smiled, Lina found no trace of the sadness lingering in his eyes.

"Then let us hope for the best, shall we? Now, if you'll excuse me. I have a call to make." With that, he stood, pretending to tip a hat he was not wearing at her, before slowly making his way out of the room.

Lina watched him leave with a smile. She couldn't wait to tell Nord about Alistair's offer. He was going to be so proud of her for managing to find someone who could help her with her little memory problem.

Her smile dimmed a little.

Wouldn't he?

CHAPTER TWENTY-NINE

Nord

"Dammit, he's not here either," Nord snarled, smashing his fist into the wall.

Finley turned away from Alistair's door, frowning as plaster rained down on the gold and turquoise carpet lining the high rise's hallway. "Thank you, Captain Obvious. Now would you like to continue throwing a tantrum, or shall we try to figure out where he *is* rather than reiterating where he is not."

After eight hours and as many locations, they'd yet to find Alistair, nor had anyone seen him that day. They might have had more luck asking around the Brotherhood, but both Finley and Nord were in agreement. They didn't want anyone to catch onto the fact that they wanted to question him. His connection to the Mobius Council was too prominent, and it would not be a far leap for anyone to make about what they were really after.

Instead, they'd settled for checking each of the frequent hangouts listed in his file, sure they'd find him at one of them since his daily routine for the last ten years was almost entirely unchanged.

They'd started with his home, thinking perhaps he'd merely left for the day by the time they arrived, so after a quick check, they drove to two parks he was known to play chess in, and then to a nearby café where he often went for afternoon tea. It was a quarter past six, and they'd just checked the last place off the list before deciding to check his house one more time. Needless to say, it was a bust.

Nord squeezed the bridge of his nose, fighting hard to control his temper. It wasn't Finley's fault the man was nowhere to be found.

"I don't understand, where could he be?" Nord asked, pleased to hear that his voice was even.

Finley's face was unreadable as he shook his head. "I don't know. We've checked everywhere . . ." he trailed off with a groan and slapped a hand to his forehead. "Could it really have been that obvious?"

"What do you mean?" Nord demanded.

"A few times we've gone to check on Lina, I've seen Alistair in the archive. I didn't think of it, because he's there so infrequently and he usually gives advance notice before coming in. I wouldn't have even thought of it now, except—"

"Lina," Nord finished, knowing exactly where his friend's train of thought was going.

"Exactly."

"What the fuck are we waiting for?" Nord asked.

Finley was already calling the portal. "Cover me, will you?"

Nord nodded, power simmering in his eyes as he created an illusion that would block passersby from seeing them.

Less than five minutes later, they were running out of the elevator toward a stunned-looking archivist.

"Can I help you?" he asked, eyes flared wide.

"No time," Finley said, racing down the hall that would lead them to the archive's central room.

Nord was hot on his heels, skidding to a halt just beside him.

Chest heaving, Nord and Finley exchanged dark looks.

Alistair wasn't there. Neither was Lina.

The room was empty.

CHAPTER THIRTY

Lina

Lina's fingers drummed a rapid tattoo on the counter as she stared at the clock. She'd been back for a few hours already, but Nord and Finley still weren't home. That wasn't necessarily surprising. Fin had warned her it might take all day, but she'd really been hoping to at least see them long enough to tell them about her chat with Alistair. It felt like the sort of thing they'd want to know, and that she should explain in person.

That's what she'd been telling herself, anyway. Why bother them while they were working if she would just catch them before it was time to go? They'd be less distracted, and less annoyed with her for interrupting them . . . yeah. She wasn't really buying it either.

As much as she wanted them to know where she was going, she also didn't want them to try to stop her. Waiting until the last possible second felt like her best chance of that. Now, even if they did walk through the door as she breezed past, there'd be no time for more than a kiss on the cheek.

Accepting defeat, Lina pushed herself upright and made her way into the living room, searching for the bag she'd tossed in the general vicinity of the couches when she'd gotten home. Spying it upended on the floor, she groaned and dropped to her knees, scrambling to shove everything back inside, taking a mental inventory as she did.

Keys. Gum. Extra hair ties. Lipstick.

Notebook . . . *that can probably stay here.*

Pens. Wallet. ID card that fell out of wallet . . .

Not seeing anything else on the floor or underneath the couch when she craned her neck and pressed her cheek to the floor, Lina sat back on her heels and frowned.

That can't be everything. She'd made sure to toss her phone back into her bag before she'd left the archive . . . right?

Lina chewed on her lip as a pit formed in her stomach. When it came to that stupid piece of plastic, she was the worst. If she weren't forgetting to charge it, she'd left it somewhere totally obscure. Like the clothes hamper, because it had been in her pocket when she'd went to shower, and it took her three days to realize it was missing. Or the refrigerator, because she'd needed both hands to pull out the pizza box, and there'd been nowhere else to put it.

In her defense, she hadn't wanted the damn thing in the first place. Who needs a phone to call someone when they're practically glued together at the hip? But then Fin had explained that phones are rarely used for calls, and that it's an easy way to look up information or listen to music—which had become the small device's primary purpose. When she actually remembered to keep it charged.

Now the one time she'd actually needed to hit the button pre-programmed with Nord's number, and her phone was nowhere to be found.

Fuck. She was totally screwed. Nord wasn't going to let her hear the end of this.

Eyeing the notebook she'd tossed back onto the couch, Lina opened it to the last page and hastily scrawled a note, pulling out Alistair's scrap of paper to double-check the name and address of where she was going, before shoving it back into her pocket.

There.

At least now he couldn't say she didn't tell him where she was going.

Not that it would make any difference.

Scrambling back to her feet, Lina rushed down the hall, trying to think of where he'd go first. Probably her room. She didn't want to leave her note lying somewhere he wouldn't notice it, so jamming a piece of gum into her mouth, she chewed hurriedly and then used it to help stick her note to the door.

She winced apologetically. "Sorry, Fin," she whispered, hiking her bag up higher on her arm and making her way to the front door.

It was weird leaving on her own. Perhaps because it was the first time she'd ever had a reason to, but even the small handful of times she'd returned to the penthouse on her own, it had left her feeling . . . off.

Stop getting yourself all worked up, she told herself as she pressed the down arrow on the elevator panel with a little more force than necessary. Lina fidgeted nervously as she waited, not sure if her anxiety was spiking because she was about to get in the elevator, or because of what might happen tonight. The answer was likely both, although now that she knew why she had an aversion to enclosed spaces, her elevator rides had become almost unbearable.

She swore she could taste dirt each time the doors slid closed, sealing her inside. If they weren't twenty-plus floors up, she might have considered the stairs, but she was running late as it was.

Finally, the elevator arrived, and Lina squeezed her eyes shut, forcing herself to take slow, measured breaths even as her heart rate skyrocketed. She could feel the pools of sweat gathering at the base of her neck and under her arms. At this rate, she was going to look like she'd stopped for a swim on her way to the Tempest Lounge.

"Almost there, almost there, almost there," she muttered, practically sagging with relief at the low *ding* signaling her arrival on the bottom floor.

She was definitely taking the stairs later.

"You feeling well, Ms. Lina?" a familiar male voice asked as she rushed out of the elevator.

Lina didn't have to force a smile for the sweet doorman. "I'm fine, Stanley. Just running late."

"Need me to call you a cab?"

"That would be great."

"Where ya headed?"

"The Tempest Lounge," she said, watching carefully to see if the name triggered a reaction.

Stanley's face remained as pleasant as ever, which brought her a measure of calm. She had the feeling if she were heading off to a place with a bad reputation, he would have mentioned it. Looks like she wasn't about to walk into a devil's lair or something equally worrisome. At least she had that going for her.

There must have been a taxi stand nearby because the cab was there in less than a minute.

Stanley held open the door for her. "Have a good evening, Ms. Lina."

"You too, Stanley," she said with a wave, climbing into the back seat of the black SUV.

The driver gave her a little wave, repeated the address, and then pulled away from the curb after she nodded her confirmation. The rest of the ride was a blur. It felt like her heart was in her throat as they sped past block after block of skyscrapers, restaurants, and storefronts.

Before she realized it, he was pulling up in front of a little hole-in-the-wall, with blinking neon lights shouting 'Get Wet at the Tempest' and 'It's Always Happy Hour Here.'

"Here you are, miss," the driver said.

Lina took a wad of cash out of her purse, shoving it in his hand without counting. His eyes went wide, telling Lina she'd more than overpaid him.

"Want me to wait for you?" he offered.

"Actually . . . that would be awesome, if you wouldn't mind."

He doffed his cap, showing off his surprisingly stylish black hair. "No trouble at all, miss. The name's Henry. I'll just be over there in that little lot. You give me a holler when you're ready to go."

Lina gave him a grateful smile. "Thanks, Henry. I don't think I'll be long."

"Take all the time you need, miss."

"Lina," she supplied, as she started to open the door.

"Oh, let me get that for you."

Before she could protest, he was out the door and running around the car to open her door.

"That wasn't necessary, but thank you," she murmured, climbing out onto the sidewalk.

He grinned at her, his amber eyes practically glowing under the neon signs. "Sure, it was. See you in a while."

She shook her head, fighting a smile. Nervous energy filled her once more as she jotted across the sidewalk to the heavy teal door with its brass handle. There was a stained-glass mural in the center, depicting a mermaid and what appeared to be a large stein of dark ale.

Lina snorted as she pulled the door open and stepped into the dim interior. It looked like a traditional pub, with dark wood everything and all sorts of random pictures and signs lining the walls. She squinted as her eyes adjusted to the light. The bar was fairly empty, but there were lots of booths on the far left side, and she could just make out a familiar crop of silver hair.

Angling in that direction, Lina was already apologizing when she reached him. "Sorry I'm late—"

The flow of words cut off immediately as a pair of unique wine-colored eyes bore into hers.

Static filled her ears as Quinn gave her a Cheshire smile. "Nice to see you again, Lina."

"Q-Quinn," she managed, blinking rapidly.

"You two know each other?" Alistair asked, his thick, caterpillar brows lifting high.

"Oh, we're great friends, isn't that right?" Quinn said, lifting her drink and taking a dainty sip.

Lina swallowed, her mouth suddenly dry. "We met last night," she supplied.

"Well, that certainly makes introductions easier. Here, take a seat." Alistair made to stand.

"No, no. You stay put," Lina said, eyeing the empty spot next to Quinn warily. She had no reason to be so nervous. Quinn had been nothing but nice to her the night before. But there was something about her, the same undefinable tension that had sent the little hairs on the back of her neck to stand on end last night, that had Lina feeling like she needed to tread carefully.

"You seem to have recovered," Quinn said once Lina was settled.

"Recovered?" Alistair parroted, his deep voice sounding gruff with censure.

Lina squeezed the bridge of her nose, feeling totally out of her depth. How much could she reveal to these two?

Quinn patted Lina's other hand in a comforting manner. "Our Lina had a surge last night."

"Is that so?" Alistair said, his eyes gleaming thoughtfully behind his glasses.

"It was a crazy night," Lina said with a dismissive laugh. "So, how do you two know each other?" she asked, trying to change the subject.

Alistair and Quinn exchanged a look that told Lina there was a long history there. It was obvious that they were debating how much to tell her. She was grateful that she was keeping her cards close to her chest. If they weren't sure how much to trust her with, she was going to follow their lead.

"Quinn and I have worked together, several times."

"You seem to work with a lot of people," Lina said without thinking.

Quinn's lips twitched up in a smile. She gave a little shrug. "What can I say, my skill set is in high demand."

"And what is your skill set, exactly?"

Quinn's smile stretched. "Isn't it obvious?"

Lina shook her head, wishing she had a drink of her own to help disguise some of her nerves. "I was just told that you're a memory weaver, but I don't really know what that means."

"I weave memories, of course."

Lina could have punched her. She gave Alistair a hard look, but one of his hands was already lifted in a placating manner.

"Quinn, enough games. Our Lina needs help. As I mentioned when we chatted earlier, she seems to be missing some memories and would like your help to recover them."

"Some memories?" Quinn asked pointedly.

"All of them, up until about three weeks ago." Or near enough without Lina giving an exact day count.

"Do you recall anything from your past?"

Lina shook her head. "Not even my name."

If that tidbit was of any interest, Quinn didn't let it show.

"Will that be a problem?" Lina asked.

Quinn took another sip of her drink and shrugged. "The brain is an interesting thing. It stores data, even if we can't recall it. Just because you're incapable of accessing the information, doesn't mean it's not still stored there. All I need to do is help reconnect the wires, so to speak. Should be pretty straightforward."

Lina snorted. "Straightforward. Right."

Quinn winked. "Memories are my bread and butter. Creating them. Removing them. Restoring them. I'm a one-stop shop."

A shiver of apprehension crawled down her spine and Lina's answering smile was more of a grimace. "Sounds great."

"The real question here is are you sure you want this, Lina?" Quinn's smirk was gone, her odd-colored eyes boring intensely into Lina's.

There was something about the tone of her voice that gave Lina pause. It wasn't so much a warning as a heaviness. She'd even go so far as to say a sort of lingering sadness, or was that guilt?

Her brows dipped low as she looked between Quinn and Alistair. "I already told Alistair. It's not a matter of want. I *need* to remember who I am."

"Why?" Quinn pressed.

Lina let out a dry laugh and threw up her hands. "Because someone out there tried to ki—" Horrified, she cut herself off, amending quickly, "tried to keep me from knowing who I am. There's got to be a reason."

Quinn and Alistair shared another look. "You think someone did this to you intentionally?" Quinn asked, her voice taking on a tinny quality.

"That's my working theory," Lina replied.

Quinn hummed low in her throat. "Well . . . I will give you the same warning I give the others. Not that anyone ever listens to me," she added under her breath. "Memories are tied to emotion. This is likely going to be a draining, and potentially painful, process. The weight of everything returning all at once, it's a lot to process. You'll want to rest for a day or two."

First her power, now her memories. It seemed to Lina that she was an all-or-nothing kind of girl.

"Bring it on," she said.

Quinn bit her lip and rolled her eyes, but Alistair's smile radiated approval.

Sighing, Quinn said, "Fine. Let's get down to business, then."

"Do I need to lay down or something?" she asked, looking around the bar. This seemed an odd place to attempt something like this.

"No, sitting is fine. I will need to touch you, though."

"Oh," Lina said, shifting a bit in her seat so she was facing Quinn head-on. "All right."

Quinn tilted her head, eyes squinted as she studied her. "If I recall, you have tattoos on your arms, is that correct?"

Lina jolted, wondering how the other woman knew, before remembering the location of her tattoos, if not the exact images, could have been visible through the sleeves of her gown. Tongue wetting her lips, Lina nodded. "Yes, two of them. One on my forearm and the other on my bicep."

"Can you remove your jacket for me?"

Lina slowly peeled off the leather jacket, shivering as the air conditioning ran over her exposed skin.

"I take it these aren't new?" Quinn asked. At Lina's confused expression, she clarified, "You didn't just get these in the last couple of weeks."

"Oh, no. They've been there as long as I can remember."

The women exchanged amused grins.

"Perfect, I'll use them as a focus, then."

"A focus?" she asked.

"It helps strengthen my magic; gives it something to ground itself to and pull from."

Lina nodded like she understood, but she made a mental note to ask Nord about it later.

"This is your last chance to back out if you are having any doubts, Lina. There's no stopping once I start. So I'm going to ask you again, are you sure?"

She wanted to groan in exasperation. How many times did she have to answer this question? But she resisted the urge. "I'm sure."

Quinn placed cool hands on both of Lina's tattoos. Goosebumps broke out at the touch, but Lina was rooted in place. Even the mental order to blink wasn't obeyed. She was fully under the other woman's control. She could feel her chest rise and fall as she continued to breathe, but she couldn't seem to look away from Quinn's eyes. The red and purple orbs looked like endless liquid pools, rippling and undulating as the color filled her entire field vision.

"Nod if you can hear me," Quinn demanded.

Lina nodded.

"Good. That's very good. Now we're going to mend what was severed. It's time, Evalina. *Remember.*"

At first, there was nothing but the cabernet-colored pools. Time seemed to stretch, and Lina was about to say it wasn't working, but before her lips could form the words, something like lightning shot through her veins, and her breath caught in her throat.

And then . . . then there was nothing but darkness.

CHAPTER THIRTY-ONE

Nord

Nord crumpled Lina's note in his hand, ignoring the slimy feel of the gum where it pressed into his skin. His heart was racing in his chest while his rage began to swell. The need to tear something apart, to dismantle a room until all that was left was him panting in the center, was pressing against him, making it hard to breathe. He was so far gone that even the corners of his vision were turning a deep, angry red.

"What's it say?" Finley asked, hovering just over his shoulder.

"You know what it said," Nord snarled, spinning around. "I could feel you breathing down my neck while you read it."

"You finished it before I did," Finley admitted.

"She asked me not to be angry," Nord said, heading toward the door.

Finley followed close behind, his bark of laughter doing nothing to calm the storm building inside of him.

"Did she forget who she was talking to?"

"I doubt it. Otherwise she wouldn't have made a point to ask."

"At least she told you where she was going," Finley offered. "Will make it easy for us to catch up to her."

"That's not the point. When will she learn that she can't just race headfirst into danger? I shouldn't have left her alone . . ."

"She's not a child, Nord. You can't babysit her twenty-four seven. The resentment would ruin any chance for you two to build something real."

"At least I'd know that she wasn't lying in a ditch somewhere," Nord snapped.

Finley eyed him and wisely kept his mouth shut. "I'll drive," he offered.

Nord nodded, internally seething that they couldn't portal to her. The location was too public, not to mention the bar was warded. The closest they'd be able to get was the sidewalk, but they'd risk being seen if they just popped into existence in the middle of a busy street.

"Fucking Alistair. I don't care how old that sonofabitch is—"

"Easy," Finley said. "If what Lina said is true, he may have helped cut our work in half."

"I don't care."

Finley shook his head. "You may not, but she will."

Nord growled low in his throat.

His partner eyed him knowingly. "You wreck my car; I will end you."

"I'd like to see you try," Nord replied, knowing his smile was more than a little crazed.

"Fucking berserkers," Finley muttered sliding into the driver's seat.

Nord climbed into the car beside him, resenting the feel of metal and leather caging him in. Even though Finley made it to the bar in record time, Nord felt like he was crawling out of his skin by the time they arrived. He didn't even wait for the car to be fully parked before he was out and ripping the door to the Tempest Lounge open.

His heart stopped dead in his chest.

Lina's familiar mop of golden hair was slumped forward, her prone body eerily still.

For one endless moment, he knew nothing but soul-crushing anguish. His mind refused to accept what his eyes were seeing. Then he was moving. He was across the room, pinning Alistair to the wall with one hand around his throat before Finley had even stepped inside.

"What did you do to her?" his voice cracked like thunder in the relative quiet of the bar.

Patrons slowly made their way out, while bartenders wisely averted their gaze. The Tempest Lounge was a favorite in the supernatural community for a reason. No one would interfere. Not if they valued their lives.

"She trusted you," he said savagely, giving the old man a shake and shoving him once more into the wall.

Alistair's nails dragged against Nord's skin as he gasped for breath. Nord loosened his hold. Barely, but it was enough for Alistair to suck in a ragged breath.

"She's alive," he wheezed.

Nord shoved a finger in the direction of Lina's body. "That doesn't look alive."

Finley moved into Nord's periphery. "He's right, mate. She's breathing."

Nord's chest heaved. The air was burning in his lungs as he struggled to make sense of what they were saying. A part of him registered that she was alive. It was what kept him from tearing out the old man's heart and flinging it onto the floor. The other, larger part of him, was still caught up on the fact that the one he was born to protect was once again unconscious and he'd been helpless to stop it.

"Helping. Her," Alistair insisted, his eyes still bulging from his mottled face.

Nord let go, stepping away as Alistair fell to the ground in a graceless heap. If he was a kind man, he would have at least helped the bastard up. But he'd never pretended to be kind. Turning away, he finally allowed himself to look at the woman fully supporting Lina's weight.

The Satori heir.

Her eyes were pits of color, her mouth slack. Whatever magic she was in the middle of performing was responsible for Lina's current state.

Nord knew better than to interfere with the spell, doing so would invite terrible consequences, like leaving Lina in a permanently comatose state. Still, being logical was the last thing on his mind. He wanted to rip Lina out of Quinn's arms and carry her somewhere safe. His body was vibrating with the need to protect her.

"She'll be okay," Finley whispered beside him.

"You don't know that."

"I do," he insisted.

Nord forced himself to breathe, to relax the fists at his sides. All he managed to accomplish was stare unblinkingly at the back of Lina's head like some kind of obsessed guard dog. It could have been an hour or minutes that he stood there. He lost track of everything but the two women sitting in front of him.

Then there was a gasp, and he about dropped to his knees when Quinn's eyes rolled back in her head and Lina took a shuddering breath.

He tried to tell himself his shaking limbs were a result of the adrenaline. But he had a feeling it was relief.

"Lina?" he managed, his voice sounding like he was speaking around a mouthful of rocks.

She didn't move, her face still obscured by a curtain of her hair.

Alistair took a few tentative steps toward the table. "Evalina?" he rasped.

Nord cut him a dark look. "What did you just call her?"

Lina's neck twisted at the sound, and her eyes were blazing with light when they landed on the old man at his side.

"Hello, Uncle."

———

Keep reading for an exclusive sneak peek at book 2 in the
Undercover Magic series,
Face of Danger, available now!

CHAPTER 1

Lina

Lina's memories returned with the force of a jackhammer to her brain. She was only distantly aware of her physical body slumped down in one of the Tempest Lounge's booths. Her attention was consumed by her past.

It was all there, laid out like a sumptuous buffet for her to pick and choose from.

Her name.

Her family . . . well, what was left of it.

Her fifteenth birthday when she received her first kiss.

Her eighteenth birthday when she received her first tattoo.

But there was one memory that outshone all the others. The one that had been powerful enough to pierce her dreams when she'd been cut off from everything else that made her whole. She focused on that memory now, immersing herself in those final, terrifying seconds, and watched them play out like some kind of twisted snuff film.

And she was its star.

Through the slashing rain and darkness, she ran into the alley, only to crash into a wall moments later. Dazed, she struggled to lift herself from the ground.

She needed to keep moving because he was right behind her.

Mataius Drake. The boy she'd grown up with. The man she was promised to.

It was too late. Above the sound of the pouring rain, she heard his dark chuckle.

"Evalina," his terrifying voice crooned. "You know there's no escape. While I do love a good chase, playtime is over. I'm here to collect what's mine."

She opened her mouth and screamed for help. But she knew there were no heroes in her story. Only devils disguised as men.

Something crashed into the back of her head, and Lina crumbled to the ground once more.

Consciousness returned, steeped in the pain of hundreds of invisible needles stabbing her eyes. The instinctive need to lift her hand to her head was halted with a rattle of noise. Confused, she squinted through the throbbing pain and looked down at the heavy, silver chains that lashed her to a chair. Her vision blurred, and she shivered at the feel of the icy rivers of blood dripping down her face and neck.

She tried to make out where she was, but the flashes of lightning outside the windows and the flicker of a dozen candles laid out on the floor revealed nothing familiar.

Harsh whispers came from somewhere behind her. She tried to call for help, but a tortured moan emerged instead. The whispers fell silent, replaced by the scrape of boots over the floor.

Mataius hit her hard across the face then fisted a hand in her hair, pulling her head up and back.

"Did I tell you you could speak?" The heat of his breath washed over her cheek. "I'm growing impatient. I've been waiting for this day for what feels like my entire life." His hand trailed down the side of her face in a macabre imitation of a caress. "Just a little bit longer now, and then you won't be my problem anymore. In fact, you won't be anyone's problem.

"The others are coming. And then . . . well, let's not ruin the surprise, shall we?"

He pressed against the weeping wound on the back of her head. She screamed against the pain, and then the world faded to nothing until a cool breeze over her damp clothes woke her.

Wax pools had formed beneath the flickering candles around her, and the sound of footsteps filled the room—too many to belong to one person. A low throbbing beat joined the footsteps. Her terrified brain recognized the source of the sound as a drum.

She tried to cry out, call for help, but something coated in the metallic taste of her blood had been shoved into her mouth.

The drumming grew louder, and a chorus of deep voices started chanting a demonic symphony. The candles guttered, and some blew out entirely. The unmistakable sound of metal scraping against metal joined the sounds.

A sob choked her as the wet slide of a tongue began to trace the damp tracks on her face.

"I don't believe I've ever tasted anything as delicious as your fear," Mataius whispered against her ear as he freed the gag from her mouth. "Go ahead and scream as much as you want, sweetheart. It only makes it better."

A dagger glinted, and fiery pain ignited just above her heart. She sucked in a shocked breath, and then her screams joined the unearthly chorus that rose in a crescendo around her.

"Beautiful," Mataius said, twisting the blade and dragging it lower. "So fucking beautiful."

Mataius carved into her chest with his dagger, drawing the symbol that would complete whatever ritual he'd initiated. She knew he intended to kill her, and there'd be nothing left for her father to find except her mutilated body.

Darkness swelled, and she welcomed the relief of oblivion.

Sound returned too soon though. Voices whispered, and Lina groaned. The burning in her chest was muted, but she could still feel the throb. Like a toothache. She tried to open her eyes, but they refused to obey.

"Shh. Quiet now, Sweetling. It will all be over soon."

A new voice but a familiar one.

"Un-uncl . . ." her tongue felt too thick to form the words.

"Yes, Sweetling. I'm here. You just rest now. You've done more than enough."

Alistair was here. She was safe.

Then another, softer voice spoke. Quinn. "We don't have much time. The damage they did was fatal. We cannot stop the severing. Already, the soul is trying to leave the body."

Whose soul? Her soul? Lina struggled to make sense of the conversation.

"*Do what you can.*"

"*Are you . . . are you sure?*"

"*It must be done.*"

"*It could take decades before the spell breaks down enough to call her back. Left untethered for that long, she'll become . . . unstable. What is left when she does return . . . she'll not be the woman we know.*"

"*Is there a way to prevent it?*"

"*Yes, but—*"

"*Do it.*"

"*She won't remember us.*"

"*Perhaps it's better that way.*"

"*Alistair.*"

"*Do as I say, heir. Or leave.*"

"*Hold her steady. This is going to hurt.*"

Lina screamed as her right forearm began to burn. The pain ignited behind her eyes as memories rose to the surface only to smolder and burn like photographs. There and gone, leaving nothing in their wake.

"*It is done,*" *Quinn said, her voice heavy and flat.*

"*And now?*"

"*And now we wait and pray to whatever god will listen that it wasn't too late.*"

The world tilted, and Lina grew weightless as if she was floating or being carried. Then, it stopped. Something cold and wet seeped into her back.

"*Until we meet again, my dearest friend.*" *Quinn's voice was so sad.*

Water splashed onto Lina's face, and something warm pressed against her forehead.

"*Sweet dreams, my beautiful Evalina.*"

More warm drops of water. And then something else started to tickle her face and neck. Dirt. They were burying her. She started screaming in her head that she was still here. But no sound emerged. There was nothing but the weight. It pressed against her on all sides, and she drifted out of consciousness, welcoming nothing at all.

"EVALINA?" ALISTAIR CROAKED.

Lina snapped her head to the side, zeroing in on a voice she never thought to hear again. With his appearance having been changed by the Brotherhood, it was a little easier to pretend that her beloved uncle—the man who'd cuddled her when she scraped her knee and gave her her first banana split—wasn't the same person who helped shovel dirt over her mutilated body.

"Hello, Uncle."

She looked away from the man who had buried her alive.

The empty tavern had fallen mostly silent, the lone bartender keeping herself busy behind the bar. Given the slightly bored expression on her face, Lina was willing to bet this wasn't the first time she'd witnessed some kind of supernatural blowout at work. Nor would it be the last.

For her, it was probably just a typical workday at the Tempest Lounge, perhaps even one with slightly less bloodshed than usual. At least, so far.

The night was young.

Part of Lina wished she could claim the same, that this was just another bullshit Tuesday. Maybe it was in the sense that her entire life seemed to be turned inside out on a regular basis—especially recently—but that kind of constant upheaval wasn't exactly something one ever gets used to.

Just when it seemed like she was starting to get her life on track, the universe went and slapped her across the face just to remind her who was in charge. Hint: it sure as shit wasn't her.

"Lina?" a deeper, slightly accented voice called.

Her eyes shot to the grief-ravaged face of her Guardian.

"Are you . . . all right?" he asked, voice tentative, pale blue eyes searching.

She wasn't sure there was a word in existence that adequately explained what she was feeling right now, so she nodded.

"Do you remember?" her uncle asked.

"I remember *everything*. You buried me alive. Why?"

"These two were the ones responsible for killing you?" Finley asked, his eyes burning with hazel fire as his voice dropped to a dangerous pitch.

"My fiancé—" Nord sucked in a shocked breath, and Lina's gaze shifted to his horrified face as she continued, "—was performing some kind of ritual, and I was his unwilling sacrifice. These two found me at death's door, stole my memories, and buried. Me. Alive." The words were ground out and dripping with anger.

Nord was ashen, staring at her in horror.

Alistair was the first to speak, dismayed when he asked, "Mataius did that to you?"

"Yes."

He shook his head as tears dripped down his cheeks. "All this time, we didn't know who was responsible. There was a ransom note. It was addressed to your father, but I got home first. I'd suspected something was going on and left the banquet early. I tried to call him, but he didn't answer. Quinn arrived not five minutes later. You two had plans that night. Do you remember?" He faltered, waving a hand like he was getting off-topic. "There was no address, but we knew a spell that could track you. We—" his voice broke "—didn't get to you in time. All that was left was your body."

Alistair cleared his throat, fighting hard to keep his voice even as he continued his explanation. "When we first arrived, you weren't even breathing. I managed to get your pulse back, but it was clear we were too late. Your body was already shutting down. We had to do what we could to salvage what was left. In order to preserve your physical self and reverse the damage—"

"My body had to be returned to the earth," Lina guessed, sensing where his explanation was going.

Her uncle nodded. "But the bigger issue was your soul. It couldn't stay tethered to a damaged vessel, and after what Mataius did . . ."

"My soul was already trying to flee its damaged vessel by the time you found me," Lina said, her voice wooden as she filled in the horrific blanks.

Again, Alistair nodded. "Quinn knew of a way to buy you time. The magic allowed your soul to heal. However, it also freed you from the pain of your past."

"If you'd retained your memories, you would have been little more than an avenging spirit," Quinn chimed in softly. "We didn't want that for you. If we could keep your mind intact while my spell repaired your soul, you would be whole when it finished. Mind, body, and soul."

That's when the last piece of the puzzle fell into place. The ball. The rooftop. Those shocked gray eyes.

"Mataius knows I'm alive," she whispered. "He's the one I saw at the ball."

––––––

DOWNLOAD YOUR COPY OF FACE OF DANGER NOW!

BONUS SCENE

Nord

Nord stifled a yawn and rubbed at his tired eyes.

I didn't sign up for this.

Since when had a man's value been determined by his ability to read a bullshit article? Finley had tried to explain the importance of staying up to date on the Brotherhood's weekly insight reports —a twenty-plus page synopsis of the open cases and persons of interest —but it was a practice in self-flagellation. Not only was the report sanitized of any truly helpful information—in case a copy somehow ended up in the wrong hands—it also read like a scientific journal regarding criminality and subsequent crime classification. Even that wouldn't have been so bad, but its author was a self-important ass whose ego was overly inflated by his bullshit job title.

Fucking desk jockeys.

How had an esteemed Brotherhood, comprised of the fiercest warriors and most powerful magic users, turned into a group of sniveling, ass-kissing bureaucrats?

He let out a little groan and forced his eyes open. These reports were complete garbage. It had taken half a page for Nord to determine that the only use they'd ever serve was to help him wipe his ass.

But that was an issue for another day.

The reality was, so long as the Brotherhood's connections led him to answers for Lina, he'd jump through their hoops. If there came a time, however, when they outlived their usefulness, there'd be no need for him to continue playing along with their ridiculous rules.

And if they tried to force the issue?

Well, then they'd learn just how formidable an unhappy berserker could be.

Buoyed by the promise of future vengeance, Nord started to lift the stack of papers from his lap but was almost immediately interrupted by the soft creak of a footboard.

A smile stretched across his face.

Lina.

He'd known she must be up to something because it had been far too quiet in the penthouse. Sure, he'd told her he had work to do, but every time he'd turned around recently, she'd been right there making good on her threat to fight dirty.

Just yesterday, Finley had commented on his self-control.

"You don't make a move soon, mate, I might have to. Jesus, just think of all the fun you could have with someone that bendy," he'd said as a half-naked Lina laid on her back and pulled her legs up and over her head.

He'd broken two of Finley's ribs with the force of the punch that comment provoked, but his partner had only laughed it off, perfectly aware that he'd been playing with fire.

Nord wondered if Lina realized the same. If she really understood what she was asking for by inviting him into her bed? The kind of insatiable appetite she'd unleash if...when...he finally caved?

Not that he wasn't enjoying her antics. He most definitely was. Already his cock was thickening in anticipation for whatever exquisite torture she had planned for today.

Nord was pretty sure Lina knew exactly the effect she was having on him, too. Even though he'd managed to resist her advances, she continued to ramp up her efforts, and it was getting harder and harder to keep his hands—and other body parts—to himself.

Despite his promise, he'd already sought out opportunities to justify touching her during their training sessions. Sure, he told himself it was all in the name of offering comfort or instruction, but the truth was that he was just a glutton for punishment.

These days it felt like his dick was in a constant state of arousal. It was almost like he was testing himself to see just how far he could push his self-control before it snapped completely. Each victory brought with it a rush of adrenaline that was drowned out only by an equally strong wave of desire.

He was wound so tightly that every accidental whiff of her sweet peach and honey shampoo or brush of her velvety smooth skin beneath his and he was rock-hard and thrumming with need. Knowing that the only thing stopping him from reaching the release he so desperately needed was the fraying strength of his own conviction only made it worse.

And yet, even though he knew he couldn't give in, like any addict, he found himself craving more. He was chasing the high that came with each new hit, even though it brought him one step closer to the brink.

If he was capable of being honest with himself, he'd admit that he welcomed the surrender. Why wouldn't he? Everything he'd ever wanted was on the other side.

But these were the rules he'd set, and his honor demanded that he obey them as long as he could. So this game between him and Lina would continue, even though he was secretly rooting for her to win.

The sound of footsteps grew louder, and Nord schooled his face into a bored mask, eyes trained unseeingly on the pages in his hand.

Even though she was just out of his line of sight, he knew the instant she stepped into the room. Just as the sea was slave to the moon, his body was wholly attuned to her. When the seconds passed and she didn't come any closer, he pressed the issue.

"I can feel you staring."

When her response came, it held a breathless quality that hinted at her excitement and stoked his own.

"I didn't know you were in here."

Nord barely swallowed back his laugh, letting out a soft grunt as he did. "Did you need something?"

"Uh, just left my brush in here."

Nord forced himself to nod and turn the page, to make it seem like he was completely absorbed in his task. If she only knew how far from the truth that was. "Don't let me stop you. Just finishing up..." Knowing his lack of attention was likely driving her crazy, and not wanting her to give up on her latest attempt, he decided to play along. Lifting his eyes, he finally allowed himself a glimpse of her.

It felt like time stopped as the air left his lungs and heat shot through his body. Fresh from the shower, Lina was all rosy skin and bright eyes, and he was consumed by the urge to help her get dirty now that she'd just gotten clean.

A trickle of water dripped down her neck from the knot of hair on her head, and all he could think about was following its path with his tongue.

Spotting her towel, her intent was obvious. Her name was the best he could do as he fought to rein in his desire. "Lina."

She took a step toward him.

Nord contemplated letting her see it through, watching the consequences of such a course of action unfold in his mind. She'd pretend to stumble, her towel magically falling away as she did, and she'd end up naked, splayed in his lap. Initially, his hands would be holding her steady, but then they'd end up moving of their own accord, following the curving lines of her body. His mouth would be quick to follow, happily taking up the cause and tasting her everywhere he'd touched her. He'd lie her back on the couch, molding his body to hers, enjoying the way they fit together only for a moment before continuing his exploration.

His cock strained against his pants, begging him to let the scenario play out. He wished he was a strong enough man to let it happen, if for no other reason than wanting to enjoy the feel of her in his arms again, but he doubted his ability to resist once she was. Which, of course, was exactly what she'd banked on.

It was a brilliant plan. Simple, but completely evil. What man could resist a naked, willing woman?

Not one.

He couldn't give her the chance to exploit the fact, or he'd be a goner.

When she went to take her second step, Nord made his move. He was up off the couch before her foot hit the ground, his hand holding fast to the top of the towel. Knowing how thin his grasp on his control was, he made a point not to let himself touch any part of her.

Just a single brush of her skin right now, and he'd come undone.

She stuttered, her eyes blinking in shock. "I...uh..."

Even though a part of him wanted to weep at the lost opportunity, another part of him reveled in his victory. He'd tested himself and succeeded once again. Barely...but it was still a win, which meant the game would continue.

Lips lifting in a small smile, his eyes dropped to hers. "Nice try."

Color stained her cheeks as she stammered, "I...I don't know what you're talking about."

He let his eyes caress her face the way his fingers itched to. "Uh-huh. So this isn't another one of your seduction schemes?"

Her eyes darted to the table beside him, and she licked her lips nervously. "I told you, I needed my brush."

Nord bit the inside of his cheek to keep from laughing. She was trying so hard to keep up her ruse but was sinking fast. She hadn't anticipated him seeing through her so quickly, and it was obvious her mind was scrambling to find a way to save face. He couldn't resist taunting her further.

"Since when do you walk around the penthouse in your towel?"

Her eyes sparkled with challenge as she tilted her chin up defiantly. "I didn't think you'd be in here."

If he hadn't known it was such a bald-faced lie, he might have bought her little show. It was rare someone could stare you straight in the eye while lying through their teeth. He wouldn't be surprised if she'd rehearsed her lines so often that she actually believed them.

"When I told you I had some work to do and I'd be down here if you needed me?"

"I still need my brush," she said flatly, looking every bit like a child who'd just been told no.

He reached over and grabbed it for her, using the movement to hide his smile. "There you go," he said, holding it out to her.

She accepted it begrudgingly, staring at the brush as if it somehow betrayed her. "Thanks."

As much as he was enjoying getting one up on her, he couldn't stand that he was the reason for the pucker between her brows or the frown tugging down the corners of her mouth.

With his free hand, he nudged her chin with the tip of a finger—the only contact he could endure without caving. "Better luck next time."

Annoyance swiftly replaced defeat on her face, and he gave her a satisfied smirk.

"If you really meant that, why don't you let me finish what I started?"

The need to claim her smart mouth and let her do just that overwhelmed him. It was time to end this. The thin thread of his self-control was stretched taut. There was no more room to play before it snapped.

"Go get dressed. We'll grab lunch before heading to the tattoo shops."

Lina's shoulders slumped as she spun on her heel and stomped off. Somehow even that display of temper was erotic. It was probably because of the seductive sway of her hips and all the creamy skin her towel dress left exposed. He wanted her so badly, it was practically painful watching her walk away.

A sudden thought struck him like a bucket of ice water dumped straight over his head. It was of Lina giving up for good, of walking away from him and into someone else's arms. He may not be able to act on his desire, but he couldn't let that possibility become a reality. So, he decided to do the next best thing...offer her a sliver of hope.

"Hey, Lina?"

She glanced back just inside of the doorway, her eyes shooting daggers at him and her lips in a sullen pout.

"Just because I didn't fall for it, doesn't mean I don't enjoy watching you try," he told her, purposely letting his eyes drift over her towel-clad body before returning to her face, hiding none of his desire for her as he stared for a beat. Then, with a wink, he gave her the truth, "Looking forward to seeing what you come up with next."

A NOTE FROM MEG

I know . . . I know . . . I did it again. The dreaded C-word. For those of you that have been with me since the Helena and Von days, you really should expect it by now. For those of you just joining me and my literary adventures, I hope you're okay. I've done worse (if that makes you feel better—it probably doesn't. Please don't hate me.) It's safe to say that any book of mine that isn't a series ender is going to have a cliffy. It's just how I roll. I love them. I promise to always make it up to you by the time we get to the end.

But hopefully, I made up for it with that little bonus scene. Who doesn't want more Nord?

If you're looking for something else to read while waiting for book 2, I have two completed, totally bingeable paranormal series for you. You can check out their blurbs and a little snippet from each on the next page.

Until next time, stay safe and happy reading!

XOXO

♡ Meg Anne

If you enjoyed this book, please consider writing a short review and posting it on Amazon, Bookbub, Goodreads and/or anywhere else you share your love of books. Reviews are very helpful to other readers and are greatly appreciated by authors (especially this one!)

Want to know when I have a new release or get exclusive access to my newest works? Join my mailing list: MegAnneWrites.com/Newsletter

ACKNOWLEDGMENTS

To my boo thangs, Amber, Heather, Jess, Kel, and Melissa. There's about 1000 things I could thank you each individually for, but I'm gonna keep it simple: Thank you for the daily motivation in all its forms (but especially the ones that involve laughter...and booze). You gals did double duty getting me through this one and I don't think I would have made it through this rollercoaster ride without you there every step of the way. Thank you for being my safe place. You are my tribe, and I adore you.

To my husband aka the Moose. You are my person <3 Thank you for making sure I'm always fed and watered. For being a willing ear when I want to talk through plot points, my teddy bear when I need a good cry, my graphics guru when I have last minute teasers or swag created, my technical support team (hell, my emotional support team) when everything goes to shit, and just all around for being my rock. I love you all of the muches.

Kayla, Roxanne, and Alex thank you for stepping up last minute to offer your help! I really value your honesty, insights, and your attention to detail. I know this book is better off because of it.

Dom and A, as always, you take my coal and somehow make diamonds. Thank you.

To my readers. You are my rock stars. Thank you for sticking with me! I hope this story is a bright spot during a dark time. I couldn't do this without you.

ALSO BY MEG ANNE

HIGH FANTASY ROMANCE

THE CHOSEN UNIVERSE
THE CHOSEN
MOTHER OF SHADOWS

REIGN OF ASH

CROWN OF EMBERS

QUEEN OF LIGHT

THE KEEPERS
THE DREAMER – A KEEPERS STORY

THE KEEPER'S LEGACY

THE KEEPER'S RETRIBUTION

THE KEEPER'S VOW

PARANORMAL & URBAN FANTASY ROMANCE

THE GYPSY'S CURSE
CO-WRITTEN WITH JESSICA WAYNE

VISIONS OF DEATH

VISIONS OF VENGEANCE

VISIONS OF TRIUMPH

CURSED HEARTS: THE COMPLETE COLLECTION

THE GRIMM BROTHERHOOD
CO-WRITTEN WITH KEL CARPENTER

REAPER'S BLOOD

REAPING HAVOC

ABOUT MEG ANNE

USA Today and international bestselling paranormal and fantasy romance author Meg Anne has always had stories running on a loop in her head. They started off as daydreams about how the evil queen (aka Mom) had her slaving away doing chores, and more recently shifted into creating backgrounds about the people stuck beside her during rush hour. The stories have always been there; they were just waiting for her to tell them.

Like any true SoCal native, Meg enjoys staying inside curled up with a good book and her cat, Henry . . . or maybe that's just her. You can convince Meg to buy just about anything if it's covered in glitter or rhinestones, or make her laugh by sharing your favorite bad joke. She also accepts bribes in the form of baked goods and Mexican food.

Meg is best known for her leading men #MenbyMeg, her inevitable cliffhangers, and making her readers laugh out loud, all of which started with the bestselling Chosen series.

Made in the USA
Monee, IL
28 July 2021